Bess

Rose Thomas

Writing on the Wall
Toxteth Library
Windsor Street, Liverpool
L8 1XF

Published by Writing on the Wall, 2018

Cover Photography and Design by Wesley Storey
Edited by The Liverpool Editing Company
Layout by Katrina Paterson

ISBN: 978-1-910580-33-2

0151 703 0020
info@writingonthewall.org.uk
www.writingonthewall.org.uk

Bess is dedicated in memory of my beloved daughter Erica, who knew I could write before I knew myself, and to Tracey, Warren, and my adopted daughter Sharon.

Bess

1

I moved in with my son Brian on a bleak evening in late October. I left my suitcase at the bottom of the stairs and listened to him blathering on about how happy I would be.

His words of welcome were no consolation to the chill running down my spine. Even before he opened the door to the kitchen, something told me it would not be the hub of the household. Spotless in appearance, without the odd burnt pan or cups ready for that quick cup of tea, it felt unwelcoming.

It wasn't Brian's fault, I told myself. He was more than happy for me to be there. It was the flat that silently rejected me. An upmarket apartment on London's docklands, it lacked the soul of life. Only the fleeting interchange of contractors and the stamp of perfection hung in the atmosphere.

I sat at the kitchen table and sipped my tea. My son whistled happily while I tried to suppress my sadness at missing home. After I'd finished my cup, Brian sprinted excitedly up the stairs forgetting the suitcases. I passed them too, happy for them to stay there ready for a quick exit if I changed my mind and returned to Liverpool. Maybe I would go back to Joe. I sighed, knowing it was pointless. What I felt for Joe was not love.

Playing with Joe's emotions was the biggest mistake of my life, a dangerous game that backfired, resulting in me seeking sanctuary with Brian. My son had no idea of the turmoil going on in my head as he pushed open the dark oak door of one of the bedrooms. 'This is your room, Mother.'

It was masculine except for the wallpaper, hideously awash with flowers of every description, a mismatch of patterns lost amongst the bottle green stems crawling everywhere. The damp odour from Brian's hasty decorating hung in my nostrils.

He had tried his best to hide the dated chunkiness of the furniture by draping a pink housecoat on the bed. Even the rocking chair stuck in the corner was best suited to an old people's home. With its thick frame and dark cream wicker seat, I certainly wouldn't be parking my backside in that.

Brian closed the door and turned to go back downstairs. I could drop the fake smile which was hurting my face. We retreated back to the kitchen to have a meal, a welcome respite, blocking my mind to what lay ahead.

That night, whilst lying in bed and smoking a cigarette to calm my nerves despite Brian's disapproval of 'my filthy habit', my instinct was to call my old neighbour and best friend, Sadie. But I knew this would make me miss home even more.

I pulled the bedcovers over my head not wanting to see the light from the full moon bouncing unfamiliar shadows around the walls. Gone were the fleeting reflections from cars and streetlights that danced around my tiny bedroom in Liverpool and the sound of the wind as it whipped frenziedly through my open window, creating patterns like a slide show on the honey coloured walls.

I sank deeper into the folds of the fresh linen sheets, turned on the radio and tried to settle. The haunting classical music lifted my mood above the flowered wallpaper, like an eagle soaring over open plains of countryside, crossing streams and meadows, gliding over dark moon-lit woods with an abundance of leafless trees. The intensity of violin strings echoed, reminiscent of a summer's day, as the eagle glided weightlessly through damp forests with a sprinkling of morning dew.

I awoke the next day in a sweat, remembering that the door was closed on my vibrant but problematic world.

As the years passed, my yearning to return home became a problem. It made me careless, a clumsiness covered in memories.

One morning I moved the duster around Brian's prized miniature glass horses. Flying Jack, a replica of a Spanish breed of stallions, stood proudly in the centre. Shining in the sunlight, its front legs were curved in dance. In a moment of distraction, slipping from my hand, it crashed to the ground. The head snapped off and the mane and legs scattered. Brian would be devastated.

From the age of eight he had collected soldiers, cars and miniature glass figurines, but he had always loved horses. His first glass horse was bought at a fairground in our local park. With his small chubby hands, he had stroked its bandy leg, hugging it close like treasure, saying, 'I'll kiss it better.'

Brian was alone most of his early years but never seemed lonely. He would skip to the shops if anyone needed a message or rock a crying baby in its pram. With a lollypop in one hand and pushing the pram in the other, he always made me smile.

As he got older, his adventurous nature began to show. He would be up and dressed early Saturday and Sunday mornings and I would not see him for hours, until he returned with scuffed knees and torn pants, his face covered in dirt. He would just say, 'I've had a jolly time today, Mummy.'

'Where have you been?' I would ask.

'On a boat,' came the answer on one particular occasion. He had caught a bus to the Pier Head, sneaked onto the ferry and crossed the river. It was no use scolding him about the danger of going so far by himself, because the next time he might not tell me.

'We can both take a boat trip, Brian, and you can show me how to catch crabs on the beach. We can eat ice cream and play on the sand.'

His eyes lit up. 'Will you?'

I nodded, smiling. 'Son, you won't go there on your own again, will you?'

'No, Mummy.'

He never let me forget my promise and for the next few years I made countless trips across the River Mersey, recapturing my memories and helping Brian build his.

I let go of the past as I held the head of the shattered glass horse. Brian's reaction could change everything. He might finally ask me to leave or make my life so miserable I would leave anyway.

'Shit,' I swore under my breath, sweeping the evidence under the chair. Brian entered the room and glared at me. 'Mother, I heard a crash! What have you broken now?'

'Oh, morning, Son,' I said fidgeting with my wedding ring, a nervous action Brian knew well.

His eyes narrowed. 'What have you dropped?'

'Flying Jack.'

'You've what!' Brian shouted. His neck jerked forward.

'I've dropped your glass horse.' I opened my hands towards him. 'Look, I'm crippled with pain which makes me clumsy'.

He ignored me and went to pick up the pieces of his precious glass horse. Cradling them carefully, he walked to the kitchen. I could hear him lift the lid off the bin and the sound of Flying Jack being disposed of. I knew apologising for his loss would be no use. He would see the accident as wilful neglect. All I could do was to wait for him to return to the scene of the crime and suffer the consequences. We were always dancing around our feelings, pent up with issues we should have addressed long ago.

But I was not sorry for other things, for the life he had narrowly escaped. I hoped that he would come to terms with the past and see things through the eyes of a man rather than a child.

In my mind the drama between us that always manifested into an argument hid the truth. I was homesick. Liverpool is where I wanted to be, sat in my tiny back yard with its whitewashed walls and plastic chairs. Down here, surrounded by pots of rainwater ready to be sprinkled on my collection of flowers and not having green fingers, was not a problem. Back home, there would be no need for pruning tools, or garden gloves. The moss-covered concrete with clumps of grass and weeds that sprouted in dark corners added to the wildness.

It was the sitting room in the flat that gave me the most distress. Whenever I looked at the mushroom coloured carpets that clashed with the dark green drapes, it took all my will power not to tell Brian how I felt.

Whenever the floor full-length curtains were switched back to reveal the view of the regenerated London Docklands it made me dizzy. I'd watch as the dark brown water swelled on the horizon, almost vomiting the deep-green waves, with a caramel coloured froth gaining momentum in the strong breeze. I longed for somewhere cosy to live, not this show-house full of nametags.

'Can I ask you a question, Brian?'

He had come back into the room, his prized possession disposed of. He wouldn't look at me.

'Depends on what it is.'

'It might annoy you.'

'Go on,' he sighed.

'Well … Liverpool's been on my mind.' There was an uncomfortable pause.

'You hassle me about Liverpool as though milk and honey flushed the toilets. Don't you think I'd like to see Grandma, Uncle Zac and Auntie Mabel? But I can't face going back, not yet anyway.' Bending forward Brian clasped his hands and muttered, 'Sometimes you make me so miserable.'

'That makes two of us,' I sighed. I tried to explain how grateful I was for the support he gave me, but he just opened the paper and turned the pages and took no notice.

Finally, he looked up. 'I assumed this place might wipe away memories of Uncle Zac's airless pit you called home. With its woodlice ridden floorboards and all the other defects. But it was, after all, an assumption wasn't it, Mother?'

I didn't blame Brian for shying away from having a proper discussion. It was his excuse that choked me with disgust.

2

Soaking in the warm water watching the sun glisten through the flimsy curtains swaying delicately in the breeze, I had the peace I'd sought. Shifting my body sideways to reach for a bar of soap, my folds of skin hugged the sides of the bath as if part of the mould. It really was time for me to stop the comfort eating and take more care of myself.

I read Mother's letter again letting me know she'd received the money I'd sent.

> *Dear Bess,*
> *Thanks for your kindness, girl. God knows I don't deserve it. Hope you are okay, I'm fine. Still managing to hobble to bingo (smile). Sadie came around last week and done some shopping for me. When you feel better I hope to see you and Brian.*
> *All my love Mother xx*

She wrote to me regularly and always sent a note for Brian. It was hard leaving her. We had both cried. But I had called Sadie when I felt strong enough against the pull of returning home, and she had reassured me that she would keep an eye on her.

Liam was on the phone as I emerged from the bathroom. He rang regularly asking if we could meet sometime for a coffee, but I always declined. His voice brought back so many of the memories that I tried to forget. As I was a good listener, it was easy for him to tell me his tales of woe, or about his failed relationship. But he never explained the reason why his girlfriend left him. He was such a charmer in his youth but now there was a slight hint of desperation, of trying too hard to please. Strange really, because that's how I had been when I was with him – desperate to please, hungry for approval. That was in the past, I told myself, and now there was no need for me to add to his pain, so I simply listened.

I was not sure of his motives at first, but after a while he asked if I would have dinner with him. I knew that Brian wanted us to be closer – at least friends – he had never really accepted our separation or the relationships I'd had since his father. Perhaps because I had never told him how broken I had been when Liam left me and how much I had suffered in the relationship. Brian had been very young and did not remember. I agreed to meet with Liam but insisted that Brian come along if only to ensure that Liam would not try and draw me into his world again.

Putting my bag under my arm I stepped into the chauffer-driven car and saw Liam smiling in the shadows. He sat with one leg stretched out in front of him. He looked drawn but still handsome.

'Hello, love. How are you?'

'Fine,' I said. He gave me a kiss on the cheek. He was still as charming as ever. He patted my knee intrusively. He would be shocked to know his action was not offensive. After all, he was my first real love, but not my last lover.

I could smell the charcoaled meats being roasted on open spits as we stepped out of the car and into the restaurant. A waiter rushed towards us. I slipped the cloak off my shoulders as we followed him towards the table where Brian was already seated looking at the menu.

'Hi, you two,' Brian said as we sat. A board smile spread across his face. 'You look so good together.'

I gave him a look. He just laughed. Liam's lips parted in a grin showing gold-capped and sparkling white teeth. Appearances meant a lot to him.

I was surprised at how relaxed I was, and I could see that Brian was happy. The tenseness that I had noticed from time to time was gone and there was hope in his eyes. It seemed to him like we were a family again. I felt guilty and torn inside – it really was too late to turn back the clock, but I would try not to spoil things at least for tonight.

Liam was taking us to see The Phantom of The Opera and I was looking forward to it. Slipping out of my chair, I excused myself and went to the ladies. When I returned, Liam was counting money in his wallet to pay the bill. 'Brian's gone, he has an early start in the morning and told us to enjoy ourselves.' I knew that I had been set up, but it didn't matter, I could handle Liam and if allowing him to try and make amends made Brian happy then it was worth it.

The curtain came down to a deafening applause. Liam turned to me. 'Fancy coming back to mine, Bess?' I paused. I was curious to see how he was living now.

In the car, I sat back on the plush seats to enjoy the journey. We drove through the countryside, silent except for the purr of the engine.

The dimly lit detached house, took my breath away. Liam had come a long way from shuffling a pack of cards in Liverpool's China Town, to living in a property where he could take a morning dip in a rippling swimming pool. I was happy for his success and grateful Brian benefited.

Chest puffed out and a smirk on his face, he turned the key and let me in first. 'You can stay the night if you want,' he said. Laughing, he added, 'In the guestroom of course.'

We stepped inside. I wouldn't mind waking up to this, I thought. One room was the total area of Brian's flat. I smiled imagining the shuttered windows open so that I could almost stroke the birds in the trees.

Liam smiled too. He had his fantasy. As long as it didn't include me, I didn't mind. He swept his way around the house turning down lights. With the flick of a switch, music played in the background. He had all the signs of a man on a mission. He poured two drinks, gin for me which was my favourite, and carried them over to where I sat. The white leather couch, big enough to put the right distance between us, was an oasis of softness.

But each time the cushions moved, he slid nearer. It was much harder for me to move away from him. I had to shift almost double his weight. He could manoeuvre with ease and made an undignified attempt to put his arm around my shoulders.

Yawning I said, 'Liam, I must go now. I have forgotten to take my tablets.' By now I'd managed to remove his arm and stand up.

'What are you taking, love? I might have some.'

'They're for women's problems, Liam. Unless you've changed your sex, you won't have them.'

'You never know.'

He had the knack of bringing a smile to my face, no matter what.

'Come on, Bess, sit down. The night is still young.'

You're not, I thought. He must be lonely in this big house. I had enjoyed the evening and his company. It was his familiarity that upset me.

'Okay, but please keep your hands to yourself.'

'I will, promise.'

I should have known he wasn't good at keeping his word. Within half an hour he said, 'I've never forgotten you, Bess.'

Trying to change the subject I told him to put on a record and fetch me another drink, a large one. To hell with the diet.

Thank God he didn't ask me to dance. It felt good listening to the music. Head back and comfortable, I'd forgotten Liam was there for a while. My mind was crammed with future plans. I realised that no one had held me captive but myself. Then I felt his icy fingers trying to undo my blouse.

I stood up. 'What the bloody hell do you think you're doing, Liam?'

He tried to make a stammering apology, but the blood had rushed to my head and I saw red.

'Do you really think I would have anything to do with you after all you've done to me and Brian? You must be mad! I know you've lost that woman you abandoned your son for.' I didn't need to say that this fancy woman had turned his head and played him like a fiddle, waited until she had his finances in her grasp then dumped him.

He began to shake. Normally I would have calmed down. But he'd assumed I was a lonely old woman who had erased the past.

'She snatched the good years. Now you want to give me the bad ones. Not this old lady,' I laughed.

'I have money again now, Bess. I can look after you.'

'It's not about the money.' I wanted the young Liam to hold at night, not some worn out old man.

'You're sitting back in your mansion now!' I spat. 'But you sold all our furniture to pursue your dreams and left me and my son to the mercy of the world.'

'Sorry.'

'Sorry? You will be if you carry on with your antics. Watch my lips there is no me and you. There never will be. So, you get off your bony backside and ring a taxi.'

Holding onto the arm of the couch to hurl himself up, he said, 'No, Bess. My driver will take you home, I'll ring him. I am sorry, you know, for what happened here but believe me tonight was wonderful.'

His voice was thick and hoarse as he spoke into the phone, 'Will you bring the car, Dave? My guest is ready to go home.'

He couldn't look at me, but I saw a glimpse of his eyes and the glistening tears within them surprised me. Perhaps he had regrets about the decision he made to leave me. Liam and I never spoke of divorce. The respectability of being married mattered all those years ago. I would never marry again, and I was sure Liam had no plans to either.

'Can I make you a cup of coffee while you wait?' he asked.

'No thanks.'

'We still can be friends, Bess. You know I have always cared about you,' he pleaded. I looked at him.

'Brian has never known the extent of your betrayal. You don't need to worry, I'm not going to tell him now.' I wanted to bring Uncle Zac into the argument, tell Liam how I really felt about him and his dislike of my uncle. But I'd tell him when I was good and ready. Liam was too upset to grasp the significance of his views and actions about black people. We were still friends and I hoped we both might benefit if the friction between us could be aired in the open without bias or vindictiveness.

With a clear mind, I walked down the path and stepped

into the car. I had wondered for all these years how our lives would have been if Liam had stayed but now it did not seem to matter anymore. I felt that a weight had been lifted from me and my anger dispersed.

I'd been in London for years and made no close friendships. I didn't fancy joining a group to keep your mind active, or a line dancing club. My friends were in Liverpool and only the thought of going back north kept me from dying inside.

In the quiet darkness of the drive home, I thought fondly of the Liam who once captured my heart. We had met on a beautiful autumn day when I attended a work colleague's wedding. I caught a glimpse of a tall muscular man in a dark suit, flocked by giggling bridesmaids. He was staring across at me and his gaze made me feel weak at the knees. I could hardly breathe as he walked towards me and asked me to dance. There were plenty of pretty girls there, but he only seemed interested in me. 'What's your name?' he asked.

'Bess, what's yours?'

'Liam.' His brown eyes twinkled under the revolving ball of light as we danced close together, but I nestled even nearer, until beads of perspiration glowed noticeably on his brow. My intention to have an impact on him was working. I wanted to feel every vein and muscle in his body.

'Ever drank champagne?' Liam asked.

'Yes,' I lied.

He went to the bar flanked by bridesmaids hanging on his arm and came back to my table leaving the bridesmaids pouting in the corner. He placed a bottle of champagne still dripping with melted ice and poured it into long stemmed glasses and sat beside me.

He was nice, so different from Slim, my previous boyfriend. Tenderly at first, then like the bubbles in the champagne, Liam showered me in kisses with lips as fleshy as mine. My head spun with desire, almost dismissing my inhabitations about having sex on the first date. I was still searching for the thrill of sex. I felt that everyone else had experienced it and I was still waiting to.

I knew even then that I could easily allow my sexual urges to overcome me, by trying subconsciously to hide from the trauma Slim had caused. Liam's gentle rebuff from my overzealousness, made me realise he was special.

He put his arm around me as he walked me home and guided me when I stumbled over an uneven curb. He picked up the contents of my handbag when I carelessly dropped it. He didn't seem to mind when I wobbled from one side of the street to the other. By the time I'd reached home after the long walk in the cool evening breeze the drunken feeling had gone. That was when all my antics of that night came flooding back. Now the shyness overtook me and without a drink to give me courage I mumbled, 'Sorry.'

'For what, giving me one of the best nights ever?'

He kissed me goodnight after I'd agreed to see him again.

As much as I'd wanted him physically only hours before, I was fully aware of the difference between infatuation and love. Liam had made me feel good and at first infatuation was all it was.

Liam and I met again a couple of weeks after our night at the theatre. We sat in an open-air cafe in the centre of London and he ordered coffee and sat back and stared at me.

'Bess, I had problems when I first moved here. No

job, no money and I was stressed. I met a woman who changed all that. She was the manager of a casino and had a lot of contacts. I asked her to move in with me out of necessity.' He went on to tell me he had never loved her and refused to divorce me. He looked down. 'I was always proud of you, Bess, especially when I realised what you had gone through. I would show your picture to people and notice the shock on their faces when they realised my wife, Brian's mother, was black'. He paused and took a deep breath. 'I admit that in some ways I was just like those people. So, love, I am sorry for the harm I caused. One day I hope to see Zac again, so I can tell him how sorry I am.'

I could forgive him now. He was a young man at the time, I reasoned. He was proving to me that he thought differently now. The hours slipped away as we talked, laughed and remembered all the good times we shared together.

3

A period of great change in my life was sparked by a phone call from Sadie telling me Mabel had been admitted to hospital with terminal cancer.

'When can you get home?' Her voice faltered. 'She's in a bad way.'

'I'll be there Friday,' I promised, my mind racing frantically.

'Will Brian come with you?' she asked.

For a moment I didn't know what to say. No, would have sounded so harsh. 'Yes, yes… he will come with me,' I answered. I knew Brian loved Mabel much more than he hated Liverpool. Meeting Uncle Zac and Mabel had changed my life forever. It was their wisdom, love and experiences which helped me grow into a confident woman. From the moment my uncle and his wife cuddled Brian in their arms I knew we would never be alone again, even though at that point in my life I was lost. Uncle Zac could never replace my father, but in some way, he kept him alive.

Brian sat open-mouthed when I told him. His voice broke, 'She won't die, will she?'

'Be prepared, son. We won't know until after the surgery.'

He left the room hunched and unsteady. Restless and anxious, I made a hot drink for both of us. Knocking on his door, I waited.

'Come in.'

I entered the room carrying a tray. 'Here you are, I've made you a hot drink.'

'Thanks.' He was sitting on a high-backed chair with his

legs fully stretched in front of him. Placing the tray on the table, I got it out quickly, 'I'll have to go back to Liverpool.'

He tapped his fingers on the table. 'I know, mother, and I'm sure you know the reasons why Liverpool is not a place I want to return to...But I have to, for Uncle Zac.'

'It holds bad memories for both of us.'

His eyes became dark. 'I remember the poverty, rooms not fit for human beings,' Brian said. 'The black children called nigger by the police. But I wasn't, they saw me as a good little white boy. It was a long time ago, but I still feel like I sold out my friends.' His eyes moistened. 'You think I am afraid of pain, don't you?'

I didn't reply. He sat beside me.

'Or I'm still scared of being left in a ditch somewhere after Fred has finished with me?' He laughed. 'It's not the blows I fear anymore.' He leaned back and sighed. 'I sold them out to their enemies. I am not the scared rat you think I am, just someone who thinks being ashamed is not enough. Words can't give me peace. That's what I'm afraid of.'

I studied him carefully, my son. The news about Mabel had drained what little colour he had. He was so fair in complexion that he was usually mistaken for being white. As a child he had blond curly hair and from an early age, he became puzzled at how white his complexion was compared to mine.

He realised that people treated him differently when he was not with me. In the 1970s colour prejudice had been a part of our everyday life. When he was able to understand, it made him feel so helpless and afraid when someone jeered at me in the street or called me names.

He would not experience those things with Liam and it was one of the reasons why I had wanted him to live with his father. Brian had gone willingly, relieved because he could now blend into white society and would not have to face the ridicule of having a black mother.

It made him sad, even now, to think about how he had left me, but spending time with him in London had brought us both healing. He was a man now and was proud of his mixed heritage and his beautiful black mother. And he was ready to come back to Liverpool.

On the way to the station, a cool evening breeze blew through the taxi's open window and I couldn't wait to be on the train and watch London disappear. Once the dock faded into the distance, a tantalising smell of food, trapped by the light wind, seemed to activate my taste buds. As we passed through more of London, I noticed people sitting on open terraces, and pubs awash with colour housed hundreds in open designated arrears. According to the numerous glasses and waiters carrying trays of lobster, shrimp platters and fruit cocktails, customers ate and drank in great volume. Nearby tramps hovered, some submerged in waste bins digging for food. Shop windows ablaze with light, displayed richly clad dummies, set against dark oak furniture, and tapestries.

'Mother, for all your misgivings about moving here, are you still sorry you left your hometown?' Brian interrupted my thoughts.

'Yes.'

'There is no comparison between Liverpool and London,' he said. 'Every time I remember leaving Liverpool I pinch myself. Here I can see black people with hope. Look!' He pointed to a black man in a bowler hat strolling along the streets. 'In Liverpool, he would be the centre of attention. In London, he is not the centre of anything.'

London had its own problems, I thought, but Brian

had a point. In Liverpool I always sensed a hatred towards black people that was as deep as the River Mersey and as dark as its waters. No amount of regeneration could fix it. Yet Liverpool was my home. I loved it with all its failings. It was a shame some of its inhabitants didn't feel the same.

4

Leaning back on the headrest watching the scenery change from London's urban landscape to cows grazing on lush fields of green and lulled by the train's rhythm, my mind drifted back to memories of my childhood in Liverpool.

I remembered my father. He was tall and handsome, the colour of polished ebony. He had a gleaming white smile and a quiet assurance about him that always made me feel so safe. He called me his little princess. He was the one who would take me up to bed at night and read me a story until I fell asleep. I loved him so much.

I was not as close to my mother. From an early age I got the impression that I had somehow disappointed her. She would plaster my hair with Vaseline in an attempt to tame my "frizz" as she called it and complain that she did not understand why I had such "bad" hair and that I did not get it from her. She would frown and stare at me as though she was trying to find something she could approve of. 'You have nice eyes, Bess,' she conceded once. 'Like your father's.' But for most of my childhood, she appeared cold and distant.

My mother was a beauty, and she had been told all her life that she could pass for Spanish, or something like that, as though it was somehow better that she did not look like a Negro. Her hair was wavy and long – 'not a kink in sight,' she would say, and she likened herself to Lena Horne, an American singer and actress famous from the 1940s. I always got the impression that her whiteness had caused a rift with my father's family, who we never saw. Or most likely, I wrongly believed at the time, that she didn't want to be associated with his black family.

It was my father who took me to school on my first day. The cold September wind was biting as it sliced through my brand-new uniform. It was a predominately white school, because of the area we lived in. Father knew I was nervous and remarked how grown up and pretty I looked. He whistled as we walked and, arriving at the school gates, he looked at me and winked. He was my confidence.

The blackened building loomed large and imposing and made me feel so very small. I clung on tightly to my father's hand whilst we were ushered with the other children and parents into the dimly lit hallway outside our classroom.

Everyone stared at us. I just wanted to shrink away but Father did not seem to notice. He kissed me on the cheek and whispered, 'Love you princess.' Then he left.

We were led into the room and introduced to our teacher, a short homely looking woman with pink cheeks and dimples who introduced herself as Mrs Jones. The tears I had been fighting back disappeared. I was suddenly excited by the array of books and toys before me and mesmerised by the beautiful dolls house tucked away in the corner.

I sat and waited for my turn in the magic box. It was full of toys. Some jingled and played songs. There were jigsaw puzzles and a host of musical instruments. I was wary of the other children who were playing in groups and tried not to draw attention to myself. I reached into the magic box and picked up a doll.

A girl, whom I was later introduced to as Hilda Jackson, decided that at the tender age of five I needed to know my place, and that she would be the one to tell me exactly where that was.

'My baby!' she demanded, snatching the doll with one hand, the other on her hip. I reluctantly let go.

Looking at me and stroking the doll's hair, she sneered, 'I don't like you.' Then added, 'Because your face is dirty.'

I had been called 'dirty face' many times by the children in my street but, somehow, I thought school would be different. Shocked that it wasn't, I decided to stand my ground and wrestled the doll from the girl's grip. We were left with an equal share. I had the top half of the doll and Hilda looked disappointed with the bottom. The interest in the toy was gone and we both looked for something else to play with.

It was after dinner when the whole class, led by Miss Jones, were taken to the playground that the taunts began. Hilda disappeared into the crowd. The boys pulled faces and scratched under their arms as I searched for a friend. The girls screeched and poked their fingers in my back asking me my name. My surname, Tobo, had them in fits of laughter and I could not understand why. I felt like a wounded pigeon, surrounded by cats. I turned around to confront the crowd as one of the boys pulled a water pistol from his pocket and aimed at me. I was left drenched and shivering, partly with fear. Some of the other children laughed. A scruffy looking boy with a runny nose piped up, 'She looks like a chimney sweep.'

Arming myself inwardly against the rampaging five-year olds, I didn't flinch when I felt water trickling down my face. Nor did I put my hands on my hips and challenge them. I was outnumbered.

But in time, other children saw me as a mantle for

their own battles and stood by my side. When we had exhausted all means of a peaceful settlement with the bullies, we had no option but to become warriors. I had a sizable army at my disposal at times, apart from when the conflict became racially motivated. I was left on my own then.

My school years were an agony of racial taunts and silent tears. I never mentioned it to my mother. I assumed that she would be indifferent to my pain and feared she might blame me. I resolved to never tell my father about it because I knew how much he would worry.

I thought my teenage years might provide me with an opportunity to reinvent myself, but no matter how hard I tried, I remained the outsider. I was never invited for tea and even school trips could be a lonely experience. The constant worry of who would like me, left me traumatised.

In fact, it was Hilda, that first day bully, who changed completely over the years. We declared a truce by the time we reached primary school, which was only a partition separating the classroom. Senior school had the same baby-faced infants. Our bodies had grown but attitudes had not changed.

Hilda and I became easily distracted and we were often caned for talking. We were both deemed to be dunces and left to do our work on scraps of paper instead of exercise books.

I was unhappy because I could see most of the teachers openly expressed an air of contempt towards me. One minute they would be smiling but as soon as our eyes met, a snarl would creep around their lips, and they'd shudder as if they could not stand to look at me.

So, I took no notice of them or what they had to say. I could read and write by the age of seven but that had no bearing on my ability to learn. As far as the teachers were concerned I was a lost cause from the beginning of my school life to the end.

That made me shut down and allow nothing to sink in for eight years because I was tired of fighting for everything. But with Hilda as my accomplice, we had a good time being rebels without a voice.

Hilda had developed into a pretty young girl with waist-length nut brown hair and sparkling eyes. Bubbling with excitement about leaving school, she would say, 'I'm going to be a nanny and live in a posh house.'

'Office work is what I'm looking for. I'll be a secretary one day,' I'd reply.

Hilda would laugh, 'Not in this life you won't, or the next one.'

The last day of term arrived. Wanting to look grown up, I wore a grey box pleated skirt white blouse and a cardigan slung over my shoulders. At fifteen years of age, I thought I could face the world. That was until the one o'clock gun, a relic from the First World War, boomed in the distance, a warning for me to start running as I was late. Scrambling over bombsites, crossing roads and dodging tired old carthorses pulling their load of coal, I thought I'd made it, but the school gates were closed. The caretaker let me in through the side door, shaking his head as I ran past him.

In my mind, the sound of the gun would no longer haunt me after that day, only the fear of the cane was left. I hated the whoosh it made when it struck on my open palm. It was the tingling aftermath of the strike and trying to hold back tears of anger that hurt the most though, but no one was caned for being late that day. Entering the classroom, the teacher eyed me with the usual contempt. 'Make sure your desk is cleared, Tobo.'

'Yes, Miss.'

During my last assembly another teacher handed me my testimonial and smiled. 'Good luck in the future, Elizabeth.' But her eyes couldn't hide her empty words. I still grinned as she handed me the piece of paper that would determine the rest of my life.

Walking home slowly, stopping briefly to read the report that held no surprises, I read that I was lazy and likely to become a manual worker.

When I returned home my parents were still at work. Putting a pot of stew on the gas ring, watching it bubble to a high temperature, I heard the front door slammed. Mother's footsteps quick and determined echoed down the hall. Slinging her bag on the back of a chair, she faced me. 'Well, where it is?

Pretending not to hear her, I continued to concentrate on the evening meal. Hoping she was too tired to ask me again, my prayer was answered when she muttered something, walked over to the sink and washed her hands. The smiling face of my father uplifted me when he popped his head around the door.

After our meal he asked to see my report. He smiled as he read. 'Well at least you are good at reading, it took me years before I could spell 'the cat sat on the mat'.'

I knew he would understand because in nineteen thirty-one when he started school, it must have been horrendous for him. Sadly, not much had changed since then he told me, and so he assured me it was not my fault. When Mother said I should have done better, Father said, 'So should her teachers.'

'I have dreams, Father.'

'I know, girl. I had them once.'

I was like him in many ways, full of dreams but difficulty in fulfilling them without a guide. Father believed in me, but still I passed through life like a ghost searching for its soul. Mother was just pleased that my attendance had been good enough to help me secure a job, and any job that brought in wages would be fine with her.

5

The summer I left school we experienced a heatwave. Mother rewarded me a few days off to rest before looking for work. I spent much of my time alternating between taking cool baths and watching the neighbours, who I called the 'bangers and mash set', lounging lazily in the sun determined to get 'brown' like us. Their ways contrasted starkly with my father who, despite all the years he spent away from his family, had never lost his taste for African food. He often visited Liverpool's dockland and would board ships arriving from any African port, returning home laden with all the ingredients he needed. The kitchen became a hub of creativity when he cooked, and the exotic smells were irresistible.

We often had Egusi and spinach soup, with an array of aromatic seasonings and hot African pepper accompanied by a plate of garri or ground rice. I loved being in his company, especially when he cooked and talked about his father who came to England as a qualified sailor, with an ambition to join the Royal Navy and help the Second World War effort. He had hopes of becoming an officer but was left shivering on the Liverpool dockside in the middle of winter awaiting orders to join a ship.

The Royal Navy suddenly changed to the Merchant Navy and he was given a job as a stoker below deck. He never returned to Africa after the War because by then he was married and settled in Liverpool. My father was born in nineteen twenty two, and his brother nineteen twenty six, but going to sea was my grandfather's life until he died. I wished he would have told me more about his brother, Uncle Zac.

But whenever I became inquisitive Mother always seemed to change the subject, stopping any further discussion in its tracks.

We ate together in traditional style, rolling the dough-like substance with our fingers before dipping it into the soup. Mother would grimace watching us eat. It seemed primitive to her.

The 'bangers and mash set' did not share her reservations and could not wait to sample the unusual meals. As the pungent aromas mixed with the fresh air, they would ask, 'What are you cooking, Mr. Tobo? It smells nice.'

He often challenged them to try his hottest dish 'pepper soup'.

'The first person,' he would say, 'to ask for a drink of water has to wash the dishes'.

If the choice was mine the kitchen was the last place I would want to be. Mother was house proud when it came to cleanliness, but thrifty when refurbishment was needed. It was now the middle 1950s, but our house was stuck in the early 1930s. There was enough space to have three lodgers, but Mother regarded their rent as savings towards buying a house in a better area. Mend and make do was her war cry. This prompted Father to hammer nails into anything that moved, from wooden kitchen worktops to jagged pieces of floor covering.

Standing on the top of the stairs, I sometimes wished to be miles away from the decaying hallway and the rot, hidden by years of scrubbing and polishing. I would cringe at the walls painted in cold blues, a variety of greens and a dominating yellow, and walk slowly to the bottom floor and the bedroom I was born in.

This is where Mother must have heard my first cry.

Was it there she chose a name that she could shorten to suit her mood? Did she use the longer version on the days she loved me and shorter one for when she did not?

Somehow whenever an unlucky neighbour washed the dishes it would evoke those memories in me. Thank God they soon became accustomed to the taste, and most of the time Father washed the dishes himself. So those memories lay dormant most of the time.

I got the impression that the women used the opportunity to come over to converse with my father. They thought he was as exotic as the food he prepared and seemed very impressed that he was so adept in the kitchen. They flirted with him at every opportunity, but my father pretended not to notice.

He knew they were drawn to him, but he only had eyes for my mother so he neither encouraged nor rebuked them, but their husbands still hovered uncomfortably, watchful. What did this black man have that they did not, they must have questioned themselves silently. My father thought they were his friends. He had an unsuspecting nature, which at times made him vulnerable.

My mother had a lot of time for the neighbours in contrast to my father who drew the line when it came to parties or going to the pub for a drink. He never drank or smoked so it was easy for him to decline their invitations.

There was really nothing in my life at that time that compared to my joy at leaving school. Even my end of school testimonial could not dampen my mood. I still wanted more for myself.

6

One Monday it all changed.

'Your holiday is over,' said mother. 'Get yourself something to eat and go to the Labour Exchange and see what jobs there are.'

Because I left school unnoticed, without any information on how and where to look for work, I had to ask where it was.

'It's in Leece Street, right facing the bombed-out church.'

Leaving the house full of anticipation of the future and walking through the door of the Labour Exchange, there were two choices open to me. I could go to the desk that said Manual or to another that said Professional. Today this is known as the Job Centre, with computers everywhere. Back then it was uniformed clerks sitting behind a desk trying to explain to fifteen-year-old school leavers what career path they should take.

I wanted to learn how to type. Feel and hear the click of typewriter keys, not the grind of machinery. With my mind made up, Professional was my choice. I hoped my willingness to work hard would show, and the years lost in my education could be reclaimed. I just needed an employer to say yes and give me a chance.

Everyone in the room seemed to either bite their nails or sit like dummies. I chose to sit next to a young girl with nails bitten to the quick. A story of someone who'd been marched off the premises for wearing a ripped blouse filtered from person to person.

'The girl brazenly had a tattoo on her bare shoulder

with the name Ted.' I overheard someone say. It was a warning to the rest of us of what would happen if we dared forget to hide our creativeness.

My turn next. Smoothing down my skirt over my hips, I stood behind the curved desk.

'Sit down, Miss Tobo,' the woman said, shuffling papers in a folder with her veined hand. She looked up. 'Firstly, what would you like to do? And can I have your testimonial please?'

Handing over the piece of paper, I babbled my uneducated enquiry regarding none manual work. She gave a hurried dismissal to my questions and sighed as I poured my heart out about working in an office. 'You have none of the qualifications required. There's no place in an office for someone like you.'

I knew what she'd said was correct. My testimonial suggested I was only fit for manual work. Something I had done all my life.

The woman's cold blue eyes rolled upwards. 'You don't have any typing experience and on your application form there are numerous spelling mistakes.' She slammed the folder shut. 'I can only offer you manual work.'

'Well, I'm not working in a factory.'

She ignored me. 'You must come here every Thursday sign your name and we can help you find employment.'

I took the form and walked slowly out of the door. Looking over at the bombed-out church, stripped of its identity, I crossed the road and entered the hollow structure. That's how I felt, empty inside with little hope of being repaired.

My downbeat mood had not changed on reaching home. Mother flushed with excitement anticipating my success. 'When do you start?' was the first question she asked.

'I'm not starting anywhere,' I said shocked at my boldness.

'What? The peanut factory is crying out for workers.'

I felt like saying, I'm not crying out for them.

Through clenched teeth my mother said, 'You're a soft cow expecting to work in an office.' Wiping her hands on her apron, she continued, 'I might have the chance, but you,' she laughed, 'have none. Just get yourself back to the Labour Exchange tomorrow and take anything.'

My silence was enough to convince her she'd won.

Later that week with the slip of paper from the Labour Exchange, I had an interview for a job in an overall factory. The building was up a steep hill, hidden behind steel gates. The gate opened as I approached.

'Yes,' a voice said from the intercom.

Stammering, I answered, 'I-I've come for a-a job.'

'Wait there.' Another man came to the gate. 'Follow me.' We walked across the yard to a small office, and we went through the formalities of the employment. 'Can you sew?'

'No,' I said.

'That's okay, we'll teach you.'

I hated sewing. Mother was always trying to push me into cutting patterns or pinning the hem of curtains. With me being no good at either task, she gave up asking.

'Right,' he said. 'Start Monday eight o'clock. If you're late you won't get through the gate.'

There was no excitement in taking a job I hated. It was a means to an end but my mother's idea of heaven. The noise in the factory left a thudding sound in my ears. Putting my hands over my ears to drown out the sound. 'You'll get used to it,' the charge hand said.

My first day passed without incident. Much of the time was spent being shown around the building and a quick introduction to some of the other women. The woman leading me around the room said, 'You can pack today. We'll try you on sewing tomorrow.'

Mandy was young like me, but more confident. She'd giggle when the charge hand scolded her untidy work and pulled faces behind the woman's back. She had the same colouring as me but with hazel eyes that twinkled when she laughed. Happy to meet someone who looked like me, I smiled for the rest of the day. The next morning Mandy waited for me at the gate. She shoved a beechnut chewing gum in my hand.

'Thanks.'

'You can buy me a loosie tomorrow.'

'Okay.'

The charge hand told us to get on with it before disappearing out of sight like a ship on the horizon, leaving me flanked behind the mountains of blue material that spilled over tables, industrial machines and the heads of workers on my line.

The clacking of machines and the sea shanty music being played made me bilious and the speed of the needles unnerved me. The charge hand returned and poked at my work pointing out it was frayed around the edge.

'Unpick!' she spat. 'Next time watch what you're doing, or you will be out.'

As I practised single lines of crude stitching, I became over confident and my finger slipped under the needle. My screams must have sounded louder than a generator. Kicking and thrashing around in pain, I saw Mandy running to switch off the main supply. The commotion brought the charge hand scurrying to my section. She eased my finger from underneath the broken needle.

'Go to nurse,' she grunted. 'She will give you a plaster.'

'Where is it?' I sobbed.

'Mandy, take this dumbbell to the nurse.' Shoving me out of the way, she sat in my place and switched the power back on.

We walked to the nurse's room in silence. Even though I had not known Mandy that long, I leaned on her arm like we were old friends.

No one had ever linked my arm until then and it felt good. It was a closeness of a friend that was missing in my life. It was my shyness and fearing rejection that might have frightened people off. Mandy liked me and had no idea of the joy she gave.

The nurse wound a mountain of bandage around my finger.

'It's a deep one,' she said. 'Keep it dry and take the dressing off in two days.' A whistle blew. It was lunch time.

'Fancy a walk to the High Street?' Mandy asked. 'We can get a bowl of soup in that place facing the butchers.'

Too embarrassed to admit I had no idea where the café was, I replied, 'Smashing, let's go.'

We looked like sisters, the only difference being Mandy's hair was tucked beneath a red polka dot scarf tied under her chin. Cracking her gum, she walked beside me.

My delight in finding a friend who not only looked like me but was also experienced, helped me to ignore the unwanted stares we got.

Returning to work, I jumped as the iron gates of the factory clanged behind us as though life on the outside was no concern of ours.

Head bent forward encouraging another enthusiastic worker, the charge hand looked up. 'You, young lady, go back to packing.'

The sewing machine section never saw me again. I folded, packed and boxed thousands of overalls in the eighteen months of my employment. The only uplifting factor was having a friend like Mandy working in the next room.

7

Mother was banging around in her bedroom, slamming drawers and cursing as I entered.

'Have you seen it?', she said.

'What?'

She continued muttering, as she tossed her handbag on the bed 'This bloody house gets on my nerves! My lipstick, of course.'

'Here it is,' I said, lifting the uncapped tube from the bed.

'Thanks.' She painted her lips with the scrapings of a lipstick, which left an uneven red line on her top lip. 'I'm going over to see my friend, she's not well. Where are you off to?' she asked.

'For a walk,' I replied. Quickly closing her bedroom door, I left before she could object and stop me from going out.

With the dust of the day kicking around my feet, I thought about working away from home. Become a nanny or a live-in domestic cleaner, anything for a new start.

Keeping Mandy a secret from my parents gave me some freedom. Being able to jump on a bus and leave Shakespeare Road even for a few hours gave me butterflies. There, in the small dilapidated property where Mandy lived, her parents seemed to have the respect for Mandy's privacy I craved. They allowed her to have the front living room as her own space. So, it was just a tap on the window and Mandy's smiling face would appear.

I loved the quietness of her house. We would talk and

play records while Mandy told of parties she'd been to, promising to take me one day. 'When you are not so wet behind the ears,' she laughed.

Mandy's clothes didn't hang - they sucked on her curves, and her cute smile and sleepy hazel eyes were captivating. She moved like a jaguar and she had something else I'd heard about - she had sex appeal. Without knowing what it entailed, I wanted to have it as well.

The journey back home was like being a butterfly one minute and trapped inside a cage the next. I didn't know what living without a domineering mother and a father worn out trying to change her would be like. It was something I wanted to experience.

In my bedroom, cold but airy, I would pick my way through the local paper, stopping at: *Nanny wanted. Experience required, but not necessary*. My hopes were always dashed because they were all too far from home.

One evening while scanning the paper I saw: *Nanny required. Must be reliable, honest and prepared to work some weekends*. It was just outside Liverpool. Opening the blackout curtains for the moonlight to brighten up the dimly lit room, I looked at the advertisement again. After convincing myself to apply, writing a coherent letter was another matter.

Waking the next morning to my mother humming, gave me the signal to relax. She was in a good mood. 'Morning, Mother'.

She nodded and continued to fiddle with the carpet sweeper. When I'd washed and dressed, and everything was clear in my mind, I sat at the table. Eating my breakfast slowly and watching mother swirling the breakfast plates in soapy hot water, my observation point was ideal.

It was Friday, pay day. Her eyes always lit up when my father and I gave her our wage packets. She'd carefully count the money, handing some back with clear instructions on how to spend it. I knew she would resist against me working away from home. It would take away the pleasure of receiving two wage packets and the rent on the same day. With fear in my heart, I blurted out the news of my pending departure.

To my surprise she did not flinch. It was not until I was halfway down the hall, I heard her reply in a raised voice, 'Don't think you can come back here.'

I laughed inwardly. It would be the last place on my list of returns. In the evening once the house fell silent, I scratched my pen on a sheet of paper to construct my first introduction letter with full stops, capital letters and commas, picked at random.

After three days of tossing half of the writing paper in the corner, a smudged crumpled letter with my crablike signature sprawled at the bottom was done.

I visualised Mrs Richardson sliding caviar and champagne down her throat and talking about me. Asking her friends, what kind of name is Tobo? Drumming my fingers on the table, I was tempted to hide who I was, removing the drama and becoming Miss Timpson or something like that. I could give Mrs Richardson a name without adjectives, so it rolled off the tongue without sticking to the palate. After considering all options, I dug the original copy from the bottom of the pile and shoved it into an envelope, hoping it wouldn't spark Mrs Richardson's curiosity. If it did I would answer her questions.

I couldn't wait to show Mandy. We met in the shop opposite the factory and bought our usual packet of beechnut chewing gum.

'Mandy, have a look at this letter I wrote last night.'

'A love letter?'

'No, soft girl, it's for a job.'

Mandy's untrained eye remarked on the artistry of my loopy handwriting. Exhilarated with her words of praise, I posted the letter that lunchtime.

Many luncheons later the reply letter arrived. It had been left propped unopened on the table. A book held Mother's attention. There was no fear of her breathing over my shoulder. Tearing the envelope open, my heart sank. Mrs Richardson's typed reply was to inform me that there were others to be interviewed, assuring me an interview would be considered if she'd found no one suitable in the meantime.

Scowling, I threw the letter to the other end of the table. As far as I was concerned it would be the last I'd hear from her. So, it was back to scanning through the newspaper, naively hoping I'd be the only candidate next time.

'Well,' said Mother, turning the radio down. 'What did the lady of the manor have to say?'

I gave her the letter.

Laughing, Mother said, 'It sounds like you haven't got a chance in hell to be employed by those people anyway.' She stopped laughing and added, 'I need you here.'

You need me, but you don't want me.

8

On Saturdays Mother usually woke me up by yanking the bedclothes from my bed.

'Come on,' she'd say. 'Get the pram out of the shed. I've got the bundles of washing ready to take to the wash-house. Have a quick wash for now, I've put the kettle on.'

I hated the steam and water-logged environment. Woman dragged wet clothes from one machine to another and ran back and forth to their own small space, which had a boiler and a tub. Then they would manually use a wooden plunger and toss and turn all the woollen clothes until clean. After a cup of tea, they placed all the clothes on warm racks and pushed them into the wall. While they sat on benches and waited for their clothes to dry, the social element of the day began. Mother would unscrew her flask of tea and sit alone with a book, while everyone else had someone to talk to.

My task was to return home and clean the house from top to bottom on my knees. Then there would be our own living area to cover, then windows and brass rods on the front stairs. They all had to be polished to Mother's satisfaction. At least it gave me some time to daydream as I scrubbed, without Mother bending over me making sure it was done properly.

The excitement of going to Mandy's house kept me motivated. By the time the work was completed, I had to go back to the washhouse and help Mother home. We would pull the old rickety pram through the side streets, keeping tight hold of the clean washing mountain until we reached our house. Now, when I put my clothes into the washing machine and push a button, I think about those days.

I would have some empathy for Mother when she would sink into her chair exhausted and make her a cup of tea. 'Thanks, girl,' she always said. For about an hour she would be smiling, and I looked forward to those moments of bliss. But as soon as she recovered, she was back to her old self which would leave me scurrying to do my last task of the day - scrub the front step. When the bucket full of black sludge was emptied down the open drain, my time was my own.

One Saturday, still in my nightdress, I entered the kitchen.

'No washhouse today, girl,' Mother said. 'There's not much washing anyway. Wiping her hands on her apron, she added, 'I've been invited to a party tonight. Do you fancy coming?'

No wonder she was being so nice. No washhouse indeed. I smiled.

It was hard to imagine Mother as insecure or shy, but she would never go to a party on her own. Now it is apparent she had the same sort of problems as me. If only she could have talked to me without being a closed book, we might have been so much happier.

My father would never go with her, so I was the next best thing. That was until she had made a grand entrance, then she would forget all about me, leave me to entertain the grannies and granddads, giving her a chance to mingle. She kept an eye on me though, and every now and then she would sniff my drink, making sure it was not alcohol. At that time there was no interest on my part to drink anything other than orange squash or lemonade. My taste changed over the years, but by then Mother had no say in my life.

At the parties, Mother would push herself forward, volunteer to make cakes or help with the cooking. She failed to see that the neighbours kept her at arm's length whenever a function was out of their comfort zone. She would make excuses for them when they sneaked off without telling her.

My father would warn her of her eagerness to please her friends, but the outcome was always the same. She would accuse him of being dull and insecure. He was never dull to me. In fact, he made me laugh, showing me all his dance moves and telling me funny stories about Mother.

The last party I had gone to with her had been bad enough. She had left me to clean up a sink full of dirty dishes. Now in an imaginary headlock because she was so desperate to go to the party and use me as her prop, she cleaned up herself. When her so called friends had consumed enough alcohol, they'd gather around her as if Mother was their blood relative and sing her praises while stuffing themselves with her food.

When shaking my hips, moving my shoulders and copying Father's flare of expression and rhythm, some would comment that I danced oddly. Those were the same people who thought they had the artistic creation of Ginger Rogers, when they had as much movement as a one-legged swan.

Mother didn't care about any of this as we headed to the latest party. The noise almost burst my eardrums when we entered the house. Children scattered like bats, stomping up the stairwell along the hallway and all exits, except the garden. That was reserved for the grownups, who transformed like two headed puppets into middle-aged woman trying to recapture taboos forbidden in their youth, fluttering their eyelashes at their pot-bellied husbands. They were almost ecstatic with merriment and performing grotesque dance moves. Some might need treatment for cracked bones or to hide behind closed doors for a couple of days. Even though the alcohol would disperse through the body, the embarrassment would linger on. As usual the girls were in groups, with a few boys dotted around. Polka dot dresses and net underskirts switched everywhere.

The boys who'd barely lost their choirboy voices stood awkwardly, holding glasses filled with fluorescent looking drinks and smiling at the giggling girls. If it was true that the world is a stage, I witnessed the greatest play of all time. Everyone, except me of course, was acting. Still amongst all the adult game playing, the little ones jumped around oblivious to the charade.

I cherished those hours dancing, drying tearful eyes and being surrounded by angels who shoved clumps of sticky cake in my mouth and laughed when cream, toffee and custard stuck to my hair.

Returning home with half-eaten sweets plastered on the back of my skirt, I sat alone in the kitchen, completely drained of energy.

9

Nearing the end of September, the nights were drawing in and the stars twinkled like polished jewels against black skies. The air was cold, but it hadn't penetrated the ground. This didn't stop me daydreaming of cosy nights around the fire preferably in someone else's house.

My wish for change was granted a week later when Mrs Richardson wrote, asking me to attend an interview. Convincing my parents it wasn't the other side of the world brought a minefield of emotions. First Mother surprised me with her tears, ones that would put a crocodile to shame. Then it was her soothing voice, with an edge of threat cleverly concealed. I laughed inwardly, knowing her Friday nights would never be the same and positive that Father saw my point of view. He sat quietly in the background until Mother rolled her eyes upwards in defeat.

Father gave me guidance on how to conduct myself in the interview and asked if he should accompany me.

'No, Father.'

For the first time, it would be me alone who would succeed or fail. It was my time to shine, but inside my nerves were getting the better of me and I kept pacing the floor to calm myself down.

I wasn't sure whether my father dabbed his eyes in sorrow of my looming departure or happiness that Mother might enjoy not having me around.

'Good luck, love,' he said, watching me walk down the steps and disappear around the corner.

The train journey taking me further away from the staleness of the city, gave an insight of what living in a rural area would be like. But it was on the bus which snaked along paths, where even hikers feared to tread, that the countryside was even more beautiful than I imagined.

The house, set back from a narrow lane, looked foreboding. Walking up the path, my legs began to shake. Managing to compose my nerves, I rang the bell. A slim-built woman opened the door.

'You're late,' she said, without looking at me. Continuing to mutter from what seemed like unmoving lips, she added, 'Come in, wipe your feet please.'

I watched the woman, who was the same slim shape from head to toe, walk briskly down the hallway. With one hand in the air, she beckoned me to follow. 'Put your coat there and go to the door on the right. I'll be with you shortly.'

Entering the cool room, painted in delicate primrose yellow with a polished sideboard angled against the main wall, I felt out of my depth. Afraid to sit on any of the chairs, I stood drinking in the grandeur of it all. Mrs Richardson swept in. Pulling out a leather chair, she gave me another quirky hand signal I assumed meant sit down. I sat with my hands folded in front of me.

Looking over the brim of her glasses, she said, 'You know there are two children. Jane the eldest who is eight and Tim is six.' She smiled, showing a row of shark-like teeth. 'They were born in South Africa, you know. I'm sure they remember little black Daisy, who proved her devotion to the children by her willingness to make herself available at all times.'

I'd heard of South Africa and saw the name on boxes of fruit. Confused about the connection between me, juicy red apples and a country so far away it might as well have been somewhere in space, I was brought back into the real world by the sound of Mrs Richardson's voice. 'They're a handful you know,' she said, tapping on the table. 'Do you think you can cope with them?'

'Yes, Mrs Richardson, I'm sure I can,' I replied, without thinking of the responsibility I'd agreed to. Now I felt scared but consoled myself quickly remembering the 'no experience necessary' on the application form. Mrs Richardson would have something in place if the situation of something like illness arose. 'I love children.'

'That is not relevant. My husband and I give the children all the love they need. Your job, my girl, is to see they come to no harm and tend to cuts and bruises. Most of all, have them tucked up in bed by seven thirty.'

My heart pounded, convinced Mrs Richardson wouldn't employ me and would rather give the job to someone like that Daisy who was always willing to please her employer.

Mrs Richardson sat without talking. Hands tucked under her chin, her eyes never left my face. 'Would you like some tea?' she asked, standing up.

'Yes please.'

She left the room.

Crossing my fingers, I hoped there would be no more questions to answer and I wouldn't be going back to Shakespeare Road as a failure, to hear Mother's condescending words of advice and 'I told you so' drama. I straightened my back against the chair and took deep breaths, hoping the exercise would calm me down.

Something shining and sparkling caught my attention. Tucked underneath some papers, a gold ring nestled underneath a folder.

Diverting my eyes helped take away the temptation to have a look and try it on. But the urge to have a look at the ring was becoming so strong my hand almost touched it, until an inner voice echoed a warning. Within seconds Mrs Richardson's footsteps trod lightly down the hall. She entered the room holding a tray and placed it on the table.

'Black or white?' she asked.

'White, please.'

'I can see you are a well-mannered young lady.' She picked up the folder and the ring and put them in a drawer.

She handed me a cup of tea. 'By the way my name is Ruth and my husband's name is Dennis. He is away most of the week in our factory in London. The weekend is his time with the children.' She bit into a biscuit. 'Only in the day though.' She wiped the corners of her mouth. 'We socialise quite a bit Friday and Saturday.' She cleared her throat and sipped her tea.

I tried to clear mine, but my saliva glands had dried up and inwardly my confidence yo-yoed from thinking positive, to sweat trickling down my back.

'I work full time,' Mrs Richardson said, clearing the table. 'In our own factory of course. It's an hour drive from here. My day starts early.' Leaning forward, she continued, 'So, I expect the children to be washed and dressed before I leave. Do you think you can manage the routine?'

Now I could feel my heart thumping against my ribs.

'And there will be housework, washing amongst other things. Can you do all that?' Almost jumping with relief anticipating the worst was over, I could only nod in reply.

'That's all I ask. Depending on references, you're hired.'

References could also include Mother and Father. My throat felt like it was closing over. Mother would struggle to say something nice. She'd certainly tell of the clothes scattered around my bedroom, and how she'd have to stand over me to make sure I'd wrung the floor cloth until my knuckles almost burst through my skin. Father, I felt, would emphasise my good points, because he only saw the finished product and he'd give the odd compliment, out of earshot of my mother. Mandy could be the friend.

'So,' Mrs Richardson said, 'depending on the references from your employer, you will start at the end of the month. Is there anything you want to ask me?'

With a sigh of relief on not having to rely on my parents or Mandy for a reference, I tried to remember what to ask. 'Wages,' blurted out before I'd had time to modify or phrase my words to sound professional.

'You will pay board and lodgings out of your wages. When I've decided how much to deduct. You will be told when you start work.'

My mind raced. 'I'll be living here with you?'

Drumming her fingers on the table she rolled her eyes. 'Where else would you live?'

The thought of being a lodger unnerved me.

'Don't think we're your parents Miss… Tobo. You will pay for things like meals and the use of my home.'

Without waiting to be reassured the same fate wouldn't happen to me, I presided to tell her the story of poor Mrs Lewis who was left on the streets in the middle of winter by a drunken landlord who wanted more money. Mrs Richardson yawned halfway through the tale. Standing up and pushing back her chair, she buried her fingers in her hair. 'You do understand, don't you?'

'Yes.'

Mrs Richardson who would be responsible for my rent and meals and the rest of my wages would be mine.

'I will be in touch', Mrs Richardson said. 'I will have a schedule of your duties soon.'

So happy with the warm handshake, I did everything but curtsy before leaving.

Back at home, I pushed open the front door and went into the kitchen. Mother had her hand in a bowl of water washing the dishes.

'Well, how did you get on?' Mother asked.

'Don't know yet,' I lied.

'If I were you, I wouldn't bank on it.'

I found my father whistling away as he swept in the backyard, his face bronzed in the evening sunshine and looking angelic. He was clearing dead leaves off the overhanging tree. I kissed him on the cheek and he asked how the interview had gone. I went into great detail of the events of the day, and he laughed loudly at all my interpretations of Mrs Richardson's mannerisms.

'Sounds like you have got it, love.' He ruffled my hair. 'Come on, let's have a cup of tea.'

We went indoors, arms around each other.

One week later, the chance to change my life came. Holding the letter from Mrs Richardson, my heart raced. She was definitely going to offer me the position and my start date was the end of the month.

My thoughts turned to Mandy. I would miss her laugh and jubilant sprit. She had changed me a little, because now I was looking ahead and leaving some of my negative traits in Shakespeare Road.

It felt like eating my last meal before being released from jail, the morning I was leaving. Both my parents sat quietly as we ate. It might have been shock or the odd chance Mother might have felt a pang of love, but she pecked me on the cheek. 'See you,' she said and scurried away.

My father's eyes were moist as he said, 'Take care of yourself, love. Are you sure you have enough money?

I assured him that I had enough cash and did not look back as I walked down the steps. If I had done, and rested my eyes on his face again, my employer might never have seen me.

Struggling with a holdall crammed with clothes, the October sun gleamed above as I walked up the steps of my new home. Mrs Richardson and her children met me at the door.

'Welcome,' she said, with a twitch of her top lip. It felt like a step into the unknown entering that house. For a few seconds the romantic view of living in Shakespeare Road came to mind but the reasons for leaving painted a grim picture. Two freckle-faced cherubs and Mrs Richardson walked towards the sitting room and opened the door. Spellbound, my eyes adjusted to the ivory and silver leaf wallpaper outlined in gold, as it glistened in the sunshine and dazzled me. Smiling and thinking how no amount of light could change my family's house, I thought of how even in the spring and summer months the tenants longed for the dark nights of winter that hid the defects. This house had nothing anyone would want to hide, certainty not the two overstuffed sofas nestled in front of a marble fire surround, which was already laid and protectively guarded by a fireguard. The duck egg blue paintwork and rich coloured rugs enhanced the cosiness and gave the room a luxurious ambiance, to feast the eyes and calm the spirit.

I smiled at the boy Tim, who was rubbing his hands together pretending to feel the heat from the unlit fire. With a cheeky grin, he moved the guard slightly as if goading his mother into scolding him.

'Tim!' Mrs Richardson snapped but Tim pretended

not to hear.

His sister Jane grabbed him by his jumper and marched him outside. He sat on the floor crying, with Jane standing over him watching for any sign of rebellion, or a hint he would defy her and scramble back into the room. Smiling inwardly, I wondered what it would be like if I had a younger brother. I'd be just like Jane I suppose, take the mother role. My life might have been different. Father would have a son and Mother would have me. Being an only child, I had to find a balance when sharing my affection. Was it the way Mother felt at me being close to my father or was it she just did not feel anything for me? Every time I thought the past was somewhere safe in my mind, it always reared its ugly head. Something as simple as two little children having a disagreement sparked my emotions.

We walked past the children as Mrs Richardson continued the tour of the house, leaving Tim snivelling in the capable hands of his sister.

'And this,' said Mrs Richardson, opening two large doors, 'is the kitchen-come-dining-room.'

I gaped at the range cooker with its polished chrome fixtures and the light wood kitchen cabinets lining glossy tiled walls. There was glass, porcelain and pottery containers filled to the maximum with grain, nuts, and spices from all over the world. It was the bowl of ripe bananas and mouth-watering pears that caught my attention and I was tempted to take a bite of any one of them. The desire soon passed when I remembered where I was.

Jane and Tim crept silently into the kitchen. Tim's tears had dried up but the twinkle in his eyes was still there, only now he was promising to behave. Mrs Richardson patted him on the head and smiled at Jane. Ahead of us, the children clambered up the stairs.

'This is my bedroom!' Tim yelled as he burst into the first room.

Mrs Richardson ignored Tim bouncing on his bed, closed his door and moved on down the hall, with Jane like a shadow following.

'This is your room, Bess.'

I liked it instantly. Putting the battered holdall on the bed, I lay beside it, sinking into the sprung mattress. I felt the pain of poverty, not envy. I had just left a house where my mother and father were fighting to live like the Richardson's. It was not apparent then if I was destined for rags or riches. One thing that etched on my mind was to try to be happy with either one.

Tim reappeared holding a little card in his hand. 'This is for you,' he said shyly, pushing the card into my hand. 'It's from Jane as well.'

'Thank you.' I studied the slightly bent cardboard and all the tiny stars that were carefully pasted in each corner. Both children sat beside me on the bed and pointed out who glued a particular section and who wrote the words of welcome. Mrs Richardson looked on. Her face softened for a few moments then returned to looking stern.

I wanted to hug the children, scoop them in my arms and shower them with kisses. But the sour expression on their mother's face changed my mind. Instead I thanked them again for their kind thoughts.

Then Mrs Richardson said, 'Right you two, let Bess settle in.'

Without protest the children stood up and walked to the door.

'Dinner will be around five o'clock,' Mrs Richardson said to me before leaving the room and closing the door behind her.

I quickly unpacked my clothes, carefully arranging creased, torn and Sunday best as neatly as possible in the wardrobe.

10

New habits needed to be formed, I told myself on my first day. I sat on the chair and waited until Mrs Richardson announced from the bottom of the stairs that dinner was ready. Hurriedly washing my hands, I took the first stairs two at a time, until I remembered myself. Then, like a lady, my feet stepped lightly on each stair.

As I settled down next to Jane, Tim's bottom lip started quivering. Smiling I assured him, 'I will change places every day.' He gave a toothy grin.

'Well,' he said flicking a crumb of bread at Jane. 'It's my turn tomorrow.'

Sitting at the table with the children made me realise what was missing in my life, that unmistakable family unity between siblings. Chewing on a piece of glazed carrot, the past somehow mingled with the sweet taste in my mouth. Yes, there were good and bad times in Liverpool. Now my life was better than my wildest dreams.

After we had eaten and cleared the table, the children helped with the washing up and Mrs Richardson was able to slip away unnoticed. I presumed she had office work to attend to. She only reappeared to give me a clock set for seven the next morning.

Rubbing her temples, she said, 'Would you turn the television off before you go to bed? We've had a long day, and my husband will be home tomorrow.' She kissed the children and outlined what tasks there were ahead of me. 'There will be a lot to do, Bess. My husband is quite a fusspot.'

It could not be worse than being hunched over a table full of coarse material that pealed the skin around my fingers until they bled. Or being shut away like a prisoner only to be let out at meal times. No, Mrs Richardson, I thought, hard work won't kill me. If it did, you would never have known me.

She checked her watch. 'Oh, bedtime can be a little later tonight we'll say eight o'clock. Your father rang. I said to call back tomorrow.'

I was not expecting the call, but I was sorry I missed it. For the first time since arriving, I missed my parents. I was thinking this as I sat in the sitting room with the children, who were wide-eyed watching a documentary about horses. I stared out the window looking at the darkness of the night sky and listening to trees rustling against the glass.

I tried to sit back in the armchair and find a comfortable position, only it didn't feel like I belonged there. Sitting amidst items that had been carved, painted or created as works of art, my black face stood out like a fly in a bottle of sterilised milk. Mrs Richardson would have to remember her magnificent home was like a stage to me, a setting only seen in my dreams. It would take a while for the fabric of my new world to embrace me.

The programme finished, and Tim darted towards the television set to change channels. I moved faster, turning it off with seconds to spare. 'Bath time!' I announced trying to sound grownup.

Both children tried the puppy dog look, followed by a short-lived flailing of arms and legs, then they turned on each other like rats squabbling over a piece of cheese. Determined not to become referee, I closed the curtains and switched off the lights as they both banged up the stairs.

'I'm a big girl now,' Jane said, closing her bedroom

door and narrowly missing the tip of my nose. 'I can bath myself.' She pointed to Tim. 'He still needs a nanny to bath him.'

I ran the bath and tested the temperature as Tim looked on. Helping him into a bath of water cold enough for his teeth to start chattering, prompted me to pluck him out. Adding more hot water and allowing him to test with his hand, I coaxed him to get back in. Tim disappeared underwater only surfacing for air and to see if I was still sitting on the edge of the bath.

Adding some sweet-smelling oils, I washed his hair with shampoo. It was while I was drying him in huge soft towels I remembered my own ones, coarse enough to grate skin.

After putting the children to bed, I ran my bath. It was my first experience of the sensation of soapy bubbles with the fragrance of jasmine oil. Finishing my bath, I climbed into bed and slept.

Opening my eyes, the sound of birds whistling startled me at first, but Mrs Richardson's shrill voice panicked me more. I grabbed the clock to stop the alarm from ringing before it smashed to the floor. Then inwardly laughing, I remembered the bare floorboards in my old room and swung my legs over the side of the bed, just to feel the soft fibres of the carpet in between my toes.

'I was calling you, Bess,' Mrs Richardson said, from the bottom of the stairs. 'In case you overslept.'

'Thanks.'

The morning passed without incident, until we stepped outside. Tim wrenched free from my grasp and happily skipped ahead, narrowly avoiding contact with a lamppost and anything in his way. He seemed to relish the fresh air, going wild with delight as the strong breeze carried him along. Jane walked serenely by my side. But

I could tell by the look on her face, outdoors was where she wanted to be. The children obviously hadn't experienced much freedom to explore.

Seeing Jane and Tim excited by something so natural inspired me to help keep their vision alive. It wouldn't fade once the front door was closed. I would teach them all my childhood games. They would dance, sing and play to their heart's content. The local park would be our starting point. If their parents had no objection to me sharing the best bits of my childhood with their children I'd be happy.

Returning to the house I heard the phone ringing. It was my father. I wanted to ask if they were missing me but decided not to pry.

'When will you be home, girl?' he asked.

'It won't be for a while. When I get a long weekend, I'll take you to town and buy you a new pipe.'

He laughed. 'Thanks, queen. I love you, girl.'

I hung on his word, love. I understood its power and what it meant to me. Not being able to see him for reassurance, the telephone was my lifeline.

Stammering I replied, 'S-so do I-I.'

'Take care of yourself,' he said.

'Okay, I must go now. See you soon.' Replacing the receiver, my eyes filled with tears. I longed for his reassuring arms of comfort and kindness.

The weeks that followed would be etched in my mind for ever. Jane and Tim fought like gladiators, almost scalping each other on a regular basis. I smashed a couple of china dinner plates, turned the Sunday roast into charcoal shavings and somehow managed to change the white items into a wine colour by not separating the clothes properly. Mrs Richardson didn't need fire coming from her nostrils to show her anger. Her lips drawn in a snarl, she suggested I take more care.

I wanted to tell her the truth.

Jane and Tim's behaviour always required my attention, with no time left to turn down the gas cooker or be attentive when sorting the washing. Allowing a red sock to hide in the white sheets as Tim was engulfed in foam sliding down the stairs was no fault of mine.

As their mother closed the front door that morning, Tim and Jane started snarling at each other. The catalyst for all-out war was when Tim kicked Jane in the shin. Jane bared her teeth as she lurched forward, grabbed the strap of his bag and drew him closer to his doom with each determined winch of stretched leather.

There was me, flailing arms, stood in the middle of them. It took coaxing and promises of sweets to stop them until, finally, coats, hats and both school satchels were strapped on, and I was able to shut the door. I walked to the school with the seemingly lovely children.

It was a ritual to be repeated daily, then it was weekly, monthly and stretched to half term. By then I was able to control the situation of inside fighting with one glance. I'd laugh inside when the bedlam switched to complete silence. The removal of their toys always won the day. I'd have them clinging onto dolls, cars, trains, tea sets and board games, or anything else I could get my hands on. I'd take them to my room and secure the booty in a locked wardrobe, vowing they'd never see them again until the kicking, hair pulling and screaming stopped

Dennis came home at the weekend. Before he'd turned off the ignition, Tim and Jane leapt into his arms. I stood in the background until Dennis, with a bouncing mane of chestnut brown hair, walked towards me. Extending his hand, he warmly greeted me.

'Hello, Bess,' he said, in a low reassuring voice.

By the time we sat down to our evening meal my anxiety had gone. The laughter and the glow on the children's faces told me happiness could be found in the house of reform. I could only grow and learn from these people. If I was willing to give my best to them, hopefully they would appreciate me.

11

After a few months, I noticed Mrs Richardson moped around the house when Dennis wasn't there. She'd become almost married to the cut glass decanter, holding it to the light of the window as if she was deciding whether to drink the alcohol or polish the perfectly crafted design. Upon deciding, she would pour the drink into a glass and gulp down the contents like water.

The doughnut shaped contraption which she wound around her hair was then snatched from the crown of her head. With precise movements, she brushed her tresses in front of the mirror until her hair fell wild around her shoulders. Wearing the skimpiest of skirts, she topped the outfit off with a pair of stilt-like shoes. She would ungracefully swan around from room to room, inspecting dust free corners and carelessly crumpled freshly ironed clothes.

Beginning to feel uneasy about my employer's behaviour brought me back to Shakespeare Road and Mother. Like Mrs Richardson, she would have spells of acting oddly and this made me wonder, was it a grown-up thing? Why can't people say when they are unhappy? It was different for me, but if I was married my feelings would not be bottled up.

Once the children were in bed, Mrs Richardson often asked me to join her. Being grateful for adult conversation, I'd gladly agree. Most times she'd be in the sitting room with a glass of gin in her hand. I'd settle in a seat, with a tumbler of juice and listen to her toneless voice.

Those times trying to block out Mrs Richardson's unimaginative chattering, I missed the hustle and bustle of Liverpool.

Here, I could hear myself breathing. Nothing happened to startle or interest me enough to look out of the window; no buses, no fights between drunken people on their way home. No soul. During the day everything seemed to come alive. It was the loneliness of the night which affected me. When Mrs Richardson said she was going to bed, I would happily walk up the stairs to my bedroom, climb into bed and pray for morning.

Six weeks before Christmas, I was looking forward to going home to spend some time with my parents and Mandy. Leaning in my chair listening to the radio, my mind flashed back to all the Christmases I'd known as happy ones.

I'd see my father have a sip of wine and convince himself he was drunk. Even mother's slash for a mouth managed the odd smile. Mostly the highlight was lying in bed on Christmas morning looking out at the snow-covered rooftops.

The telephone rang. A crackling sound followed by, 'Bess, is that you?'

'Yes, Mandy. It's me.'

'We're having a party on Saturday, are you still coming home? Can you pinch a bottle of booze?'

'No... No, I can't.' No one had ever asked me to steal. Mandy did not really mean for me to steal, I convinced myself. But I didn't want to lose my best friend or my job. I would buy a bottle.

Whenever the children were preoccupied with their parents playing board games or watching television cuddled up on the couch, it made me crave friendship more than ever. It would be nice to have someone who liked to watch Ready Steady Go and share a bag of popcorn.

When Dennis returned to work, Mrs Richardson was back performing like she was auditioning for a part in the musical Hair. I snapped at everyone that day, thinking of how I'd felt hours earlier, recalling the image of the Richardson's together as a family. Before my frayed nerves got the better of me, I yanked the children's coats off the banister.

'Let's go to the park.' They ran half way up the street before I caught up. Letting them run loose in the park, I sat on the grass. Keeping them in sight but letting them go far enough to feel free, I watched the sun high in the sky. Wrapped in my own world of nostalgia, an angry woman's voice made me jump.

'Are those two monkeys with you?'

'Yes, why?'

The young woman stood over me, almost shoving a snapped umbrella up my nostril. She had legs a stork would be proud of.

'Look what they've done!' She was pretty, but this was lost in her thick growling voice, which also didn't suit her carefully made up face and trendy clothes. The spikes of the umbrella bent around the frame.

Scrambling to my feet, I called the children. I watched as they changed position, trying not to be the first to face me.

'Who is the culprit? I asked firmly.

Jane pointed to Tim. 'He did it. I tried to mend it.' Both children apologised, and Jane began to cry.

'I will deal with you both when we get home.' I turned to the woman. 'I am so sorry. I will replace it.'

Jane's sobbing softened as the woman's attitude changed. 'There is no need.'

'Will you be here tomorrow?' I inquired.

'I can be.'

'I will meet you here at four thirty. What's your name?'

'Abigail.'

'Mine's Bess.'

After an awkward silence she walked away.

The rain lashed down the next day. With one umbrella keeping me dry and the other tucked under my arm, I walked to the park. Abigail was there sheltering under a tree. The bottom half of her dress was soaked with rain.

'Well, give me the bloody thing!' she snapped.

I handed it over.

'Thanks,' she said, opening up the umbrella. 'I must admit it's nicer than my other one.' As we stood in silence a bolt of lightning flashed across the sky.

'Get under the tree for Christ's sake!' Abigail shouted. 'We could be struck standing in the open.'

Before long we were deep in conversation, mainly about music, boys and going out. At last I'd found someone who listened to Radio Luxemburg and knew nothing of the Archers.

'Do you like dancing?' I asked.

'Love it,' she replied.

She reminded me of Mandy. It was the way she threw her head back when she laughed. Her eyes looked sad but kind.

'Smoke?' she asked, taking out a packet of cigarettes.

I shook my head. 'No, thanks.'

She lit up and blew smoke through her nose. 'Hope you're not one of those goody goodies.'

'No,' I said awkwardly. 'I have my moments.'

'Like what?' she laughed. 'Bunking in the pictures?'

'Something like that,' I replied, smiling. The rain began to trickle and then it stopped. Abigail put up her umbrella and stepped from under the tree.

'Do you want to?'

'Yes,' I managed to reply. 'I would.'

Scratching a telephone number on the edge of a cigarette packet, she tore it off and handed it to me.

'I'm off,' she said, and was gone before I looked up from staring at the number. I held the piece of cardboard as though it was gold dust that could blow away with the slightest change of atmosphere. Reaching home, I skipped up the stairs to my bedroom and put the number away.

Mrs Richardson put the children to bed early that night, informing me as she ran down the stairs that she was going out. Slamming the door behind her, she stepped into a waiting car. Peeping in on the sleeping children, I saw Tim was asleep clutching a toy gun in his hand with a cowboy hat on his head. Smiling, I removed Tim's toys and placed them at the bottom of the bed.

Jane was curled up with a teddy bear that looked as though it had been hit in the eye with a bullet, a gaping hole and a wad of cotton wool poking through the socket. Silently tiptoeing to my room, I closed the door on the night.

12

I rang Abigail the next day, after asking Mrs Richardson for permission.

'Don't be long!' she called out just as Abigail picked up.

'Who's that old cow?' Abigail giggled.

Embarrassed by her remark, I didn't answer. Instead I began to explain I'd be away for the weekend, but I would like to meet up with her soon.

'Okay,' Abigail piped. 'See you when you get back.'

It was Christmas Eve when I saw her again. Doubling back to the pastry shop I was walking past, I peered in the window. My eyes weren't playing tricks. It was Abigail sitting there. She looked glamorous in a short skirt and a shocking pink jumper to match.

Glancing down at my own skirt hanging limply around my legs, I sighed. Enviously craning my neck to see her shoes convinced me that Abigail hadn't borrowed them from her mother or aunt. Her painted lips and matching nail varnish glistened like fluorescent lights.

Abigail turned her head as I knocked on the window. At first she screwed up her eyes, but then she leapt from her seat and ran into the street and caught hold of my arm.

'Why didn't you ring?' she asked, leading me into the cosy tea room. Before I'd removed my coat, she was at the counter and returned with a mug of coffee.

'Thanks.' I sipped my drink.

'So,' she said, 'did you go home?'

'Yeah,' I replied. My weekend had been a disaster. I'd foolishly assumed Mother's erratic behaviour might have improved, or at least her mood swings would have been less lengthy. And by the time I'd arrived at Mandy's, the party had been in full swing. I was too tired and sat in the corner, thinking of how I would enjoy the Sunday train journey back to the work.

'You going back for Christmas then?' Abigail asked.

'No.' My mind was made up on that.

Christmas flew past and spring came early that next year. The sun seemed to kiss the flowers, opening their petals and bringing them alive.

Abigail and I met regularly in the park and would sit on the grass and talk. The gruffness of her voice could not disguise how caring she was. I would laugh when she said, 'I hope old snooty arse is not working you too hard.' She never commented on how I dressed, like Mandy did, but she thought I should treat myself to some new clothes.

'You need some makeup on that gob of yours as well,' she laughed. 'Next time you have a day off we will go and buy some. You have lovely skin, Bess, make the best of it.'

It was a compliment that made me blush, imagining myself wearing lipstick and getting admiring glances, like Abigail did.

The following week I met Abigail in the park again. She suggested we buy the makeup before we had a cup of coffee. There were no guidelines then, to the shades best suited for dark skin. Abigail chose a colour between a murky beige and red pepper, then she matched it with a light blue eyeshadow and a lipstick that would look like I'd eaten a box of oranges. A black pencil was the last thing the shop assistant put into a bag and handed it to me. We spent the rest of the day window shopping and Abigail telling me about how she had her own room.

'Next time when old misery guts pays, would you like to go and buy some new clothes? Afterwards I'll take you to mine.'

'I'd like that.'

A few weeks later, we sat in a snack bar with the sound of coffee being violently shaken into a frothy mass.

'I had to get away from my mam and all six of her squawking kids,' Abigail revealed. 'So, one day I just walked out. Got myself a job and now I'm happy.'

I didn't intend to delve any deeper and she gave no more details of her life. The pain of leaving home was etched on her face.

Wanting to open up and tell her something about myself would only overwhelm her. She did not need to hear the confusing details of my life. She needed someone to cheer her up. Telling her all about my interview with Mrs Richardson had her laughing. The sadness in her eyes was gone and her smile was back.

Returning home to the privacy of my room, I unzipped my bag. I opened the compact and lightly brushed my cheek with powder. With pouting lips ready to apply the lipstick, my heartbeat quickened with the sound of Mrs Richardson's voice.

'Dinner is on the table, Bess.'

Shoving everything in the top drawer I shouted that I was coming.

The children sat facing each other at the table.

'Did you have a nice day off?' Mrs Richardson asked.

'Where did you go?'

'Just for a bus ride.'

She might prefer the children's nanny to be fresh-faced, simply dressed and quiet in manner, but a change was coming. Brimming with my secret hopes and expectation, I focussed on my next day off.

The following Saturday I was up early. I was washed and dressed before anyone else. Pulling on my skirt, a jumper and a coat, I tiptoed down the stairs. Too early to meet Abigail, I took the bus going in the opposite direction of the town centre, to the countryside.

It took over an hour before the bus returned to the depot. Getting off the bus, I could see Abigail in the distance. I waved and shouted her name until she saw me.

She towered over me in her stepladder shoes. We crossed the main road to reach the market, holding our noses as we neared the fish stalls. The ones with the latest fashions caught my eye. A short skirt to show off my legs was what I chose, with a blouse as sheer as a pair of nylon stockings. Looking at Abigail's shoes, I thought about how I could easily balance on the spiked heels. It couldn't be any harder than learning to ice skate. Without any hesitation, I tried on a pair of black pointed shoes that had heels as high as Mandy's.

Stepping lightly on a broken paving stone, I took no notice of Abigail's lack of enthusiasm. I tried to convince myself that it wasn't a deterrent when I wobbled.

'I'll have this as well,' I said, picking up a matching bag.

'Will you be here next week?' Abigail asked the market stall holder.

'Yes, love. Same time same place.'

Finishing my shopping spree with a combination of wooden bangles, glittering headbands and chains of flowers, I gave a satisfied look at Abigail. She rolled her eyes and lit a cigarette.

'Shall we go to your flat now?' I asked.

'It's not a flat. It's a bedsit.'

It didn't matter if it was a cave. A fashion parade, playing records and maybe have a drink would be ideal. Walking towards the house with Abigail emphasising how it looked like Dracula's mansion while I peeked at my new clothes, her talk fell on deaf ears.

'Here it is.'

I lifted my head to see the house, like a giant statue, stood in front of me.

'There's my room…well, bedsit. Right at the top.'

I felt like a midget entering the hall. Clip-clopping on the tiled floor, I expected to see mushrooms growing on the walls. I could smell something that I recognised - it was Shakespeare Road.

We climbed the stairs and looked down at the floor below the grimy panes of glass on the front door.

'Ready to reach the summit?' Abigail laughed.

She was right to laugh. It was the climb of my life. Half-way to the top we rested. My mouth was open. I was gasping for oxygen and dreading the next flights of stairs. I hoped that she would have a big armchair with plenty of cushions I could snuggle into. She'd serve ice cold, lemonade and serenade me with the latest pop records.

'This is mine!' Abigail announced turning the key and opening the door.

I entered the dungeon in the sky with some apprehension. The curtains were hanging like torn ship masts and almost reached the bottom of the ten-inch skirting board.

With a mocking grin Abigail said, 'You can sit on the best seat in the house.' She pulled out a battered wicker chair and pushed it towards me. Plastering the thick foundation and powder over my face, she twisted the lid of the blue eyeshadow and smoothed the powder over my quivering eyelids. Gently rubbing high over the brow, she stood back to admire the result and reached for the eye pencil. I gave a piercing screech as the pencil made contact with my eye.

'For fuck's sake!' she snapped. 'Keep still and stop fluttering your eyes.' Another attempt to draw a straight line failed.

'I've gone too far down,' she hissed. Rubbing, smudging and blending the pencilled area, finally she said, 'That's perfect now.'

She painted my lips with orange lipstick. 'Now kiss the tissue and lick your lips.' She studied me carefully. 'Before you look at yourself, you could try on your new clothes.'

Taking her advice, I put on the skirt, blouse and stilettos.

'Now walk from the kitchen back to the living room,' Abigail said.

The catwalk felt more like an old tomcat's walk. Stumbling on the stiletto heels, I tried to balance without holding onto the table. Abigail dragged a full-length mirror from under the bed. I opened my eyes. When I looked at Abigail she was holding her sides laughing hysterically at the sight of me with one foot pointing south and the other foot twisted inwards and the blouse hanging limp around my shoulders. The worst was my face, painted as though it was a dereliction of war. When the laughing stopped, I took off the clothes.

Abigail put on a pan of water, filled a small bowl and handed it to me.

'Here,' she said, 'I need all that crap. You don't.'

I washed away my fantasy.

Reverting back to what felt comfortable, I combed my hair but couldn't resist adding a faint touch of lipstick. I slung all the other cosmetics in the bin but kept the jewellery.

'We will take the things back next week. Get your money back and buy something that suits you!' she shouted from the kitchen.

'I won't be here, I'm going home.'

'I'll take them back,' Abigail replied.

I smiled to myself, remembering Abigail's question to the stallholder. 'Will you be here next week?' She must have had a premonition that my new look was going to be a disaster.

It was a lesson learnt the hard way. Trying to be like everyone else was harder than being individual. Yet the easy and most enjoyable part was the journey of discovery. I'd thought I'd look like a princess when in reality a court jester stared back at me. It didn't matter. A friend had shared those moments.

13

Soon after becoming friends with Abigail, I met Slim. Mandy had convinced me to go to a local club with her when I went home for the weekend, and being desperate to get out of Shakespeare Road, I'd agreed.

You Give Me Fever was playing on the radiogram. My heart leapt as his dark brown eyes, long and slanted, met mine. He was dancing with a woman a lot older than me, holding her close as they swayed to the music.

I felt special that night. Mandy had leant me one of her off the shoulder blouses, which took the emphasis off my drab pleated skirt. A hint of red lipstick gave me confidence.

Mandy was standing behind me. 'Stop drooling over him, he's mine.'

'So, he's your feller then?'

'Not exactly.' She took a swig from her glass. 'I'm with his friend but he is going back to the States soon so…' she laughed. 'I'm on the lookout.' Mandy was always telling me about the men she liked, so, ignoring her comment, I continued to stare at Slim. I watched him move his hips to the music and admired the way his head was the same height as the light.

I let the thick wine slide down my throat before Mandy told me a couple of glasses would make me tipsy. It didn't take long for me to feel the effect. Tipsy felt good and I wondered what three glasses might do.

Slim came over. 'Hello, you need to go easy on that stuff.'

I wanted to shout, I'm doing it for you. I'm sick of being a girl, like Mandy is always telling me I am. I want to be a woman like her. But instead I pulled Mandy up to dance.

'You drunk?' she asked.

Throwing my head back. 'Yes,' I said. 'With love.'

'Stop talking shit, you soft cow.' She twirled me around.

It didn't matter what she said, I wanted Slim to notice me. I pouted my lips trying to look sexy, and it worked. Slim smiled.

Picking up the glass, I poured another drink. I was hoping it would make me appear older, but forgot wine stopped me thinking rationally. It was like all my dreams had come at once. Feeling glamorous, my shyness had disappeared, and I could step outside of being Bess for tonight at least.

Slim walked towards me. 'Wanna dance baby?' In seconds I was in his arms. No one had ever held me so close. I'd never experienced a man's hot breath in my ear.

Slim whispered that he liked me. I danced closer and he responded. Something happened to me that night. Between my wish to explore and Slim's warm sensuous lips on my neck, I wanted to feel his mouth, have his hands roam over my body, grasping at that secret place. The heat of his body so close to mine, meant my feet hardly touched the ground.

Suddenly, like a long-playing record had stopped, I felt dizzy. All I remembered was Slim catching me before I hit the floor. He stayed with me until I recovered my senses. Mandy was too busy dancing to worry about me.

When I was able to stand without toppling over, he asked if I wanted to go home.

Yes, home was the safest place. Never before in my

life had I thought of Shakespeare Road as my sanctuary. But tonight I wanted to be under the same roof as my mother and father.

Slim draped my cardigan over my shoulders and walked with me to the main road. He hailed a taxi and took me home.

'You got a phone, honey?' he asked.

I jotted the phone number down and handed it to him. He kissed me, and the taxi sped off.

When I walked up the steps and turned the key with some trepidation, the door opened. Thankfully nothing stirred within. I stepped on the wrinkled carpet, digging my heels into the grooves for support, crept to my room and hobbled to the bed and criticised myself for drinking so much. That was until I remembered the thrill of meeting Slim again.

I returned to the Richardson's a few days later.

Mandy rang as I stepped through the door. Mrs Richardson, hovering in the hallway, made some remark on the amount of calls. 'An American rang asking for you yesterday. I told him you were not available.'

'You coming over at the weekend?' Mandy asked.

'No,' I lied. 'I'm babysitting.'

Mrs Richardson was staring at me, so I put the receiver down and got on with my chores.

She wasn't at home the next time Slim rang. He told me where to meet him, at a house tucked away in a side street not far from Mandy's.

'It's number ten, don't be late, honey,' said Slim down the phone.

'I won't.'

The gold leaf brocade curtains slightly drawn together,

shimmered under the streetlight when I tapped twice on the window. Slim opened the door. He stood with the hall light behind him, holding a bottle of beer.

With no preconceptions of love and marriage on my mind, Slim being in the American Army and not a boy next door, a mixture of basic ignorance and not seeing further than my nose, for that night and the time after with him, I lived in the present.

14

Two months later, the past came back making me wish the blackout I'd experienced after the party had been permanent. My period was late.

I could feel the nip as autumn beckoned. The smell of dying flowers, limp with water, stems breaking and rotting in their coffins of soil, hung on the wind. Even though I wrenched at the smell of food, the garden became my sanctuary.

I never wanted what was growing inside me. It was happening without my consent, I consoled myself. There was no looking in mirrors to admire any expansion of my stomach. I was afraid to face the consequences. I was haunted by tales of young pregnant mothers being shut away in homes and babies taken from them. I was scared out of my wits about Mother knowing my dirty secret, as she would be the one to take me to the home herself.

Wondering what my father would say made me physically sick. Mother would take the reins and lead him in her direction, and he would follow.

I only saw Slim a few weekends after he'd changed my life. He would invite me to the odd party that I convinced myself were dates. I managed to keep my pregnancy secret, but my baby's fate was sealed. Just before the third month Mrs Richardson found me thrashing around the bed in pain.

Blood soaked bedding lay all around me, as I tried scrambling from the horrifying scene. Panicking from the pains engulfing my body, I cried out in despair. My screams had stirred Mrs Robinson.

Rolling me gently to the other side of the bed, she slipped the sheet from beneath me. In silence, she disposed of everything and took away a part of me that I would never hold.

Returning to my side, she handed me a clean nightdress and then changed the sheets. 'The bleeding has stopped now,' she assured me. 'There is no need for a doctor. You have lost the baby, Bess. Shall I contact your parents?'

Still weak from the shock of what I'd experienced, I managed to whisper, 'Please don't.' In the stillness of the night and the glow of my bedside lamp, Mrs Richardson looked angelic. Her soothing voice, without any haughtiness and stiffness, was kind and gentle. She straightened the pillows behind my head. 'I'll make you a cup of drinking chocolate, Bess. You rest, I won't be long.' Closing the door she left the room.

I had mixed emotions, but gratitude that no one but Mrs Richardson would know what happened that night. I would always remember the life I'd wished to be rid of. The tears flowed for my baby.

Mrs Richardson returned with my hot drink and left me alone with my thoughts. As much as I tried to block out what happened, the guilt flooded back in my mind. Not telling someone and hiding my pregnancy must have done something to my child. My stomach was constantly in knots and the fear was overwhelming. After falling into a fitful sleep, the next morning brought no closure to the ache in my heart.

Nothing seemed to go well for me after that night. The input with the children became rarer. Mrs Richardson piled more and more domestic duties for me to adhere to and talked of employing someone else to help with my role as nanny.

'Will you come into the dining room, Bess?' she said one morning. It was the day the children would usually go to the park with me. I had been making sure all my duties were done, and I was about to put on the children's coats.

Her forehead was wrinkled and creased with frowning. She slapped a piece of paper on the table. 'This is the amount of phone calls you have had over the last four months from undesirable people.'

Feeling stunned at her actions, but not forgetting she had been so good to me by keeping my secret and looking after me, I said nothing.

'Bess, I do not want my children to be cared for by someone with low morals. It would be in everyone's interest if you leave.'

I knew it was not her being spiteful. It seemed I'd rocked most people's view at the time: children should come after marriage. I'd shaken her own romantic notion of love and marriage. Mozart should be playing in the background with Champagne corks popping, heralding the joining of hands in holy matrimony and babies should be conceived on feather beds. To her, I was no longer innocent, just someone who hadn't learned the rules of love, only the need.

Heartbroken, I went to my room and packed all my clothes ready for my fate. I felt numb for the days to follow. Trying to keep my distance from the children was the hardest part. I had no thoughts of returning to Shakespeare Road because my mind was empty.

I could feel Mrs Richardson's sorrow when she dismissed me. Her lips were unsmiling, but the sadness in her eyes brought tears to my own. Handing me my wage packet, she said, 'I've paid you up to date, Bess. Take care of yourself.'

I rang Abigail from the station and promised to visit as soon as I could. The train ride back to home filled my heart with dread, in contrast to the bright morning when I started my new job. Now the rain lashed against the train windows. I was returning to Liverpool in defeat. Instead of moving forward in life, I was going back to the darkness.

'Coming, girl!' Father shouted, fiddling with the lock as I waited outside the door. Shocked at his appearance, my instinct was to put my arms around him, but he looked so frail I kissed him lightly on his forehead.

'What's the matter?' he asked, seeing my crumpled face. He spoke as though his voice had to travel through a twisted windpipe.

'You don't look too well. What's wrong?' Both our questions overlapped. I wanted his answer first. Mine could wait. Father was in trouble.

'Oh, it's nothing, girl, just something to do with my old ticker. He shuffled along the hall. 'Let's have a cupper before moaning Minnie comes in.'

I was panicked by the thought of him dying. Would he be frightened? Trying to put negative thoughts about Father's health to one side, I kissed him again.

Picking up my case, I followed him - back into the past which was to become the present again, gift-wrapped by my own foolishness.

Yet as I watched my father's bent back taking baby steps and not his usual stride, a feeling of compassion came over me.

'Here she comes,' he warned as Mother's heavy footsteps thumped up the hall. Shaking out her rain-soaked coat, she regarded me. 'Been sacked, have you?'

I didn't want to deal with her at that moment. 'I'll stay

in Mandy's, but I'll come and see Father when I can,' I replied, gathering my things.

'By the way,' Mother said. 'Why have you come back?'

I wanted to be flippant and say I'd been sacked but instead I told her, 'They're moving back to South Africa.'.

Father's eyes rolled helplessly, swimming around glistering membrane. 'You going to be okay, girl?' Looking over his shoulder, he shoved five pounds in my hand. 'Don't tell your mother, girl. I'll give you a few bob next week.' He managed to wink at me, but his smile did not make his eyes twinkle. They looked tired and sad.

It was an odd feeling walking back down the steps. I was free but there was a safety net. As bad as Mother was, I knew the door would always be open if I chose to return, even if this was only because she would have an extra pair of hands. I just hoped to God I would never need to go back.

I suppose Father convinced himself I was just staying in Mandy's for a bit. It was not unusual for me to spend the night there and return the next day. What he didn't grasp was that my departure was permanent.

15

The rain started as I jostled my way down Smithdown Road to reach Upper Parliament Street. Slipping through the side streets, I reached Mandy's house and banged on the door. Through a small window, I could see Mandy moving down the badly-lit passage. Her shadow sleeked across the wall.

'Who is it?'

'It's Bess. Open the door! I'm wet though.'

The door squeaked open.

'What the bloody hell has happened?' asked Mandy.

I stepped inside, shaking out what seemed like a million raindrops trapped in my curly hair,

Mandy, uncharacteristically, helped with my bag. By the time I'd removed my coat, the smoke-encrusted kettle had been placed on the fire. Burying the knife deep into a crust of bread, she cut four slices and dug a long steel fork into the soft dough and toasted the first slice.

The flame of the fire licked at the bread until it was brown and crispy, enough to soak up a thick layer of margarine. I was so hungry that every bit of toast was eaten, even though it was covered in soot. As Mandy handed me a long-awaited drink, she asked why I'd left.

'The family are moving.' I kept up the same lie.

She did not need to know the mechanics of what happened to force me back to Liverpool. She would never understand how heartbroken and disgusted I felt. Losing my job was bad enough, but it was as though I'd left part of me behind. If only I was like Mandy, who wouldn't turn into a quivering mess whenever the wheels of life changed course.

There I was sitting in someone else's house being ousted by my mother without a hint of resistance on my part. If that's not being a coward, what was? No, the blame had to be with me. I was too afraid to stand up and be counted.

Mandy was too busy painting her nails to ask questions. All she wanted to know was how much money I had. Blowing on her manicured masterpiece as the clock struck twelve and pointing to the couch she announced, 'I'm off to bed, kid. You can sleep on that thing.'

I wanted to close my eyes to the events of the day and wake up to find it was all a dream. Rolling a makeshift pillow with my jumper and skirt, my eyes closed but my mind was alert to every sound.

The next morning Mandy poked her head around the door before entering. 'You awake?' she inquired, pushing the door wide enough to slip through. Picking up the poker, she scattered the ashes. 'Did you manage on the couch?'

'Just about.'

As soon as I get this fire going,' Mandy said, rolling up some old papers, 'we'll have a cuppa. Your feller is in town, he asked about you.'

It felt like a stab in my heart when she mentioned Slim. Everything came flooding back: my baby, the Richardson's, my lovely bedroom and Abigail. Holding back the tears and sitting upright on the couch, I watched Mandy clear the ashes. She made the tea and handed me a cup.

'Can I ask you something personal about your plans?' she said.

'Go... on.'

She walked towards me with a glint in her eyes and

threw my bag at me. 'When are you getting up?'

Ducking to avoid it, I jumped out of my comfort zone.

'The kitchen's free now. There's a flannel and bowl under the sink, don't forget to put the latch on the door,' said Mandy, smiling. 'We can go to the club tonight to see if Slim is there.'

The sun was setting as we walked through the dusty streets on the way to the club. Mandy's fish-tailed skirt emphasised her toned shape.

'What else did he say?' I asked.

'Who?'

'Slim of course.'

Screwing up her face she replied, 'He just asked how the heifer is.' She laughed. 'No, he didn't. We had a dance that's all.'

I'd heard Mandy always danced with Slim and he was often seen whispering in her ear, calling her a sexy momma. She'd laugh and snuggle closer to him. Somehow Mandy teasing Slim didn't bother me. It was her way of getting attention. Reaching Upper Parliament Street, Mandy fussed with her hair and constantly asked if she looked okay.

'For the umpteenth time, you look great,' I told her.

With little money in our pockets, we walked past the parked cars and up the steps of the club. The owner, who looked half asleep, eyed us as we stepped into the lobby. He snapped open the hatch and sucked his teeth as we walked past him. We found two empty seats in an alcove.

Mandy went to the bar, returning with two bottles of Brown Ale and two glasses. We sipped our drink. With a good view of the stairs, we could see Slim when he came in. Mandy slid her glass towards me as the tall handsome man she'd been ogling pulled her on the dance floor.

Slim appeared next to us. I could see him brush against Mandy, who had her arms locked around the man's neck and seemed oblivious to Slim's presence. He pretended not to see me until Mandy returned to the table.

'Hi, babe,' he eventually said, with his eyes firmly glued on Mandy's bare legs. The air was hot and stifling with blue cigarette smoke almost hiding the crowd. Mandy was up dancing again and I felt isolated until Slim said, 'Want a drink, sugar?

'Yes.' I thought he'd wanted me in his arms and would lead me onto the dance floor, but he handed me the money to buy the drinks.

'I've changed my mind. I don't want one,' I said.

Slim disappeared to the other side of the room. Mandy returned and sat next to me. 'Don't worry about somewhere to stay you know, Bess. You can stay at ours for as long as you want.'

With no job and therefore unable to contribute anything towards household bills, I considered returning to Shakespeare Road for a second, but then You Give Me Fever started playing on the jukebox. Mandy pulled me onto the dancefloor. Slim was dancing with his arms around another woman. It was like a scene from the past. Slim performed the same actions, the only difference was his partner.

'That woman dancing with Slim is no Rita Hayworth,' Mandy said, twirling me around. 'She looks more like Old Mother Riley to me.'

I don't remember if it was the word Mother or old which disturbed me. Was that how Slim saw me? Maybe not old in looks, but old news to him. I stumbled forward as Mandy gave me the last spin and fell into a crying heap in her arms.

'For fuck's sake, everyone is looking at us,' said Mandy, escorting me back to my seat with Slim at our heels. The more she tried to calm me down the more I wailed.

'This is all I need,' I heard Slim say as Mandy led him to my side. 'Some old broad playing the arse and making a show of me.'

'Come on, girl. Pull yourself together,' said Mandy.

'Do you know what?' I said. 'I don't care. I have lost more than you know.' I pointed at Slim. 'He doesn't even want to know me.'

The club owner looked like he was on skates as he charged over to us. 'You come in here looking for men. Get the fuck out before I throw you out.' He began to drag the empty chairs away from the table.

'It's okay, man,' Slim butted in. 'They're with me.' Slim shuffled his feet with a look of concern as the club owner's face settled into a rubbery mask twisted with bitterness.

Taking my arm, Slim led me towards the door calling the man a motherfucker under his breath.

'I'd like to rip that motherfucking bully's heart out,' Slim growled between clenched teeth and one hand jammed into his trouser pocket. 'If I draw this knife he'd call the military police and get my arse thrown in jail. Fuck him, he's nothing but a fool.'

I was scared. Knives. Jail. I shuddered.

'Look, man,' Slim was struggling to keep the explosive edge in his voice under control. He pointed to Mandy. 'Let her stay. We'll go outside.'

Grudgingly, the owner agreed. 'No more trouble, you hear me?' Then he turned to Mandy. 'She's not sitting in here without buying more drinks.'

Fishing in his pockets, Slim handed over some money to her. 'Here you are, honey. Buy whatever you want.'

As we were leaving the club I heard the owner talking. 'These fucking black people born in England are no fucking good. Them don't know what hardship is, man.' The other man shook his head in agreement.

The night air, damp and murky, didn't help the situation. I felt hot and unclean as the sweat seemed to be coming out of every pore. Still crying, I asked Slim if he wanted to be with me.

Lighting a cigarette, he inhaled and then looked at me. 'Of course I want to be with you, baby. Mandy can tell you how I feel about you. I don't want to fool you, but I'm in the military.'

'I know.' I wondered where this was leading.

'I'm far from home, miles away from the problems I've left behind. I just want some fun. You understand?'

I told him about the baby, my words tumbling out. For a moment I saw sadness in his eyes. But his attitude changed when he heard my job as a nanny no longer existed. He asked what he could do.

'I want to be with you, Slim.'

He shuffled his feet. 'Baby doll, you know I am only in Liverpool at weekends. The landlady won't rent to a woman, you know how it works, babe?'

I didn't. I wanted to walk away and leave him in peace, but something in his eyes told me he liked me. Clinging to the hope he'd help me, any self-respect I had was left on the pavement. Without saying a word, I was pleading for his support and unconsciously begging for his pity.

'Okay, I'll talk to the landlady. See if something can be worked out. I'll tell Mandy you're staying with me tonight.' He raced up the steps and disappeared into the club.

16

A face appeared at the window as Slim fiddled with the lock. 'Shit, the old bat is still up.'

The door flew open and the landlady, ready with her house rules, blocked the way. She stared at me. 'Slim, this is a respectable house and female visitors are not allowed after ten.'

'I know big momma, but she's my girlfriend.'

'Mrs Polanski,' said Slim, keeping his voice low and seductive. 'I swear on the holy bible she's my girlfriend.

The landlady's beady black eyes twinkled in the shadow of the light. 'Make this the last time. You won't be able to sweet talk me again.' Her face softened as the door opened wide enough to slip through

'Okay.'

'Did you bring the usual, Slim?' she asked.

'Yes, it's in my room. I guess it's better to talk business tomorrow.'

'Alright, leave it until the morning.'

Almost every article in Slim's room was transportable, from the transistor, to a plastic suit holder hanging on the door. When the distinctive rumble of my empty stomach became embarrassing, food was the only thing on my mind. Pulling out drawers and looking in cupboards searching for something to stop my craving, I asked, 'Don't you eat?'

'There's candy and crackers to eat, honey.' He held a paper bag he'd taken from his suitcase,

Sitting on the only chair in the room with the salted

crackers and the nut filled bar moulded together in my mouth, I crunched and munched until they were gone. Puffing on a cigarette, Slim watched me eat.

'Honey, I love the way your eyes, as well as mouth, enjoy eating,' he said, pouring a glass of Thunderbird. He handed me a glass and fixed another one for himself. After this, he lay down on the bed. 'Come over here, sweet thing. Lie beside me and give me some loving.'

I avoided his request by asking where the bathroom was.

'Up the hall on the left, baby. Hurry back. I'm waiting for your sweet kisses.'

I needed to freshen up because Slim looked immaculate against the grey blankets. Before leaving the room, I took a bar of soap from his overnight bag. I crept down the landing. I was looking forward to washing away any trace of perspiration caused by the trauma of the last few hours.

Slim was naked and the overhead interrogation light was off when I got back. There was just a bedside lamp with a bulb no bigger than a fairy light casting ghost-like shadows on the wall. The atmosphere was a mixture of secret thoughts and desires.

'Oh baby,' he murmured, as his fingers searched from the nape of my neck to my breast, swollen and taunt from his caress.

My lips brushed against his ear, whispering how I'd missed him. I felt him slipping something onto his private parts. Afterwards, in the darkness, I could hear his shallow breathing and hoped he would not forget his promise to speak to the landlady.

Opening my eyes to a new day, the bottles clinked together as Slim tried to retrieve the holdall from under the bed.

'I'm going downstairs to see the old bat,' said Slim, dragging the heavy bag. 'Come with me if you want.'

We knocked on her door. 'Who's that?' the sleepy voice inquired. 'I'm in bed.'

'Big momma, it's me.

'Me who?'

'I have your booze here.'

'Wait there, let me put some clothes on.' There was a coughing spasm before Mrs Polanski shuffled to the door and appeared in full view with pipe cleaners in her hair and a cigarette hanging from thin lips.

'Come in, excuse the mess.' She checked the bottles. 'How much do you want this time?'

'Mrs Polanski, you're like a mom to me. I have received my pay check early this month. So those bottles, of finest, and I mean the finest bourbon, are yours free of charge.' He then picked up the drinks as though he was about to change his mind. 'But I need something in return.'

I could have sworn she pulled her dressing gown together when she asked what it was he wanted.

'It's my girlfriend, she has nowhere to live.'

'So?'

He looked into her large staring eyes. 'Would you let her stay in my room?'

Before she had the chance to answer, Slim pulled out a roll of notes. 'Look, I can even pay the rent in advance.'

'Slim, you know the rules.'

'I know, Big Momma, but Bess is a great gal. She has few friends and she would be company for you.'

Who in their right mind would want me as a friend? I thought. But I said nothing.

'Okay, she can stay. The rent will be three pounds a week and I want two weeks rent in advance.' She wagged her finger. 'She must keep the place clean. The stairs and landings must be brushed and scrubbed twice a week.' And that was that.

Slim returned to base after the weekend leaving me to face Mrs Polanski and her orders. But the honeymoon period was thrilling. Slim would return on Friday afternoon and we'd close our door to the world. His kisses and lovemaking convinced me that I was everything to him. With nothing to compare it with, I was not curious enough to realise it wasn't fulfilling.

We would go out quite a lot in the beginning and always met up with Mandy. It was, at the time, the happiest days of my life. I was working with her again, back in my old job, but at least I could go home to my own space, have peace of mind and look forward to my father visiting me. He never wanted to meet Slim. Maybe he was afraid my heart would be broken. He never expressed his thoughts, but I knew he had nothing to worry about, apart from me getting on a plane to America with Slim when it became my home. Mother refused to visit, but it wasn't about me. It was the area she didn't like.

Life was good but within eighteen months, Slim changed. He would go out on his own and sometimes didn't come back until late. The naive young girl I was believed what he told me.

'Honey, I was playing cards with a few pals.'

One Monday evening after my tasks were done and I'd brushed out the clumps of dust gathered in the hem my skirt, I decided to go to Mandy's.

Mandy opened the front door. 'Has Slim gone then?' She tossed her hair. 'Left you in the lurch, has he?'

I wondered why she should ask if Slim had left me, but I shrugged it off.

'No, but it feels strange when he's not there.'

'You're not on your own though. You have the old witch to keep you company,' said Mandy, putting the kettle on the fire.

'Don't remind me.' Mrs Polanski had almost caught her nose in the branches outside her window when I left.

Mandy poked at the bread in the frying pan and laughed. 'Her beak's long enough. I bet she can see around corners as well.'

'She'll probably see the dirt I brushed under the mat.'

'There is so much shit in that house even Christopher Columbus would have difficulty finding a clean space.'

'Fry us an egg, girl?' I asked.

'Duck or hen?' she joked.

'Does the old cow still close the door at twelve?'

'Sometimes. Can you come back with me later? Maybe stay overnight?' I asked.

'Not if that old sow has anything to do with it.'

'Do you know her?'

'Yeah, that's why I dodge her when I go to yours.'

We ate and decided to go back to my place after all. After Mandy changed, she cocked the latch, pulled a string through the letter box of the front door and we set off.

Mrs Polanski opened the front door and stared at Mandy. 'You have been here before, I never forget a pretty face…When it looks like a fox.'

'Who are you calling an animal?'

I could tell Mandy was vexed but I managed to calm her down.

'So, this is one you call your friend?' Her eyes were still fixed on Mandy as she spoke to me.

'You have never liked me since Frank Powell.'

Mrs Polanski lowered her eyes.

'Remember when you wanted him to sell you booze and I told him to say no and you're still at it. You've always thought I'd shop you.'

Mrs Polanski lips twisted into a grimace.

'That's right! don't go around calling me names Mrs. …whatever your stupid name is, or else.'

Without saying a word Mrs Polanski turned on her heels and walked away.

'Has she got Slim bringing her drink?' asked Mandy.

'No.' I didn't know why I'd lied, it just came out. Maybe I secretly thought Mandy had a vindictive streak and I wouldn't like to see Mrs Polanski in jail.

Mandy slipped of her shoes and lay on the bed. 'What side does Slim sleep on?'

'We don't have sides.' I took off my coat.

'When is he coming back to the love nest?' she asked.

Seeing Mandy sprawled out on the bed annoyed me. Her hands were all over the place. She looked like she belonged there, cat-like and provocative.

I tried to see myself in that position, but the image wouldn't come. 'He'll be down at the weekend.'

'I'll come around then.'

17

Slim left me some money before he went back to the base. The plan was to buy something to brighten up the room. Friday night, after scrubbing and polishing until I was satisfied Slim would appreciate my effort, I went back to Shakespeare Road to see my parents.

When my father opened the door, he looked healthier and he moved more robustly with the aid of his stick. His face lit up when he saw me.

'Come in, girl. I'll put the kettle on.'

I smiled as he tried to walk quickly. The stick wobbled in front of him as his legs tried to keep up.

'I've got loads to tell you,' he said, putting the kettle on the stove. 'We're leaving soon, got a house in Penny Lane, girl.'

For a moment I felt thrilled for them. But as much as I hated our old house it was the place of my birth, and even though a lot of my memories were bad, there were many good ones as well. It was always their ambition to move somewhere nearer to their idea of heaven and away from their damp house in Shakespeare Road.

He poured the tea and continued talking. 'There's room for you, if you want to come with us. What do you say, love?'

Not bloody likely, I thought, but instead I replied, 'Wait until you move in, then we'll see.'

He seemed satisfied with my answer and chatted on how hard-working Mother had been. With the rent coming in, she had saved up for a deposit on the new house.

The Sunday after this news, my hopes and dreams came apart, when Mrs Polanski told me something that should have been no surprise, but still was.

While I was gone she'd opened the front door to Mandy. Using her foot as a wedge she'd told her I was out, but Slim shouted from the landing to let her in. Mrs Polanski stepped back and watched Mandy as she climbed the stairs. Swinging her hips, she'd put two fingers up to Mrs Polanski who shook her head in disgust. She followed soon after and listened at the door. She recounted what she'd heard.

'Not here, Slim. She might come back.'

'But I'm hungry for you, babe.'

'Not hungry enough because you're still playing the arse, sleeping with her and playing fucking house.'

'I wanted to tell you, Bess, but I couldn't.' Mrs Polanski said, touching my shoulder gently. 'I thought he liked you and only wanted one thing from her.'

Looking back, Mandy had seemed extra flirtatious lately. She'd smiled at Slim a lot, fluttering her eyes and bending over him when she had no need to. But I thought that was just how she was and that she meant no harm.

I gave Slim the chance to tell me the truth. He lit a cigarette and I could hear him drawing in deeply, before he spoke. 'There's someone else, babe.' I don't know if by calling me babe he'd thought it would soften the news. It didn't.

'It's Amanda. I love her.' Standing up, hands shaking, he plucked another cigarette from the almost empty packet.

I sat up dazed and stared at him. 'You love her? You love Mandy?'

I hadn't expected love. I wanted to smash the chair

over his head. My tears refused to flow, but I was wringing my hands in despair telling myself not to lose control and run out of the house and find Mandy. I'd never experienced hate but in those moments, I hated them both. The most hurtful aspect was that I'd let it happen instead of challenging Mandy about her flirting with Slim. Like a fool, I'd turned a blind eye to her capers.

Slim's breathing came in short gasps as he moved with deliberate accuracy, packing his belongings and trying to avoid my questioning eyes. Was he shutting out the image of me engulfed in pain and reeling from what he'd told me? He was still talking, but only bits of it sank in. He tried to reassure me the rent had been paid and Mrs Polanski would take care of me. He wanted to leave no loose ends and convince himself that he wasn't abandoning me. But he had.

The moment the door closed behind him, a barrier came down in my heart. I wouldn't be the first to be deceived by a man. How could I believe it would never happen to me? Laughing, crying and throwing things all over the room, the commotion brought Mrs Polanski scurrying up the stairs. She banged at the door, shouting if I was alright.

'No!' I shouted. 'He's left me.'

'He's gone, just like that? You stay here with me. I'll drop the rent.' She picked up a shoe. 'Next time throw this at his head.'

Mrs Polanski showed me so much kindness over the next few months. There was no way Mandy would be part of my life again, so the job had to go.

My father never said the words that he saw it coming. Instead he would say, 'He did not deserve you.'

Nothing changed. The parties and the noise at weekends didn't diminish because I had. The invites to join in the fun were there, but I always declined.

Slim must have seen me as a leech he had to shake off. It was me who snared him, getting drunk and throwing myself at him.

It was no use trying to mend what could not be fixed. From that day forward, I swore no man would ever hurt me again. It was not only a new me, it was a new identity.

18

My mother didn't welcome me with open arms, but she did ask how I was. I was moving back in with them, to their new house. It would be a clean break then. Slim and Mandy could be erased from my dreams and slotted somewhere in my memory, where I hoped they'd lie until the anguish no longer existed.

Not since childhood had I seen my parents so happy. It wasn't long before Mother established herself as a seamstress, making curtains and alterations from suits to school pants.

I was looking for work in local advertisements but spent most of my free time with Father when he needed a helping hand. Going up and down stairs would lock his spine through spasms of pain, rendering him incapable of moving. Mother's compassion came to the surface. She'd rub my father's back and wipe his silent tears then lead him to his favourite chair. Mother and I were getting on fine as well. She had her odd moments, but they didn't last for long.

Even though Father walked with a slight stoop and his legs bowed with the pain, women were still comfortable in his presence. They would giggle at his jokes, while their husbands pretended to prune the roses outside. My father wasn't aware of his own magnetic presence, which left him vulnerable. He referred to the men as his friends, unaware they might have seen him as a savage with a high sex drive.

With Mother's willingness to turn a blind eye to racist comments, she interpreted the culprits to be joking. 'It's no good me fighting for the little bit of black running through my veins,' she said, slamming a piece of paper on the table. 'By the way I got you a job. You start on Monday.' I wanted to say thanks, but the speed of the material being pushed under the foot of her machine indicated it was the wrong time.

I started work in a local electrical factory, doomed to packing miles of wire and minute plugs and adaptors ready to be shipped overseas. Using Mother as my covert mentor, I too made friends and was invited to many parties, church dances, weddings and most events taking place in my area. With Mother and me thinking we were social butterflies, any tension between us played an insignificant part in our lives.

I settled into my job and learned to hide my insecurities by refusing to challenge hostile colleagues. I laughed at what should have annoyed me. It was the cover I needed. I wanted to develop into someone else, anyone but good old dowdy Bess. Now I had the chance to live, learn, copy and grow after the experience of losing Slim and my best friend. The new home at Lambert Crescent would be my stage, my job would become my audience and I would oversee the costumes.

And then I met Liam.

I agreed to have a meal with him after we had danced briefly at a wedding. I couldn't wait to tell my workmates. It was the topic of conversation for days, until the supervisor put an end to our giggling, telling us to shut up and get on with our work.

The Friday of our first date, I was up before the birds to choose something to wear. Leaving a trail of clothes scattered around the room, I made a final choice. With my clothes folded neatly on the bed and grabbing a piece of toast in transit, I left for work and watched the hands of the clock move slower than a worm. The weekend started the moment I pushed my clocking off card into the machine and raced home.

'Don't want any tea tonight, Mother!' I shouted from the landing.

'You can bloody well have it tomorrow then,' was the reply.

Wriggling into an orange mini-skirt and a black jumper and pulling on my tan coloured boots, I slung a long black coat over my shoulders and added my black skull cap, decorated with an orange flower.

The bus stopped a few yards from the restaurant, which gave me time for a quick glance in a shop window. I smiled at my reflection and was ready to make my grand entrance into Raymond's top-class restaurant.

Liam spotted me and waved as I walked in. 'Over here, love,' he said, standing up and taking a rose from a silver vase and handing it to me.

'You look nice, Bess.' Blushing, I thanked him for the gesture and sat down facing him.

'You don't look bad yourself in your city suit,' I replied.

Liam handed me the menu. I didn't want a heavy meal.

'What are you having?' Liam asked.

'Number seven.'

With a grin, he said to the waitress, 'I'll have steak and chips, and a prawn salad for my girlfriend please.'

'Why did you call me that, Liam?' If I was a flower, I am sure the leaves would have opened, as though the morning dew had sprinkled the petals with magic formula.

'Because soon you will be.'

'Not unless I say yes.' I laughed.

He folded his napkin. 'You will.'

Playfully, I pretended to stab his hand with my fork. He stopped me as the steel prongs brushed lightly against his skin. I felt the heat from his fingers.

The waitress brought our meals and we ate without taking our eyes off each other. Finishing with a glass of white wine, Liam loosened his tie and relaxed back in his seat.

I sat like I had a steel rod in my back. Was he toying with me? Could he tell I'd had some experience with men but was not experienced? I was all mixed up inside. Was I just a curiosity?

'Penny for your thoughts?' he asked, leaning forward.

I snapped back from my inhabitations. 'They're worth more than that.'

Pushing his plate away, he beckoned the waitress and paid the bill.

'I have something to show you,' Liam said, and he led me outside.

19

The night was starless, and the pavement wet with rain. Liam was jangling a set of keys.

'My car is parked in the side street. It's not far,' he said. We walked over to where it was parked, and Liam opened the passenger door of a brand-new Hillman Imp. 'Hop in, your carriage waits.'

As we drove along, he cleared his throat. 'My flat is just a few miles from here. Do you fancy seeing it?'

I nodded but I was out of my comfort zone. He was taking me somewhere only sheep lived, after fattening me up for the kill.

'Stop this car!' I yelled. 'Take me back, now!'

He halted to a screeching stop.

'What's the matter, love? Do you feel ill?'

'No, scared.'

He laughed. 'Of me? I'll take you home if you want, or let's just sit here and talk for a while. I'm sorry I frightened you.'

He opened a packet of cigarettes, and I relaxed back into my seat. 'Want one?' I shook my head and watched the flame of the lighter play shadows on his face. He was so handsome, and something in his soft brown eyes and the gentle touch of his hands put me at ease. He restarted the car, letting the purring of the engine shunt slowly forward along the tree lined avenue until we stopped at a row of houses.

'Here it is. I'm on the second floor.' Kissing me lightly on the cheek, he put the key in the lock and opened the front door.

The apartment was not what I'd expected. I stepped into a room that didn't have a frayed tapestry settee, dog or cat hair everywhere or wallpaper coming away at the seams. Instead, there were two orange armchairs with delicate steel legs that moulded to body shape and curved around the bottom of the spine. Pictures were carefully arranged against a backdrop of sunflower patterned wallpaper, which had purple stems and red leaves. The only sombre piece of furniture was a long coffee table.

'Take your coat off, make yourself at home. Drink?'

'Yes, please.'

Liam rolled up his sleeves and prepared the drinks, shaking the ice bucket to loosen the cubes, before tossing them into a long-stemmed glass.

'This will warm you up.' He switched on the lamp and the radio and sat next to me. His dark eyes looked sleepy as he stretched his arm, touching my bare leg and letting his fingers snake along my thigh, leaving me unable to object when the wetness from his mouth stirred me with passion. I still wanted to feel what my friends bragged about, so I laid back and let him explore, until I had to pull away.

'What's wrong?' he asked, stroking my back.

I pulled my jumper down, smoothed my wrinkled skirt and stood up. 'It's late, Liam. I think I should go.' My heart pounded, eager to feel his lips again, but I bottled everything up. If he wanted me as much as I wanted him, he'd wait until I was ready. I asked if we could go home.

We drove through the empty streets in silence. When I opened the front door, Mother was at the bottom of the stairs.

'Well, who is he?'

Taking off my coat and hanging it on the stand, I tried to avoid the question. 'Is Father still up?'

'I know you've met someone at the wedding. Nothing stays hidden around here,' Mother continued. She followed me into the kitchen, niggling about where I'd been and if he liked me.

'Yes, and for your information it depends on if I like him.'

'You should. He's got a job and a car for God's sake, what's wrong with you? And he's white.' She was wringing her hands. We were about to go over old issues, about how lucky I'd be to find someone, anyone. I didn't want to hear it. Liam had made the evening special. I wasn't going to let Mother spoil it.

The next morning, I heard Father humming in the bathroom. It sounded like 'Here Comes the Bride', which made me smile. Mother must have had him up all night telling him about my new boyfriend, forgetting Liam could dump me overnight. But I was strong enough to handle rejection and not be swayed by words of love. Liam had opened the tenderness in my heart, but around the edges there was a ring of fire. He rang that afternoon. 'Hi, sweetheart, fancy going out tonight?'

'No, I'm washing my hair and getting things ready for work on Monday.'

'Okay, we can have a coffee on Monday night. I'll pick you up at seven thirty. I know your address.'

Before I had a chance to say he could meet me on the corner, he blew a kiss down the phone and was gone. I could picture my parents with their noses pressed against the window like two school kids waiting for a big picture to start. They sat by the fire grinning at each other as I set about my chores.

On Monday morning the assembly line was buzzing

with questions about Liam, but my lips were sealed.

As we sipped creamy coffee in a local cafe and looked into each other's eyes, he told me about his work in insurance and that he'd lived in America for a few years. I wanted to know more about his time there, but he never delved too deeply into that part of his life and I put it at the back of my mind. He joked about having permanently wrinkled hands after washing pots and pans for hours on end to subsidise his college fees. He then wanted to know more about my life.

I told him little as possible regarding Slim and Mandy. He didn't need to know what I'd put to rest, and I didn't need to be reminded. Looking back, we were both secretive. So later, when we had nowhere to hide, our revelations were devastating.

Months after our first date, I took him to see Abigail and received a welcome fit for royalty. The kettle was blowing steam within minutes. Daintily cut cakes and biscuits were arranged on matching tea plates.

'Eat up,' said Abigail and poured the coffee.

I looked around, impressed. There was more than one chair to sit on and a modern settee, and flowered curtains gave light to the once dingy room. Abigail had a home to be proud of.

'Have you seen Tim and Jane?' I asked her, when Liam slipped out to buy some cigarettes. I longed to see them again and hear their giggles. I even missed the danger of pulling them apart when fists, feet and the odd toy became weapons when a fight broke out. The best times were when they'd be friends, heads locked together, sharing sweets and laughing at nothing in particular.

'No, not for a while. The last time was in the town centre, but they didn't see me.'

Liam was gone for about an hour, but it gave me and

Abigail a chance to catch up. We laughed about the silly things we'd done and reflected on how we'd grown. Liam returned with a box of chocolates for our host and a bunch of flowers for me. We left, promising to keep in touch, and drove back home. Sure enough, my parents' noses were pressed against the window.

'I'll have to meet them soon.' Liam smiled and waved to them.

'Not yet.'

But it was inevitable. Mother and Father somehow wormed themselves into speaking to Liam. They waylaid him one evening as he waited for me outside the front door. Watching the charade from my bedroom window, I saw that Mother was the first to poke her nose through the open car window. She was beaming, looking around, trying to catch a nosy neighbour spying on us. Father stayed in the background eyeing up the car. Prodding one of the tyres with his foot.

'Bess must bring you around for tea,' I heard Mother say. 'Shall we say Sunday?'

Liam quickly seized on the invitation, telling Father that he'd take him for a spin too. I dashed downstairs and jumped in the car and rescued Liam from another round of questions. Mother, being naturally inquisitive, would want to know where he worked, where he lived and if he liked homemade pie before he had time to blink. Sunday would be here soon enough. There was time to fill Liam in on Mother's behaviour and Father's sometimes intimidating silence.

My parents surprised me on the day. They both relaxed, and Mother discussed subjects that Liam knew about. She openly blossomed talking about rare books and art.

'Did you have a university education, Liam?' she asked,

pouring the tea.

'No, Mrs Tobo, but I do have qualifications equal to degrees, which I gained in America.'

'Oh, in what subjects?'

'Accountancy.'

Father rolled his eyes 'Sure your qualifications didn't come from the duck pond,' he chuckled.

Liam tried to laugh it off, but I could see he was a little taken aback by the joke. But besotted with Liam's love and attentiveness, I soon tossed my concern aside.

The chair squeaked as Father excused himself from the table. 'I'll put the kettle on,' he said, looking at Liam as if to warn him that Mother would have him scrutinising her books before he knew it. But within a couple of hours they'd warmed to each other and conversed about their life ambitions.

'Qualifications in America can be a bit tricky, son,' said Father, making up for his earlier 'duck pond' comment.

'I know, but I assure you I'm a highflyer, Mr Tobo. My job in insurance is just the beginning.'

'It's the best place to start, son.'

'In the insurance business?'

'No, from the bottom.' Filling his pipe and taking a deep drag on the stem, my father continued, 'I worked hard. Up every morning at four. Now I have a good pension and a lovely wife who spends all of it.' He winked at Liam. 'What more could a man ask for?'

Liam laughed and pulled me towards him. 'Well, Mr Tobo, in the future Bess will be spending all my money. What do you think about that, Bess?'

'Shut up, Liam! You're embarrassing me.'

Father poured himself another cup of tea. Mother sat with her ears cocked, seemingly engrossed in her sewing.

20

By the time we returned to the flat, we were hungry for each other. We burst into the bedroom, stripping off in transit. I tried to mimic Liam's moans and groans as he trashed around the bed, even though I was content with kisses and caresses. Yet I was still waiting for the explosion that others likened to an earth-shattering moment when Liam rolled off me, smiling from ear to ear.

'How was it for you?' he asked, pulling me towards him.

Having Liam in my arms, feeling his heart pounding in his chest, I knew I had done something for him and I loved it. I wriggled my feet to the end of the bed. 'What did you think of my parents?'

Snuggling into my neck, he murmured, 'Nice people, real nice.' He sat up then and looked at me with a serious expression. 'Bess, can I be part of your family?'

'Do you mean you want to be adopted?' I laughed at first until I realised he was serious. 'Who would want to be adopted by my family unless they were stark raving mad.'

'No, don't be silly. I want to marry you.'

I was stunned. 'Liam, let's wait awhile,' I said eventually.

His face clouded over. It wasn't a sulky expression, just hurt. I could see his chest rise and fall. His cheeks were red, but the rest of his face was as white as bleached stone. 'Please, love,' he pleaded. 'Just say you will.'

I wanted to be with him, but marriage was different

to romancing about the big day, that's for the innocent. Slim took that away and shredded my heart in the process. Liam would surely not be capable of such cruelty, but common sense weighed heavily in my mind.

'No, let's wait,' I repeated, then thought of something. 'What about your family, Liam? When will I meet them?'

'You won't. I'm an orphan and lived most of my life in Northampton.'

I held him close that night, afraid he might wake thinking I was not there.

For a year we dated. I learned that he couldn't boil a potato or conjure up a simple meal like corned beef hash. He found out that I had a knack of turning white clothes into red or blue and shrinking anything made of wool. But we were in love.

We enjoyed driving through the countryside at night, hearing the hooting owls high up in the trees and watching the sunset. We'd rise on a weekend, get dressed and decide where we were going with the jab of pin on a map of the local area.

Mother constantly warned me about becoming pregnant. But I was happy now, secure with the man I loved. I'd never forget my baby with Slim, no matter how many children I would have, but I felt safe. However, at times, old memories would resurface. Once this came in the form of an airmail letter. I slit the edges open, revealing Mandy's scrawling handwriting.

> *Dear Bess,*
> *I am in North America. Got your address from that girl we used to sit with who looked like she'd break in half in a high wind. She lived around the corner from you. Slim has left the forces and we are living with his parents. The house is no better than what I left.*

The only good thing is the weather. Charlotte Town it seems to be over-run with bloody chickens. Slim works on a farm and he is the biggest chicken for miles (smile). The wages are not good. To make matters worse his lovely mother cannot stand the sight of me. And to top it all, the baby is due in a few months. Anyway, Slim promised we would move to Raleigh, that's like London, bright lights and all that, so I might have some good news in a few months.
Love
Mandy Xx

Were the two kisses from her and Slim? Did she think I needed them? The wastepaper bin was where the letter ended up, shredded, soaked in water and left to disintegrate. I washed my hands as if to rid them of contamination while Mother looked on.

'When you've stopped scrubbing your hands, peel those potatoes,' she said, handing me a knife.

I smiled. 'Chipped or whole?'

'Chipped and not too skinny.'

I could not wait to see Liam that night. I still had butterflies in my stomach each time I saw him. My parents told me to slow down, that I wasn't rushing for the train.

'No, but I could be taking a ride in a wedding car.' It took a few minutes for the news to sink in. 'Liam has asked me to marry him,' I said, to make sure they knew what I meant.

Finally, they both reacted. 'You love each other, girl, and you have our blessing,' Father said. Mother insisted on a white wedding.

'No, I've decided cream and red accessories.'

'Red? My God! What will the vicar say?'

'He's not invited.'

Putting her hand on her forehead, Mother tried to wear me down. Liam hooting the horn saved me from a long drawn out argument.

Putting on a hint of lipstick, I gave Mother a reassuring pat on the shoulder and left before she could drag out some off-white lace material, a boxful of tangled cotton reels and insist she'd make my wedding dress.

Liam sat in the car with a grin on his face as we sped off towards the flat. He was still grinning when he opened the flat door and Abigail jumped out of the shadows with her new boyfriend trailing shyly behind her. Stunned to see her, I was rendered speechless. After the initial shock, we settled down to catch up, leaving the two men fussing about in the kitchen.

Liam struggled with a tray of drinks leaving Abigail's boyfriend to bring in snacks of cheese, crackers and packets of crisps. I could see a tiny box hidden behind the glasses. Eyeing the box, I wondered if it was something for me and apprehensive it might be something for Abigail

'Hope you like it,' Liam said, handing me the leather-bound object. With shaking hands, I opened the lid exposing an engagement ring nestled on a cushion of blue velvet. Liam leaned towards me and slipped the small diamond ring on my finger. With tears rolling down my cheeks, my words became jumbled trying to thank him and crying at the same time.

Abigail had tears in her eyes when she held up her glass to toast our engagement. We danced until the early hours, only turning the music down when someone banged on the wall.

After Abigail finished showering us with kisses and we'd closed the front door, we were alone planning a life together. First though, we swore that we would live every day like it was the last - laugh, sing and dance for a couple of years. I wanted to have fun with Liam by my side.

'Fancy a nightcap?' he asked.

'Just a small one, love. I don't anything to take away the picture in my head or distort the image of us on our wedding day.'

'I have a snap of you,' he laughed.

'Where is it?'

'In my head and you are naked.' Without warning he lifted me up and we laughed all the way to the bedroom.

I chose my wedding outfit alone. A cream brocade suit was draped on a lifelike dummy in the window of Nannette's on London Road and I knew I had to have it. I liked the area because TJ Hughes was over the road, where I often browsed through the trinkets without assistants breathing down my neck. The suit fitted perfectly, hugging my slim waist and sitting around my thighs without creasing.

Shoes were the difficult item to purchase, but there were so many shops I found a pair within the hour. They were plain except for a delicate daisy pattern around the sides, and they were pillar box red. Mother would be horrified, I smiled, putting them in the box.

The only other stressful thing I had to do was choose who to invite from work. Four weeks before the event I was bombarded with excuses, which mainly came from the previously most enthusiastic guests. Some delivered the news at break times with a slice of toast and a friendly chat. But I was left with a few faithful colleagues who had no concerns about what other people thought.

21

On the big day Mother was make-up-assistant-come-hair-dresser. She was in her element, whizzing around from the dressing table to the kitchen and scolding me and Father for not eating breakfast. Father scratched his head as Mother screeched when he accidentally snapped one of the flowers. I was too happy to let Mother's ear-piercing voice bother me. Father picked up the flower, tied a bit of tape over the stem and stuck it on Mother's cheek.

'You bloody old fool,' she said. 'Messing about on a day like this.'

'Toni,' Father said. 'We will never have a day like this again. Let's have fun, woman!'

Mother sucked her teeth and playfully pinched me. Yes, it was a day for happiness.

Liam had asked Abigail's boyfriend to be his best man. As I wanted Abigail to see how far I'd come from my hideous dress sense, we decided she would be waiting for me at the registry office holding a bag of confetti and a large handkerchief to dry her tears.

Mother and Father stood at the bottom of the stairs as I descended, hands outstretched ready to catch me if I tripped on the way down. Father was in his black suit, white shirt and, of course, a red tie. He looked so handsome.

The mother of the bride looked stunning, her face twenty years younger as if all her frown lines had been left in the jar in her bedroom. Best of all I wouldn't be there when she slapped on her usual face that night.

'What a lovely outfit!' I heard someone say as I gripped my father's arm, taking care not to lean too much on him. Mindful of his frailness, we walked slowly towards the wedding car.

Shivering in the midday sunshine, it seemed everyone from Lambeth Crescent came out of their houses to see me on that crisp Saturday afternoon. Beaming faces smiled, while trying to endure the slight but biting wind that made their eyes water. Still they stood in huddled groups holding bags of shopping. Children stood by their mothers waving tiny hands. Taking a gulp of air, any resentment of past experiences left me - to the children I was just another bride. I ducked my head and stepped into the wedding car, as Mother sped off ahead of us in a taxi.

The small room was packed to capacity and Liam couldn't take his eyes off me as we stood together waiting to take our vows. There was a hush as the registrar cleared his throat and began speaking. My thoughts were of the present. It was like being baptised. I'd emerge cleansed from the baggage I'd carried. Liam looked so handsome, but most of all warm and caring. Even with all my flaws and recklessness, I was the one he had chosen.

After we'd exchanged rings and were pronounced husband and wife, Liam said, 'I love you. Whatever happens, from now on, remember that.'

We walked as one into the fog. Like I had always imagined, the white sun managed to slice through the dense mass, then it disappeared leaving nothing but a clear bright day.

We drove to the hotel, which was nestled on the top of a hill. Fires glowed in every room. The tables were arranged intimately with bowls of flowers set against crisp white linen, and staff dressed in black and white uniforms stood nearby.

When everyone was seated, I could see who the shy ones were. They fidgeted with napkins or smiled nervously.

Father stood up. 'Come on you lot, this is my only daughter's wedding day. We are here to let our hair down!' He lifted his glass. 'This will help.'

A ripple of laughter was the tonic everyone needed. The smiles on everyone's faces and the chatter of voices had the waitresses on their feet and serving. We sampled all the dainty side dishes including sliced pork seeped in apple juice. The roast was arranged like a work of art. Nothing like Mother's Sunday roast, which was often slapped on a plate and swimming in gravy

'Quiet please,' Father said, tapping on his glass when it was time for the speeches. 'Many thanks to all of you and I know all your names, so this is personal. Again, many thanks to Linda and Jim…' Leaning forward he called all the guests names and raised his glass each time.

After he'd finished, Father grinned and took Mother by the arm. 'Come,' he said. 'One dance.' Mother smiled and led the way to the middle of the room, while Father took baby steps towards her and slowly they moved to the music. He held onto her as they danced.

'Just like old times,' I heard him say.

The best day of my life drew to a close as dawn moved like a shadow across the sky. Tipsy well-wishers smothered me and Liam with wet kisses and backbreaking hugs. They departed, swaying down the driveway to waiting taxies or to their hotel rooms. We stood in the silence of the room surrounded by tables and the disarray of half-eaten food stuck to the tablecloths and drowned in alcohol. Liam carried me down the carpeted hallway.

He held me close to him.

'I love you,' he said, undoing the tiny velvet buttons of my jacket. I noticed a serious tone creeping into his voice. His eyes were dark and passionate as he put me down. Opening the door to our honeymoon suite, a bottle of champagne was on the table. While Liam opened the bubbly, I showered and wrapped a towel around myself.

Liam was kneeling by the bed when I came out. 'Bess, I have something to tell you.' There was a thickness in his voice and he struggled to get the words out. 'I've lost the flat.'

'How? 'Don't tell me there's been a fire.'

'No, Bess, no fire.' His head was bent. 'It was my own stupidity…I'm a gambler.'

Father always said Mother should be happy he wasn't one of them. It ruins people, he'd say, and they end up living on the street.

I tried to stay calm. 'What on, Liam?'

Avoiding looking into my eyes he replied, 'I played cards and lost the lot, even the car but I was winning, Bess. I was …winning.'

I knew what it was to have nowhere to live and the consequences. I remembered how I'd trampled alone to Mandy's house and was grateful for somewhere to lay my head, only to end up making the wrong decision by moving in with Slim.

'Liam, what are we going to do?'

'I'm sorry, Bess. We'll have to live with your parents. Only for a while until we get another flat. I promise.'

I sank back on the pillow in disbelief. We'd be going backwards, away from the light airy flat to the claustrophobic world my parents lived in. I started to tremble. 'How could you dash our dreams with a pack of cards and rip me inside out?' I felt hot as I swung my legs to the edge of the bed. Liam bent forward to hold me. I pushed him away. 'Don't touch me.' But he did and helped me to reach the toilet to be sick.

Drifting into a fitful sleep and grateful for the hush of night to block out our dilemma, I woke up to Father knocking on the door telling us breakfast was ready. I pulled the covers back and tore at my nightdress, ripping the lace garment I'd chosen for our wedding night. I never wanted to see it again. It was like I was tearing Liam from my mind and heart, but I knew that would be impossible. 'I'm going to need a double gin and tonic before I can face anyone. You'd better go down and smooth the way for me,' I told him. He attempted to come back in the room. 'Get out or you will be sorry!'

Everyone was assembled at the bottom of the stairs waiting for me.

'Let's eat,' I said faking a laugh, but my heart felt like stone when Liam looked at me.

After breakfast, Liam was in deep conversation with Father who kept nodding his head. Eventually he came over and sat by me. 'I've told your father about the flat but not everything.' I had a feeling he'd leave out the gambling.

'Bess, we still have the furniture and we can stay in the flat for a couple of weeks.' Looking proud of himself, he added, 'And I can get the car back.'

22

At least our sunshine flat hadn't been snatched without warning. I was left with time to pack, wrap and store my dreams, like the furniture. I'd have a chance to come to terms with going back home, back to my old room to wake each morning to the chattering of old minds. The car would be our means of escape, but the magic had gone.

My love for Liam hadn't altered but my belief in him had. Now I would watch his every move, question him more, throw any unbelievable yarns back at him and demand the truth.

We moved later that month.

As I entered my old room, it was like opening a page of a book I'd read but hadn't enjoyed. We acted like a honeymoon couple in front of my parents but once we were alone we never had sex. I was cold to Liam's touch, refused to face him in bed and slept in a housecoat.

For months we'd return from work and greet each other with a kiss. Once out of sight of my parents, I'd wipe my mouth with the back of my hand and make sure Liam saw me. He brought me bunches of flowers every Friday, ran my baths and even tried to comb my hair. Nothing he did worked.

But then one night he came home from work sweating and tired. I felt sorry for him and gently put my hand on his forehead. I, instead of Mother, made him a hot lemon drink and cradled him in my arms all night. The next morning, I watched him sleeping, his eyelashes long and damp curled at the ends. I stroked his face and traced the line of his mouth with my finger. At that precise moment the sun steamed through the bedroom window highlighting fine specs of dust sparkling on a rainbow of colour.

Laughing inwardly, I thought of how Mother would only see dust, forgetting the beauty of nature when it interacted with the atmosphere. This reminded me of our relationship when we clashed. She would explode like a volcano, but I would bubble under the surface.

Liam slowly opened his eyes. Something within me stirred. It was like a wave of longing, excitement and love that made me open the top of his pyjamas and kiss his chest. He caressed and kissed me with so much passion that I was left breathless but wanting more. He climbed on top of me, and from that point I was lost as a tingling sensation ran through my body. Then the explosion came from him and mine collided, merged, melted and erupted at the same time. We were unable to speak for at least twenty minutes after. Then it was only words of love and a lot more sex, but now I knew the real joy of being in love.

Liam rubbed his eyes, drawing me close under the snug blankets. I would never forget that morning, so when I got pregnant I knew that was when Brian was conceived.

I did not want Mother's advice on morning sickness. But when it came, I was grateful for it. I'd vomit clinging to the rim of the toilet in a lather of sweat.

'What you need, love,' she'd say, 'is dry biscuits and a cup of weak tea.' I knew she meant well, but the thought of food made me wretch more.

Father stayed in the background but was always ready to prop my swollen feet on a stool or make a concoction of food I'd fancy. This was unlike Mother and Liam who'd squirm as I spooned cooked rice swimming in tinned tomatoes into my mouth.

Yet Mother was always there when I needed her, while Liam and my father did their best to keep calm. The slightest twinge would send them into a panic. Mother and I would laugh at them fussing over me.

'You never worried over me, Hal Tobo,' Mother would scold.

'Yes, I did,' Father replied.

My waters broke at the same time Mother was mopping the floor. She was frightened at first but soon reassured me she could cope. She rang for an ambulance then called Liam's workplace.

Twenty-four hours later Brian lay in my arms. I just kept looking at him, his hands stretching as if to grasp at his new world. He was part of our world now.

Mother cried that night. It might not have been the first time, but I'd never seen her happy tears. She held Brian so tenderly. She did this without her usual grip of steel and stroked his face with fingers as light as a feather.

'Be careful, he is so precious,' she said, passing him to Liam.

I thought of my first child without doting grandparents or a loving father, my baby who died struggling to live in my womb. I closed my eyes in pain.

After the birth, we had no option but to find somewhere to live. Mother still tried to bind Liam to her side, feeding him each night. It was my promise of sultry evenings together when we could be alone that moved him. We found a small affordable house in the same street.

I set the rules from day one. Mother came around and tried to march past me.

'I'm busy at the moment bathing Brian, see you later.' I said.

With a surprised look on her face, she replied, 'Okay, see you later.'

I had gained her respect. Standing with my back against the door, I relished in my new-found freedom from my mother. There was no going back.

23

I awoke on a glorious September morning hearing Brian gurgling playfully in his cot. Still warm from Liam's love-making, which had been unusually emotional, I slipped out from the tangled sheets and stepped on the thick carpet, instead of cold lino. This made me tingle with joy.

We were the only ones with keys to our sanctuary. No one could disturb our private moments. The days of Mother hovering and giving her unwelcomed opinions on everything was gone. Only the subject of sex on Mother's part had always been taboo, but I realised now that a few tips would have been helpful. Without blushing, she'd ignored any questions on martial revelations. God knows what she'd have thought of my pill popping ritual each morning to make sure only the patter of two tiny feet gladdened my heart. This would give Mother more reason to say I was useless at multi-tasking and bully her way into our lives. But I loved it when she let her guard down and played with Brian. I'd watch the joy in her eyes when he hugged her neck or fell asleep in her arms. Rocking him she'd say, 'Babies need something to cuddle into.' Despite this, I still relished my freedom from her.

'You okay?' Liam asked.

'Hmm fine.'

I wanted to climb back in bed with him, but I stopped myself.

'Don't take hours preening yourself,' I said. 'Will you get the baby up? And I'll cook.'

When I crept into Brian's bedroom he had gone back

to sleep, so I went into the bathroom and washed. I was sure the running taps were Brian's alarm clock. Straight after I turned them on he would want freedom from his wee-soaked nappy and start to cry. Once I'd washed and changed him, he played while I cooked breakfast.

At the table we were bright-eyed and alert, with Brian sitting in his highchair picking at his food, with most of it around his mouth. I'd burned the toast, but Liam still chomped on it without comment and left for work soon after.

With Brian cleaned up, I put him outside the front door while I got myself ready for our usual walk to the shops.

'Do you need anything from the shops, Mother?' I shouted, lifting the letterbox of my parent's house.

'Yes, a few things. I will write a list.'

'No Mother, no list. My brain still functions.'

Mother laughed as she opened the door. 'Leave Brian with me,' she said. 'We'll sit out in the garden.' As she often did, she commented on his ice cream complexion and the silkiness of his hair. 'He's his father's child,' she'd always say.

'Yes,' I'd reply. 'But I am his black mother. As far as I'm concerned Brian is as black as me.'

'But he could pass for white. I am sure Liam has a say in this.'

'Yes, he agrees with me.'

I would know if Liam had an issue regarding how Brian would see himself, wouldn't I?

The air had become hot and sticky and Brian began to toss and turn. It would be better to leave him with Mother, to cool in the shade of the garden.

'I'll be back in a couple of hours,' I said, kissing Brian and taking the list Mother insisted on giving me.

With nothing to do with my hands except for constantly jerk the string bag over my shoulder, I walked as far as Allerton Road. I was undecided whether to buy something different for our tea or spend time looking for a sexy bra. I walked a bit further but my interest in shopping began to fade. The underwear could be bought next week. Food was essential.

I finished shopping and took my time walking home. A group of women were gathered a few doors away from my parent's house. I only recognised the woman from number ten and the woman from number two. They kept looking at me. With quickening steps, the adrenaline increased my heartbeat and I was out of breath when I reached them.

'Bess,' one of woman said, twisting her hands. 'Two men were banging on your parent's door shouting for Liam. The shouted all kinds at your dad when he answered and then tried to force their way in, but your Dad managed to shut the door.'

'We shouted at them,' the woman from number two said. 'They scarpered down the street calling Liam a motherfucker. But they said they'd be back.' I raced up the street. Only Americans used that kind of language.

Mother opened the door ashen-faced, Brian in her arms. Throwing my bag on the floor I grabbed hold of him.

'They… they,' she said, 'threatened to hit your father. He was so scared.'

'Where is he?'

Hands shaking, she pointed to the living room. Father was lying on his back clutching his chest. I put Brian on the floor beside him and shook Father gently to let him know I was there.

He opened one eye. 'Where's your mother?'

'She's here, and she's okay.'

His eye closed and his hand slowly slipped to his side. I cradled him like a child, while mother looked on and wept. He was breathing easier and began to tell me what happened.

'Two yanks came looking for Liam,' he gasped. 'They called him a nigger lover and asked if I was the gardener.' He coughed. 'You don't think they'll come back, do you?'

'No,' I assured him. 'Now lie still.'

'Don't send for an ambulance, girl,' Father said. 'It's only a little turn, just help me over to the settee.'

I didn't want to move him, but he became agitated with my reluctance to jostle him to the other side of the room. It was his fear of hospitals that gave me the green light to take charge.

'If you get worse, I'll call an ambulance.'

'You always were a fusspot. I wouldn't mind a cup of tea, girl, nice and sweet.' He waved his hand and tried to get up. I covered him with a blanket and went to the kitchen, leaving Mother in charge of Brian. I brought all of us a hot drink.

My parents seemed to have recovered enough for me to relax but I kept an eye on Father. I had no time to think of Liam while the drama unfolded. Now sitting by the window with the heat of the day surging through my veins, I thought of the trouble he'd caused. Deciding to spare my parents further trauma, there was no need for more questioning. Even though my father appeared calm, he still looked pale.

'Father, are you sure you are okay?

He nodded. 'Funny,' he said. 'I was just thinking of Zac.' He hadn't mentioned his brother for a long time.

'I could just see us as kids playing together.'

I'd imagined they were different personalities. Zac receptive and likeable, while Dad was quiet, thoughtful with his hopes and dreams of escaping his poverty-stricken life. I knew by his expression that he longed to see his brother. But looking at Mother's twisted lips at the mention of Zac's name, it wouldn't be an option. I never ventured to ask what the issue was, but I did know that Father's family had cut him off.

'Mother, will you keep an eye on Brian? Once I've sorted things with Liam, I'll stay with you overnight.'

Mother's eyes lit up. 'All night, girl?'

I nodded. 'First let's get Father to bed and give Brian something to eat.'

24

I slipped into my house hoping to go unnoticed.

'Where the hell have you been?' Liam shouted. 'Where's the baby?'

He must have known Brian was only a few doors away. We wouldn't leave him with anyone but my parents. I turned to face him. 'You have some explaining to do! Two men are looking for you, two yanks.'

Liam's face was bloodless. 'Sit down,' he said. 'I'll tell you the truth.' Shifting his position and crossing his legs, he reached for his cigarettes. 'My mother died while I was in the States. I'd flittered away most of my money and I couldn't come back for her funeral.'

'You didn't say goodbye to your own mother?'

'No.' He bowed his head, holding the cigarette at knee level. 'I've always regretted not being there.'

I gripped hold of the table to steady myself. I wanted to get away. I knew he could see the anger in my eyes. But it must have been my look of disgust which prompted him to tear at his tie gasping for air. Rushing past me, he threw open the back door and sat on the steps sucking in mouthfuls of air.

My eyes searched his face. I wanted to find out more. 'Did you have family in America?'

'Yes, distant cousins. They were supportive at first. But when the cash ran out so did their hospitality.'

For a moment I felt sorry for him being alone in a strange country.

'Why did you go there?'

'I wanted to travel, see the world and make money.'

'By gambling?' I asked. Inside I wanted to vent my feelings on him for allowing his wayward ways to interfere with our idyllic life, but I took a deep breath and listened.

'I survived by washing dishes in restaurants and waiting on tables. That's when I met Tyrell and Shane and started doing some running for them.'

That's the part, I thought, that's going to push me over the edge. He is calling them, so calmly, by name. He should call them as cowards and racists. I poked him in the ribs. 'You expect me to know what you mean by running. The marathon, a bloody egg and spoon race, what?'

'It was only a few items at first. But that increased, and I became worried because they wanted me to deliver drugs.'

'You didn't, did you?'

'No, no way, but I knew it was only a matter of time before I'd be forced to.'

Shuddering at the thought, I let him carry on talking. Pulling another cigarette out of a packet, Liam took long deep drags.

'One night they asked me to mind some cash. It was then they told me they were part of the mob. I had to hide, make sure they couldn't find me.'

And then he'd seen me, the soft cow sitting alone at a wedding. Was I someone to hide behind?

'First you trick me into marriage Then you withhold the fact you are on the run from God knows who!' I screamed at him.

There were tears in Liam's eyes as I spat out my rage. He tore at his hair looking wild eyed and scared. 'Don't, Bess. The neighbours can hear us arguing.'

Standing with our noses almost touching, I hissed, 'Let them all know how I married a liar and a cheat, who conned me with trinkets from his ill-gotten gains and left my parents to wallow in his mess.' The stench of resentment seemed to hang in the air. I ran upstairs and hastily stuffed a bag with clothes for myself and the baby. I shoved Liam out of the way. 'I'm staying with my parents tonight. Don't even let me smell you when I return. Get out of this house and don't ever come back.'

I found my father in the kitchen sitting on his stool. Forcing a smile, I chose my words carefully, 'The thugs were men who tried to pressurise Liam into joining their gang.'

'It's a funny sort of gang who come all this way looking for Liam,' Father replied, wobbling over to the sink to help wash the vegetables. 'Unless they were partners in America.'

'Father, Liam is beside himself with worry.'

'Why isn't he here then?'

Again, I acted like Liam's partner in crime. 'He's gone to try to find them, so they don't return.'

He relented then. 'It's all been too much for me, God knows how Liam's feeling.'

Father's words humbled me. In my anger I'd forgotten Liam's pain. I didn't mean half the things I'd said. Maybe we could overcome the obstacles and face them together.

'Bess, if anything…should happen to me promise something?'

'Please, Father, stop talking like that. You're scaring me.'

'All I want you to do is tell Zac.'

'But why now, after all these years?'

'It's a long and complicated story, love. Promise you will let him know.'

'I will carry out your wishes, Father. It could be at least a twenty year wait though,' I said trying to lighten the mood.

He gripped my arm. 'Don't let your mother put me in the house of rest. Zac will know what to do. The key to my writing desk where you will find all the instructions is in that old tartan waistcoat.'

'Okay, sit down and let me get on with the tea. Then I'll pop back to mine and make sure Liam is okay.'

Outside in the stillness of the night I tried to understand the urgency in Dad's request. He sometimes had difficulty breathing and always looked pale. Apart from that he seemed fine. Putting my concerns to the back of my mind, I turned the key of my front door and entered the dark hallway.

'Want a cup of cocoa, love? Liam asked, tentatively.

'Yes,' I said, curtly.

'How is your dad?'

'Sleeping I hope, but he was talking about dying, who he wants me to contact and stuff like that.'

'Don't worry too much, love. He's a strong old man.'

'I suppose he is. I'm just overreacting.'

Liam mixed the cocoa, pouring the water over the thick chocolate and handed me a mug.

'Thanks. Liam, take no notice of some of the things I said. I was so angry.'

'I know you had every right to say those things, it's my mess.' As he bent down, the tears flowed. I stayed silent wishing to find words of comfort.

We sat for over an hour, neither of us speaking, until I prised myself from Liam's arms and returned to my parent's house. Mother was still up cradling Brian in her arms.

'I'm off to bed,' she said, handing him over to me. 'Turn

off the lights before you go up.'

I watched her climb the stairs, holding onto the banister and taking one stair at a time. It was the first time pity for her struggling to cope without Father crossed my mind, wondering what she would do without him to draw strength from. She would never admit it, but he kept her focused by giving her confidence.

Walking up the stairs with Brian asleep in my arms, I thought how Mother liked me a little bit more than I'd thought. Maybe it was Shakespeare Road which turned her into a monster. It must be hard if you don't have a strong mind. It would be easier to band together with the masses and forget who you are. It was only through my experience of heartbreak that standing up to my husband came naturally. But outside the security of my own home, I sometimes became the same little girl starting school many years ago.

I returned to Liam the following morning and tried to put everything in perspective. After convincing ourselves the men from America would not return, our lives returned to normal for the sake of our son.

25

Around three in the morning, six months later, the phone rang. Springing out of bed with Liam close at my heels, I picked up the receiver with shaking hands.

Mother's voice seemed to echo. 'It's your father, love. He's in the Royal. You'll have to go to him.'

While I pulled on a pair of slacks and slung my coat over my shoulders, Liam threw my purse in a handbag and within minutes managed to find the car keys. We had no alternative but to ask our neighbours to look after Brian.

As we drove through the quiet streets, we only saw the odd stray cat scurrying to feast on the contents of upturned bins. Clasping my hands together, I prayed my father's life would be spared. I hoped he'd be sitting up in his hospital asking for a cup of tea. Liam parked the car opposite the hospital and we walked towards the entrance.

'Mr Tobo was brought in this evening,' Liam said to the woman on reception. I stood behind him prayed silently that it was all a dream.

'Oh,' the woman said. 'Here he is. I thought I'd heard the name before. He's such a gentleman. He's in ward six. Take the lift to the third floor and it's straight ahead.'

The terrifying squeak of a trolley being pushed by the hospital porter unnerved me enough to cling onto Liam. Still gripping hold of him and slowing his brisk walk, I caught sight of Mother sitting outside the ward. She was fidgeting with her wedding ring and didn't move as we approached. The redness and sorrow in her eyes confirmed the worst.

'He's gone, love,' she said in a hushed voice.

My throat muscles spasmed. Even though my mouth was open, there was no sound. The rush of blood made my head spin as I crumpled to the floor. Liam helped me up, wiping his eyes on the sleeve of his jacket.

'It's my fault he's dead,' Liam sobbed.

Mother stood by the door watching her only child stiff with grief and Liam shouldering so much guilt. 'Liam, my husband was a sick man,' she said.

My mind was whirling, remembering how thin he had looked the past few months. 'Mother, did he have cancer and not tell anyone?'

'No, it wasn't something eating away at him. It was his…heart and his lungs. They were finally unable to cope.'

'He knew he was dying, Mother. He tried to tell me, talking about his last wishes and all that and how he wanted Uncle Zac to be told if anything should happen to him.'

Mother stiffened. 'He mentioned Zac?'

'Yes, he must be told.'

Biting her lip, Mother nodded. 'You're right, after all they are brothers.'

'I want to see him,' I said, slowly walking towards the door and waiting a few seconds before opening it. Liam and Mother followed. I didn't know what to expect, but those chocolate brown eyes were what I wanted to see. I also wanted to hear his voice and see that smile whenever Mother stalked him around the house.

Making a small opening in the curtains around Father's bed, I was expecting to see his lifeless body. Instead I saw a gentleman who looked like he was asleep.

Tiptoeing towards the bed like a child creeping into their parent's bedroom, I kissed him. 'What will we do without you?'

We walked in silence through the long corridor which, by now, bustled with activity. Quickening our step, we were all eager to reach the exit door, as though the fresh air might bring some relief.

'You go to your mother's and I'll pick up the baby,' said Liam.

I nodded and helped Mother into her seat, wondering if I had the strength to climb into the front passenger side. The silence was awful. Liam sat straight-backed and he constantly looked into his mirror watching Mother staring out of the window clutching the treasured paper bag of Father's belongings. When we reached the house, we made no attempt to get out of the car.

'Come on, you have to go in,' Liam said, eventually. Entering the house was strange. I kept expecting Father to appear and say hello and offer us a hot drink. I brushed past his coat, and I could smell his tobacco. Even in the kitchen, I expected to see him sitting on his stool, pressing the ignition on the cooker. It was just a room without Father; he'd brought it alive.

Mother opened the kitchen cabinet. She stretched to retrieve the cup with 'Dad', painted all over it. She froze for a second and then ran her fingers around its rim, before carefully pushing it out of view.

The tray rattled as she carried it over to the table and poured the tea into the cups. 'Sorry,' I said. 'I should have told you about the key.'

'Key?'

'Yes, the one to get into his desk.'

'Bess, me and your father couldn't hide much from each other. I've always known where he kept it.' I looked up. Here was a woman who once found conflict over the smallest of issues but now made little fuss. She was calm like the ocean on a clear night. Yet it was hard to reach her and impossible to predict the storm which lay deep in her eyes.

The next afternoon while Brian took his nap, I found the key. Following me through to the living room, Mother watched as I opened the cabinet. Tucked in-between a mountain of papers, two faded snapshots of a stern bold-faced woman fell out. She was standing on the steps of a small house with a little boy either side. Although I'd never seen her before, I knew who she was. Her grey hair hung limply around her shoulders and she wore a long and faded print dress covered with a pinafore. The woman looked so much like Father. My Grandmother.

'I would never let him put any of these pictures up in the house, so he put them back where they belong, hidden and forgotten,' said Mother.

I wanted to ask her why, but there was too much pain in her face.

One photo was of Father swinging on a rope tied to a lamppost. I laughed at the ragged little boy with his impish smile. I was then startled to find two envelopes addressed to Mother and me tucked in the corner.

'Just like him to write what he could never say to my face,' said Mother.

She read hers aloud, her voice shrill and emotional with each word.

> *Well, old girl,*
> *I've gone. I love you, but you always knew that. Thank you love, for our life together. Without your love, I might have died long ago. Look after yourself. Stay close to Bess. Love Hal.*

Kissing the letter, Mother placed it alongside the pictures. She turned to me. 'Leave it there until after the funeral. It will only remind me that he's not here. For now, I want to believe he's still with us.'

Listening to Mother had delayed the opening of my own letter. Finally, carefully tearing the end of the envelope which revealed Father's distinctive handwriting, I read with misty eyes and a quivering mouth.

> *Sweetheart,*
> *I often dreamed of both of you being at my bedside when my time came so I could tell you, in my own words, how much I love you. The words would come from my own mouth not written on a piece of paper. Just in case my wish is not granted, I love you dearly. You and Mum stay close. Remember me in your thoughts. Love Dad.*

Waving her hand like a fan near her eyes, Mother said, 'If I could have one wish, it would be for him to be here with us.'

I could feel my mother's despair, but my own grief seemed to push everything into the background. Still, I felt pity towards her and my anger from the past seemed to set like the evening sun.

It was then I noticed the other letter, which had been inside my envelope. It had fallen on the floor by my feet. I picked it up. It was addressed to Zac.

Mother hadn't noticed, so I quickly shoved it into my pocket. Standing up, I caught hold of her hand. The long strong fingers felt lifeless as we walked through the door and into the garden. Outside in the warm late evening sunshine, I felt renewed. But my mother seemed more subdued. Refusing to sit on the garden chair, she stood and stared into space.

Liam returned from the shops and took Brian home, so I could spend some time with Mother. She spent most of the day lying on the bed. The heat was unbearable, and her dress clung to her damp body.

'I can still smell his cologne in the air,' she said.

Smiling, she told of his nightly ritual of a warm bath, leaving his skin soft and supple. She loved seeing him propped up in bed with his glasses perched on the end of his nose completely absorbed in one of his cowboy books. Every now and then he would say, 'Are you asleep, love?' He would nudge her slightly, so she'd snuggle closer to him. As long as she was near him, he would settle with his hand on her thigh and read for hours.

I could see the tears hanging on the end of her eyelashes as she spoke. Slowly, she calmed down and her eyes became heavy. Shifting to Father's side of the bed with his pyjamas clasped to her breasts, I left her to sleep.

Sitting in the kitchen caressing a cup of warm milk, I wondered what Father wanted me to say to his brother. Why had he waited until he was dead, leaving me alone to break the bad news? But most of all, I wanted to know the people who had shaped his life.

26

Creeping past Mother's room, I saw that the door was ajar. Her soft breathing assured me she was still asleep. Liam was taking care of Brian, giving me the perfect opportunity to find Uncle Zac. There was no need to tell Liam of my plan. I wanted to be alone to clear my head. Father must have wanted me to visit his brother, otherwise he wouldn't have included the letter within mine. But it also meant that he wanted to protect Mother from something.

Closing Mother's door inch by inch to keep any noise to the minimum and with one hand holding the banister and the other brushing the wall, I trod lightly down the stairs. Unlocking the front door, I stepped into a mountain of crisp golden-brown leaves swirled around my ankles.

'A single to the top of Upper Parliament Street please,' I said to the bus driver, as if it was my regular route. I'd vowed never to return to the area but something deep inside me always wanted to. I had the love of a good man, a beautiful son conceived in love - what more did I want? Why did I feel as if this area was like coming home? It was only when I stepped off the bus and black faces appeared like a glorious painting that had been hidden away, that I realised. Opening my bag and touching the letter, I wondered what my uncle was like. Would he be the image of Father? Have his considerate nature? Could he cook? I remembered that I'd not eaten for hours. But something else replaced the desire to eat - the thought of seeing relatives I'd never got the chance to meet.

Mother always told me that the Boulevard and the surrounding streets, was where unemployed, drug smoking, black men lived.

'It is an area no respectable woman would visit,' she'd say.

But I felt connected to the gravelled-lined path, even though I'd only been as far as Upper Parliament Street in the short time I was involved with Slim.

Standing on Uncle Zac's doorstep, I wondered if I should knock with short blunt strokes or a timid tap. I decided on the latter, knocked gently and waited. The white net curtains ruffled, and dark green drapes poked out from an open window. Fixing any stray hairs blown by the breeze, I grew restless waiting for someone to answer. Suddenly the door opened, and my instincts told me that the man standing before me was my uncle.

'Yeah?' he said. 'What do you want?' He was far smaller than I expected, with a boyish face and an expanding waistline. But his eyes twinkled like Father's.

'U-Uncle Z-Zac?' I stammered.

'What the…bloody hell. Uncle?' He scratched his head.

'I'm Bess, Hal's daughter.' I inched closer.

'Hal!' He beamed. 'Our Hal's girl?'

'Yes.'

He opened the door wide. 'Come in, come in, girl!'

I entered the house as Uncle Zac flew down the hallway with his hands flapping in the air shouting, 'Mabel, look who's here!'

Following my uncle, I saw a woman emerge from the kitchen.

'What's all the shouting about?' Her dark brown eyes fixed on me without blinking. She leaned on the kitchen door watching Uncle's frenzied actions.

'Sit down, girl,' he said, leading me to a small dining table. 'Make yourself at home. This is my Mabel.' He waved Mabel to his side as he sat down. 'How is my brother, the old goat? She's a looker just like her uncle isn't she, Mabel?'

Mabel held my gaze as though she knew there was bad news to come.

My mouth felt dry. 'My father is... dead.'

'Dead. My brother is dead?'

'Yes, Uncle Zac.'

Mabel couldn't save his head from hitting the table. I ran out of the room and sat on the stairs. Mabel's soothing voice, as she comforted my uncle, gave me some peace as well.

But the feeling of isolation still haunted me whenever I thought of not seeing Father again. Mother was racked in pain. This left me in awe of the love I sensed in Uncle Zac's home, and I wished it could be scooped into a ball and I could take it with me. When I ventured back into the room, Mabel was in the kitchen making tea. Uncle Zac sat with his head in his hands.

Mabel came in and put a teapot on the table. 'Sorry about your Dad.' Her voice cracked with emotion, but I was unable to read her eyes. What lay behind the sea of darkness? Did she resent me being here? Uncle sank into Mabel's arms like a lost child who'd been overjoyed one minute then had it shattered into sorrow.

He looked up. 'Sorry, love,' he said. 'You've lost your Dad and I should be comforting you, instead of crumbling.' He put his hand on his chest and tried to stop the tears. 'Was it his heart?'

'Yes, it weakened over time. He had a heart attack.' I paused. 'If Father had died without leaving me a letter, we wouldn't be sitting here now. Here is yours,' I said.

He seemed calmer, as though being strong enough to deal with the contents was all that mattered. His tears fell, and I could see the wet patches soaking into the page. He shook his head as he read it. Pushing the letter towards me he said, 'You can read it if you want to.'

I read aloud. Mabel listened but said nothing.

> *Zac,*
> *for many years I've wanted to get in touch. You know me, leaves everything until the last minute. This time though I left it too late. Please tell everyone that I have hurt that I'm sorry, but I had to follow my heart. I am sure that you and Mabel understand that now. I want you to organise my funeral. Only you would know what I want. Cover me well, brother, and don't throw any rocks into the hole. Say a prayer for me. Hal.*

Mabel picked up the used cups. Patting Zac on the shoulder, she said, 'I'll leave you two alone for a while.' Uncle Zac and I sat in silence, the memories stored in our hearts. When he finally looked at me, his eyes were red from crying and he was trembling. 'I am so ashamed of myself, girl'.

'Uncle Zac, we all make mistakes. I've made a few.'

He bent his head.

'What happened between you and my father?' I asked.

'Hal wanted a different life and we wouldn't accept it,' he said, then seemed to be thinking something over for a moment. 'But I can carry out his wishes in death. My brother wanted an African style burial. Do you think your mother will agree? What if she doesn't want me near the house? I wouldn't blame her.'

My face flushed, remembering how bitter Mother was towards him. For a moment I wished I'd spoken to her first. No, I told myself, it was time for making my own decisions.

'You were his brother. Mother would never turn you away now.' I didn't want to know about the issues between them. That could wait. Only Father was important right now.

'Okay... I will have to take whatever your mother wants to dish out.'

It seemed to me he wanted some reassurance and I hoped his mind was free from torment.

'Call Mabel will you, girl?'

I found Mabel washing the dishes. Her hands were red and crinkled as she wiped the suds on a tea towel.

'Uncle wants you,' I managed to say. Without a word, Mabel brushed past me. Thinking Uncle might want a private conversation with his wife, I did not follow. The kitchen was spotless. It was big, but there was a cosy feel about it.

'Bess?' Uncle Zac called. I ran to the room. There was a slight hoarseness in his voice. 'We've started making the arrangements.' He pushed back his chair and stood up. 'An African wake is not like putting someone in a funeral parlour. There's a lot to be done.'

I chewed the inside of my mouth. 'Okay, Uncle.'

Mabel picked up her coat from the back of the chair. Sliding her arm into the sleeve, she turned to me. 'Where do you live?'

Her question seemed to cut Zac to the core. He sat down wearily. 'To think I couldn't even remember my brother's address, girl.'

I rubbed his shoulder. 'Try to think of the good times because I will need to know everything about what you and my father got up to when you were young.'

His face lit up. 'Yeah, I suppose you're right. Let me look for a pen, girl.' Shuffling towards the sideboard, he opened the drawer. 'We haven't got any writing paper, girl…but the Liverpool Echo could come in handy.' He ripped a corner off the paper and handed it to me. I wrote the address and gave it back to him. Tucking it into his waistcoat pocket, he said, 'Thanks, girl, thanks for everything.'

It was dark when I left Uncle Zac's. I pondered the idea of calling Liam. But the vibration of being in this area was like a magic carpet beneath my feet, so I decided to stroll to the furthest stop and catch the later bus.

Uncle Zac was on my mind. We had been thrown together by circumstances beyond our control. I didn't know what had happened between my father and the rest of his family, but I wanted to find out. But when I'd reached home it was late, and all I wanted to do was hold my son.

27

The day I'd dreaded came with clear blue skies, and hot with a light breeze. Normally, on such a glorious morning, I would embrace my daily routine. Today, though, it was different.

Slipping on my black dress, I heard a car coming to a halt at the bottom of the path. Hurrying down the stairs, there was no need to wait for the doorbell to ring. Father didn't need any introduction; it was his home and he'd be welcomed with love. To have the house invaded by people who laughed and cried in their grief and told tales of Father's past and Mother's too, would seem an invasion of privacy to her. But he would have felt perfectly at home by it all.

'Put him over by the window. It's his favourite spot, apart from the kitchen,' I found myself blurting out. One of the bearers took my arm. 'You can still see him,' he said. I avoided the man's eyes, not wanting his rehearsed sympathy. 'This comes off. We don't screw it down until the last minute.' He went to slide off the coffin lid and then a blackness came over me. When I opened my eyes again a neighbour was leaning over me. She brought me a cup of sweet tea and held it to my lips while I drank some.

'You're still a bit wobbly, Bess. Lie on the sofa until you feel better. I'll stay for as long as you need me.' She was someone I hardly spoke to. As my eyes closed, I wished I had made more of an effort to get to know her.

'Thank you,' I managed to say before I fell asleep.

'The house is too quiet,' I heard Mother say as I woke up. 'Is it because my Hal is dead or was the silence always there?'

I managed to persuade her to lie down. Flopping on the unmade bed, the skin on her arms and legs hung loose on her shrunken frame. She'd been acting oddly since I told her about meeting Uncle Zac and that he'd volunteered to arrange everything. I wanted to change her bed linen earlier that day, but she had drawn the sheet up to her chin. 'No, not yet.'

I understood Father was still with her. His smell, his very being, were her memories now. Within an hour the doorbell rang, and four vigorous black women bustled in, carrying pans full of swollen rice. Others carried large enamel pots and cast-iron pans. The smell of cooked meats left to marinate in cayenne pepper took over the house, ready to be stewed, fried, or roasted to perfection. As Mother retired to her bedroom, she missed being kissed by greasy palm oil lips or hugged by strangers with alcohol fuelled breath. So many chairs were stacked in the hallway and the kitchen I could hardly move. Boxes full of glasses, cutlery and dinner plates were piled high.

The neighbours gaped with bewilderment at the droves of proud Africans wearing flowing gowns, shimmering with gold thread, beating their drums calling Father's name. Later, the neighbours came to pay their respect and their own memories of my father. It was time for Mother to see him.

'Mother!' I called.

After a few minutes she creaked open the door. 'Help me to the bathroom, girl.'

I led her back into the room to gather some toiletries and clean clothes, then took her arm and guided her to the bathroom. I left her to freshen up while I made her bed. When she'd finished and returned to her bedroom, she stumbled back to the dressing table and sat down. With trembling hands, she brushed some lipstick on.

'I'm ready to see him now.' Dismissing anyone who tried to approach her, she walked slowly to where Father lay, lifted the veil covering his face and kissed him on the forehead. 'God bless, Hal,' she whispered and sat with her arm draped over the side of the coffin.

It seemed like hours before Uncle Zac arrived, with a crowd of other people behind him. His face was gaunt, and his eyes had lost the shine. I hoped he would see how happy I was to have him here. Pointing to the door ahead, I said, 'Father's in there. Mother's with him, go through.'

An elderly man held up his hand, signalling the others to wait at the door. 'Bring me the cloth he ordered,' Uncle Zac said.

A young man stepped forward, bowed to the elder and gave him the square of material embodied with fine silk. He turned to face the crowd.

'This', he said, 'will be placed on the coffin.' He gave the cloth to Uncle Zac. 'Take this, son, and cover your brother. Let Zac have a private moment,' he urged.

Without looking at Mother, Uncle Zac walked towards the coffin. He seemed apprehensive, the closer he became. Seeing Uncle Zac with white hair must have been a shock to Mother, and she winced at his cries of pain. But she must have known his tears were real and the sorrow in his dark brown eyes had an impact on her. Yet she sat tight lipped with her head down.

Leaning over the coffin, Uncle Zac shook his head in disbelief. 'Hal, Hal,' he repeated as he held Father's ice-cold hand. He turned to Mother. 'How are you, Toni?'

'Bearing up.'

He sat down next to her. 'Can you forgive me?' Taking a handkerchief from his breast pocket, he wiped his brow keeping a tight grip on the wet piece of linen. 'You know I loved my brother.'

Mother nodded. 'I am sure you did. But there was no need to disown him. You can't justify that, can you, Zac?'

I held my breath. I wanted to know more about this too, but I couldn't face it yet. He stared at her. 'We won't go into all that, some other time maybe, but not now, Toni, not now.'

Mother rose from the chair. As she stood up to escape his presence, other mourners gathered around her. That's when the first lips touched her cheek, and she backed away from the sweet smell of alcohol on their breath. But I was sure she was grateful for any physical contact, as long as Uncle Zac kept his distance.

The sound of drums brought the house alive. The eerie atmosphere was gone. Despair was replaced by joyfulness and peace. Even Mother managed to smile at everyone dancing around the coffin singing African melodies and calling Father by his African name, Adebeyo. I was sure that he was listening.

Later, as the sunset faded into blackness, hymns rang out. Family members, friends and neighbours seemed satisfied their presence calmed the grief-stricken mother and daughter. The room became hushed and still with silent thoughts. Bottles with only a pub measure left in them lay discarded. Tea and coffee were being served now.

The elders sat on easy chairs. Some had loosened their ties, taken off their jackets and kicked off their shoes. Others, with their heads bowed in prayer, sat next to the coffin. Weather-beaten bibles lay on the knees of old men, who sang songs of the land they had left. They whispered, 'Africa, welcome your son before his final journey.'

The smell of burnt candles made the room hazy. The tales of youth had all been told, gone were the agile smiling elders. Now they hobbled around the room on their wood and ivory sculptured walking sticks or found a younger and stronger arm to lean on. Later that day, their friend would be gone forever. But, for now, he was still with them. Uncle Zac started to collect the empty glasses.

'Sorry Mabel couldn't come tonight, Toni, but she will be at the funeral.'

Mother nodded. Mabel not being there would normally have her on her feet in confrontation. It was a snub, no matter what Uncle Zac said. Instead she sat and stared into space. With Mabel's absence, I realised that the main problem was between her and my parents, and Uncle Zac had been caught in the middle. One day I would find out the truth. But right now, my mother wouldn't be able to take any more trouble.

'You and Bess should get some rest. It's going to be a long day. We are staying up with Hal,' said Uncle Zac. He took hold of Mother's arm. 'Have a little sleep.'

Slumping forward, she agreed, all the fight in her gone.

28

I woke the next morning to a heap of bedclothes at the side of my bed and the terror of a dream. I'd seen Father floating towards me. His presence was comforting at first, then something flickered at the far end of the room. The light seemed to entice me to grasp at the colours dancing before me but when I stretched my hand out, the light moved away, and Father's face appeared in the haze-like mist begging to be rescued. I tried to reach him. I couldn't.

He hasn't gone, I told myself, he's downstairs. Stepping over the jumbled mess and wiping the sleep from my eyes, I bolted to the door. Taking the stairs three at a time, I saw that the door to the front room was ajar. The brass handle of the coffin glistened in the sun. Yes, he was still there.

I shook Mother gently. 'You have to get up now, it's getting late.' Opening her eyes, like a weight was slowing the process, she squinted to bring me in focus. 'What time is it, girl?'

'Ten o'clock. I've made a pot of tea. Uncle Zac has gone. There is only a couple of women cleaning up.'

She pulled back the bedcovers. 'I'll be down in a minute.' She searched for her slippers with her feet.

'I'll put a couple of pieces of toast under the grill.'

She waved her hand. 'No, Bess, nothing to eat.'

Downstairs I sat at Father's side. It was only ten fifteen and the undertakers were not due until two that afternoon. Mother came down and ran her fingers on the side of the coffin. 'My Hal,' she said.

A woman came in and offered us tea. 'Do you two want to be alone with him?' she asked.

'No, it's okay. Sit down,' I replied.

Mother raised her eyebrow, but I knew she wanted some company too. I asked the woman what her name was.

'Joy,' she replied. We sat together in silence until the coffin lid was being closed. Mother was supported by Uncle Zac holding her arm, with me and Liam standing close by, as we walked out of the house.

Whether the men's suits were made with wool from the Shetland's, from the silkworms of Sudan or Paddy's Market, each wore black. The women brought their own individual styles: from headdresses and skirts sewn with pure gold thread, to coats and jackets made from Polyester and cotton. They craftily accessorised with beads, bangles and rings on their fingers. They looked wonderful.

I watched as the flowers in the hearse moved gently, balancing delicately on fragile stems, with the purr of the engine. Each movement they made was as though Father was sending me thousands of kisses sealed with a million hugs and one trillion goodbyes.

I relived some of my precious times with him as we moved slowly along Smithdown Road - how I'd skip down these streets alongside him feeling so proud. He'd be wearing his old felt cap that Mother hated and the raincoat with his tobacco pouch sticking out of the pocket. Every now and then he'd stop and say, 'Just having a quick fag, girl, then I'll buy you some sweets.'

We drove past the cemetery, which was hidden behind a black wall. There was only a glimpse of the sunken gravestones, long forgotten, but complementing the highly polished ones, that sprung up like new shoots.

Arriving at the church reminded me of the Bible, when the prodigal son returns home. Father was returning home. The crowd milled around welcoming him. Now he could be laid to rest in peace.

After the service, we buried him in a quiet space under the shade of a tree. With shirt sleeves rolled up, the men filled in the grave themselves. Mother was led back to the car in tears and was still upset when we arrived at the hall. I knew we wouldn't be staying too long. She had already expressed she was only going out of respect for Father. We left an hour later.

Mother stayed in this state of mind for a while. Sitting together one morning, a few days later, I asked her if she was looking forward to spring.

Pushing her hair back, she stared into the fire. 'No,' she answered. 'I'm not. When your father was alive then, yes, I loved to hear the birds twittering away and see them nesting in the trees.' She changed the subject and picked Brian up.

At lunch she moved the vegetables around her plate. Her hands trembled slightly as she put the fork down.

'I'm not ready to push the memory of your father to the back of my mind,' she said. 'Your father isn't ready either.'

Spring came and went. I'd sneak to see Uncle Zac and Mabel whenever I could, never mentioning his name to Mother or daring to tell her. But she knew.

Then, just before Christmas, Mother seemed to be on the mend and spending more time with her neighbours and going to bingo. Liam and I spent so much time encouraging her to accept she was only alone in her thoughts and assure her we were there for her. I gave

Mother unlimited time with Brian, and that seemed to work, but she couldn't forgive my contact with Uncle Zac and Mabel.

On Christmas Eve, after she'd wrapped Brian's presents, she poured herself a drink, laughed a lot and was even invited to a party a few doors away. Mother, I felt, had begun a new phrase of her life, which made me happy. That was until New Year's Eve. With her little finger curled around a glass of sherry, she swayed and stood inchers from my face. Her lips were twisted. 'You!' she spat. 'Think more of Zac and Mabel than you do of me.'

Liam swirled the whisky in his glass, oblivious to the argument brewing. Lips dry, I feared answering. Brian, cuddled up asleep, reminded of my responsibility. I sat and waited for her next sentence. Mother staggered towards me with her wine-stained teeth clenched together. 'You chose to get close to my enemy, so I am moving on.' The alcohol she'd poured down her throat slurred her speech and from then on it was a jumble of incoherent sentences. Eventually she fell to the floor in a drunken stupor and I put her to bed. Picking Brian up and rolling a blanket around him, I crept to the front door. Leaving Mother grinding her teeth and Liam asleep downstairs, I was glad to get out of the house.

The next morning Mother left. I'd heard her knocking, but I turned over in bed until she'd gone. Liam was snoring beside me. Brian stirred from his sleep as I kissed his damp face. Snuggling into my angel who always brought hope for the future and the strength to face the coming years, my spirits lifted.

29

Christmas passed, leaving rows of houses stripped of their twinkling fairy lights and windows rattling against the cold winds of winter. The frosty look on Mother's face when she opened the door was cold enough to set a jelly.

'Oh, you've finally come.'

I wished I hadn't. She tossed her head and I could see a cigarette dangling from the side of her mouth. She hated tobacco. Father was always pushed to the back door whenever he lit his pipe. Now there she was, turning the curtains from cream to nicotine brown, brazenly crossing her skinny legs and letting the ash gather around her feet. 'I'm off to bingo tonight so don't bother coming back,' she said blowing the smoke like a halo around her head.

I put the kettle on, hoping a cup of tea would act like an antidote, maybe bring her back to reality and forgive me. But no sooner had the tea slipped down her asbestos mouth, Zac was mentioned. From then on, she left me dizzy trying to make sense in what she was saying about him. I heard dog, rat, snake and every creature she could think of.

'I've got to make a life for myself now,' she said, finally. It was Liam banging on the door that interrupted her from carrying.

He was stood there with a face drained of blood holding Brian. He put him in my arms. 'They're back,' he said.

'Who?'

'The yanks.'

I could hear Mother shouting, 'What's going on out there?'

'I'm coming home in a minute, just let me calm her down.'

Liam disappeared before I finished speaking, his shirt- tail flapping in the wind.

'I'll be back in a minute, Mother, something has propped up.'

'You needn't bother!' she shouted after me.

I ran home with Brian.

My mind raced. 'Did they see you?'

'No, I hid.' He avoided my stare. 'I stole the money. I should have told you.'

Stealing was unheard of in my family. Now this gambling thief dared to bring this into our home and disrupt our child's life. We would have to move. The look on my face was enough for him to grab the newspaper and begin searching for somewhere to live. He spoke as if his vocal cords were still in the embryo stage. 'They're all too expensive, Bess.'

I pretended not to hear what he'd said. I busied myself feeding Brian, leaving Liam sweating and mopping his brow and wondering what to do.

The following evening Uncle Zac called. Liam was upstairs taking a bath and didn't hear the bell ring.

'I thought I'd come and see how you are,' he said, wiping his feet on the mat. Taking off his coat, hat and gloves, he warmed his hands by the fire and gently held Brian. He smothered him in kisses.

'Where's lover boy and Moaning Minnie?' he asked.

'Oh, one's in the bath, and the other one's probably arguing with herself.'

I made a drink for both of us, leaving Liam's to cool.

'You look strained, girl. Sure you're alright? How's

your mother?'

'Missing Father so much.' I tasted salty tears rolling down my cheeks. I tried wiping them away but to no avail.

'What's wrong, girl? Tell me.' I started at the beginning and ended as Liam walked in.

'I'll make some fresh tea,' I said, dropping the cup. It smashed to the floor. Liam helped to clear the mess then sat down with Uncle Zac.

'Bess has told me everything,' I heard him say. 'If you want my help in any way I'm here for you. I have people who can take care of those two. So, let me know if you need me.'

'Thanks, Zac, but I'll sort it out.' When he left Liam bounced into the living room, slamming the door behind him. His face was red with rage. 'You didn't have to tell him everything.'

'I wanted to.' Looking into his eyes, narrow and threatening, I didn't hate him, but there was no desire to reassure him either.

'My uncle will be involved whether you like or not,' I said.

'You've only just met him, for Christ's sake.'

'Yes, so I have many years to make up.'

He sat facing me. His tone changed, and he looked worried. 'What are we going to do Bess?'

'I'm going to see Uncle Zac tomorrow.'

'Is that to finish my life story?' he was back to raging at me.

'No. To ask if he could tell me something.'

'What's that?'

'Why I'm married to such a fool.' I stormed off to see to Brian. After putting him to bed and switching off the hall light, I found Liam with a bottle of whisky in his hand. He half-filled the glass, and I winced as he swallowed in one gulp. Even with the glow of the fire, the room looked dull. The radio had been turned off. The televisions blank screen did nothing but deaden the atmosphere.

'Will you stop biting your nails!' I snapped, as he gnawed his teeth around the soft tissue. In the silence of our bedroom, I watched the hands of the clock, waiting for daylight.

The next day I went to Uncle Zac's. Mabel opened the door and they both struggled up the steps with the pram. A young girl ran down the stairs. 'So, you're the one my Dad keeps yapping about.' She glared at me.

I realised it was Ruby, Uncle Zac's daughter.

'You look nice,' I said to try and hide my embarrassment.

Ruby flicked her head and didn't reply. I couldn't blame her for her rudeness. She didn't know me, even though she looked a bit like me with her tumbling flaxen curls. She had skin like milk and almond shaped eyes, but her features were from the Tobo clan, as Mother would say.

'Don't be late!' Uncle Zac shouted as Ruby closed the door behind her.

Mabel made a pot of tea and disappeared to the kitchen with Brian in her arms. Uncle Zac sat in his chair and filling his pipe. 'You seem to be on edge still. Do you want my help?'

'It's the trouble with the Americans, Uncle. I can't think straight, and we don't know what to do.' I poured the tea.

'Thanks,' Uncle Zac said, reaching for the cup without taking his eyes off me. He took a few sips. 'Don't you think you should leave the bloody house? Move from the area all altogether?'

'Oh… I don't know,' I said. 'What about my mother?'

'She could live with you. She's no spring chicken. She is going to need you eventually.'

The thought of Mother being dependent on me turned my insides. But it also gave me the determination to do whatever I wanted to do now before she'd bang her walking stick on a room above our heads.

I quickly shut the image out of my mind. I concentrated on how sturdy she was at present and hoped she'd want her independence for as long as possible. But in my heart, I would always be there for her and I was sure she knew that.

'My mother wouldn't leave her home yet. She loves the house and the area.'

Stretching his legs Uncle Zac said, 'You and Liam could live here.'

'I'll have to ask Liam.'

He stood up, reached for a box of matches, and relit his pipe. 'You'll have to put your foot down. Liam put you and the baby in this position. He should have no say in the matter.'

I knew I had to do what made me feel safe. Liam had lit the fuse. Now he just wanted to sit there hoping the nothing would blow up.

Returning home, I suspected Liam had given Mother a running commentary about my betrayal. It was written all over his face.

'We're leaving here,' I announced. 'We're moving in with Uncle and Mabel.' I walked out of the room, leaving him to digest what I'd said.

Brian had fallen asleep. Slinging the toy car Liam had bought in the corner of the room, I went downstairs to face him. I waited for the long confrontation and all his objections on why we shouldn't leave. I put my head in my hands waiting for the show to begin, but to my amazement Liam touched me lovingly on the shoulder and asked me when we would move.

'We could be out by next week,' I said.

'Next...week,' Liam replied. 'It will take time sort things out. Put the furniture in storage and... all that.'

'I know.'

What about your mother? And there's my job.'

'Yes, she'd be safer without us. We have a car you know, and Uncle Zac is not living in another country.' An excitement was building up inside me. As if my soul finally found something I'd always longed for. An Uncle who I knew loved me. Someone in the family who'd not been conditioned or frightened to show how much he cared was offering me the chance of another life. Neither, Liam or Mother would snatch that from me. I was even prepared to leave on my own, take Brian and run.

Liam was all talked out. Defeated and tired, he went upstairs alone.

30

The next afternoon I found Mother in her garden holding a pitchfork and digging holes in the frozen earth. She looked radiant with a winter blush on her cheeks as she lifted her head and glared at me. 'As long as I see Brian, you can do what you want.'

'Mother, we're not moving abroad.'

'No, just moving in with the enemy.' There were no words to ease her pain. I stood and watched her toss tufts of rain sodden grass as far as she could. 'I told you I'd know when I was ready to start again. Well, you've helped me make my mind up, the moment Liam told me you were moving in with Zac.'

I put my arms around her and held her close. She didn't shrug me off. In an unusually calm voice she added, 'I don't want to see Brian in any danger.'

With a promise to visit every week, I left her in the garden.

That afternoon, wrapping clothes in brown paper and washing my little china ornaments, I realised how little I'd brought to the marriage. I wondered if Liam ever thought of it too, but no, I told myself, ownership wouldn't enter his mind. I sealed the first batch and had a cup of tea.

The happiness I felt at leaving escalated, until I was almost bursting with joy. Liam came home from work and sulked at my enthusiasm. The urge to tell him the decision to move came from me and no one else was on the tip of my tongue. Not the two Americans, me, me, me, I wanted to shout. Instead I smiled inwardly.

Mother clung to Brian on our last few moments in the Crescent. I checked the back door, ran my fingers over the tops of window sills and, without a backward glance, closed the door on the past.

Liam sat tight-lipped in the car. He revved the engine so hard that black smoke billowed from the rear end. Mother waved us on our way before disappearing into her neighbour's house, leaving me content that she would be safe and had good support.

The rattling of pots, pans and the thump of plastic bags falling off the back seat gave Liam something to moan about. He looked at me as if wanting a reaction, only to see my lips curled in a smile.

Uncle Zac was standing on the bottom step of his house, with Mabel rigid in the doorway as we arrived.

'Welcome, queen.' Uncle Zac beamed. He led us in and opened the parlour door. 'You get accustomed to your room and we'll bring the rest of the stuff in won't we, son?'

Liam looked around the room, narrowing his eyes at the cream and brown flowered wallpaper. I was sure I saw him sneer at the pink lampshade dangling overhead. The cracked lino on the floor held his gaze and he kept standing on the sunken parts, trying his best to bring this to my attention.

'Yes,' he finally replied.

I wonder what he would have thought of Mrs Polanski's, I smiled to myself.

When our bits and pieces were put in place and I'd patted my favourite eiderdown on the bed, we went into the kitchen where Mabel had cooked a meal. Afterwards, she insisted on bathing Brian, leaving me and Liam to wash up while Uncle Zac snoozed in his chair. I held my breath as Mabel swished Brian around the sink, fearing he would slip and crack his head. But I saw how her big chubby hands held Brian steadily and how gently she washed his hair.

Ruby came in, her bottom lip jutting out, as she saw us making ourselves at home. 'Is that my dinner?' she asked.

'Yes, do you want me to put it in the oven for you?' I replied.

She snatched the plate and went over to the oven. Her baby face was caked in makeup, making her look older. Her mini-skirt was like a belt, and she had a skimpy top on that I was sure would fit Brian. When her food was ready, she sat alone, chomping noisily. I was sure she had an arsenal of tricks to throw at us. After all, we were the intruders. But I was confident we would eventually become good friends.

After dinner, we all gathered in the large back room. Mabel sat flicking through a book. The gas fire hissed from the draught, which filtered through a gap under the door and projected a cosy glow on the highly polished furniture. Uncle Zac filled his pipe. Striking a match on the side of the grate, he turned to Mabel. 'Our Ruby is not going out again, is she?'

'Don't know, she might.'

He snorted at her curt reply. 'Mabel!'

'Can't you see I'm reading?' Marking the chapter by turning the corner of the page, she slammed the book shut and glared at him.

'If you weren't so soft with Ruby, she'd be working by now,' Uncle Zac replied.

'Oh,' she said, screwing her face up. 'Working where?'

Uncle Zac stood up and placed his pipe on the mantelpiece. 'Anywhere.'

'If, and when, our Ruby gets a job, Zac Tobo, it won't be any old job. It certainly will not be in a bag warehouse, or a peanut factory, and she is not interested in working in an overall factory either.'

Uncle snatched his pipe again. 'Ruby seems to forget she larked around in school. So, woman, Ruby will be a manual worker and won't be sitting at a desk doing paperwork'. He banged the ash from his pipe and sat down.

'I'll just go and see if Brian's asleep,' I said, desperate to escape, but they didn't hear me.

'That doesn't mean she should work anywhere!' I heard Mabel shout.

'It does! Because if she didn't spend so much time in front of the mirror or hanging around boys or listening to stupid music with you filling her head with rubbish, she'd be earning her keep.'

I peeked in at Brian and returned to see Mabel stand up and fling her book on the floor. 'What rubbish do I tell her?'

'For one, you tell her she isn't black!' Perspiration slid down my uncle's face.

'I never tell her that,' Mabel protested. 'I just tell her she looks more like me.'

Uncle Zac laughed. 'What! With a flat nose like hers?'

Mabel lowered her eyes.

'Mabel, you know as well as I do that Ruby will only get hurt.'

'I know, Zac, but I am only trying to make her strong,' she spoke quietly. 'You know what it's like to be black.

'Yes, but it doesn't work like that, love. No matter how light skinned someone is, white people see the black first and maybe the qualifications second. That's where the employers have the upper hand. Most of us don't have the qualifications to get a good job and our Ruby is one of them.' He leaned forward and turned the fire down, making the room dark. Mabel returned to her book.

Uncle Zac's words played on my mind, especially when he rubbed the back of his neck and complained how he'd strained it lifting heavy coal bags. He confessed how he gave Ruby money from his work's pension to buy a bit of makeup and recognised that he also spoilt her. It wasn't just Mabel who was trying to shield her daughter from the world. Then he would tell me about Mabel.

'She's so prim and proper now. Hard to believe she thought it was okay to wash nappies in the same pan she cooked scouse in.' He pretended to shudder and rolled his eyes. Then he mentioned his Father who'd wash chickens with a scrubbing brush. He dabbed the tears from his eyes. 'By the time he'd finished, the chicken was hairless, featherless, and gutless then dropped into a pan of boiling palm oil.'

'What's amusing you two then?' Mabel appeared.

'Just told Bess about my father, love. Remember him and his chickens?'

'How could I forget? I was the one who had to catch them. They'd run around the yard clucking their heads off. I was terrified!' She smiled. 'I remember that big old pot which was always full to the brim with a thick red sauce.'

'So do I,' said Uncle Zac. 'How Father would put the lid on the pan and turn the gas so low that the flame was almost invisible.

Mabel leaned back in her chair and rolled up her sleeves. 'Look, I still have the scars, from moving the chicken around that cast-iron contraption and being splashed with grease.' She laughed.

'Those were the days, old girl.'

'Yes, Zac. I wouldn't change them for the world.'

I left them alone to talk about the past, sitting knee to knee, forgetting the arguments and lost in their memories.

31

Some weeks later, when Mabel and Ruth were out, and Liam had gone for a walk, I seized the opportunity to talk to my uncle.

'Do you fancy a drink, queen?' he shouted from the pantry.

'No thanks. I've drunk enough coffee and tea to sink the Titanic.'

'It's a drop of the hard stuff I am talking about - my special concoction of Guinness with a splash of rum.'

'Okay,' I replied. 'No ice.'

'The only block of ice in this house is Mabel!' he laughed.

He placed both glasses on the table. 'Those two have gone to the creepy church where they talk to things that go bump in the night. They probably want to find out my life expectancy.' He raised the tumbler and sipped slowly.

'You were quite angry with Mabel a few weeks ago?' I ventured.

'That's not something for you to worry about.'

'What I don't understand, Uncle, is she never seems relaxed?'

'Mabel's always been hyped up. Don't get me wrong I love her, and as hard as it is to believe, she cares for me. It's just that her love is like a ladder. If you miss the step, you could find yourself swinging in mid-air.'

'Mother tends to have similar problems to Mabel. Is that why you and my father fell out?'

He leant forward. 'Mabel has always been honest. She can't hide how she really feels. There were a few...issues with how your parents got together.'

'Because my mother was too white?' I asked. 'But that doesn't make sense as you and her-'

'It wasn't a colour issue that made her disapprove of them,' Uncle Zac cut in. 'That was a problem between me and Mabel though.' He toyed with his drink and reached for his pipe, banging the stem against his tobacco tin. He refilled our glasses. 'I am of the opinion, girl, that white people have instincts they are not aware of.'

'What do you mean?'

'Well, if black people are concerned about who their children marry, then they often tell them verbally. But with white folks it's not necessary for them to be so blunt. Because, I believe, most of their kids subconsciously know their parent's view on black people.' He swallowed his drink. His fingers tapped the thick glass. 'Somehow the message would be clear - black people should keep their genes to themselves.'

I was so glad I had this man's genes. I wanted to shout about how proud I was of them.

'So, when the rules are broken, family links are often severed. In most cases family ties are broken beyond repair,' he concluded.

I thought of the times I'd felt alienated when the revulsion of others could barely be hidden by a smile, when their actions told me what they truly felt. Mabel loved him, but she felt unsure around other black people, and that would have included my father.

He told me, as he'd told Mabel, that this wasn't her fault. She'd been influenced by others and the uneasy feelings would pass. But he always knew her impression of black people was like a dye engrained into nylon fibre.

And no matter how he'd try, there was no solution to removing what would be engrained forever.

He loosened his collar, 'Do you know what? There are some black people who, behind closed doors, call their own children black bastards. So, you see those sorts of insults were not exclusively used by white people.' He stood up and walked over to the window and sighed.

I was beginning to understand my parents and how they tried to run away from their identity to avoid being rejected. What the ears didn't hear, I presumed, was their way of coping. I also thought of Liam and the way he acted around Uncle Zac. He'd accepted me and my father as we had integrated ourselves into a white world. But my uncle didn't conform.

There was a rustle at the front door. Mabel and Ruby bustled in. Taking off her coat, Ruby put the kettle on while Mabel plonked Brian on her knee. The glow of the fire caught the happiness in her face. Brian looking into her eyes with wonder was a sight that would stay in my heart. Mabel was a good woman, and the love she gave my son was not rehearsed or false. So, no matter what her instincts about colour were, and her issues with my parents, I loved her as well.

Liam came in about an hour later. Uncle Zac pulled out a chair for him to sit on. 'Do you fancy going out at the weekend?'

'Oh...no, Zac. I'm working overtime on Saturday, need the money,' he said, smiling. Usually when Liam smiled, his eyes did as well, but now they crinkled into slits.

'Let's set a date when you can meet the gang then,' Zac offered.

A look of panic spread across Liam's face as Uncle pulled out a chair and asked Mabel where the bottle opener was.

'Hal used to drink in the Sefton Arms. You know the one?' Liam asked. I assumed Uncle would say yes and they would have something in common. It was a predominately white pub.

'Nope, don't know that one,' replied Uncle. 'Is it posh? I don't do posh.' For about an hour Uncle yapped about himself but Liam revealed nothing. When Liam felt comfortable in his surroundings he would be the first to tell a joke or two, now he sat straight backed and observed. 'Well, son, shall we say next weekend then? I'll show you around and I know you will have a good time once the yanks have been seen to.'

'I'll let you know,' replied Liam. He beckoned me to follow him into our room. As I walked behind him, I saw the slouch in his movements and how his jacket hung limp around his shoulders. He sat on the bed. 'I can't do this Bess. Live here, in this hut, with him.'

Stunned by his coldness, I shrank away from him. He let his arms drop to his sides. 'Okay, if you want to stay here I'll go to London find us somewhere to live and get a job. All the stuff with the yanks should have died down, and when you're ready, you and Brian can join me.'

My head reeled trying to make sense of it all.

'Do you have a problem with Uncle Zac?' I asked.

'He's just...not like us,' he said and turned away from my rage.

To Uncle Zac and Mabel nothing had changed. But whenever Liam and I were alone, I'd freeze if he even brushed passed me, or tried to cuddle up to me in bed. The following Friday he handed me an unopened wage packet, packed a small bag and left in the early hours of Saturday morning.

32

I didn't want to see the empty place at the breakfast table that morning. Asking Mabel to wash, dress and feed Brian, I stayed in my room, too ashamed to face Uncle Zac.

He tapped on my door. 'Come on, girl. Stop moping and have something to eat. You have a child to look after.' I heard him walk away then return a while later. 'Me and Mabel are out on the tiles tonight, so there's no babysitter.'

I creaked open the door and stuck my head out to see if he had gone. He hadn't. He stood with his arms folded, pipe dangling from his lips. 'I saw him leave this morning. Are you going to tell me the full story?'

I lied and said it was to do with the yanks, and not my suspicions that my husband was racist.

With Liam gone to London I settled in my new home. Because there was no urgency to worry about the conflict with the Americans I was able to push those events to the back of my mind. Spring arrived, and I took Brian to visit mother regularly but always glad to return to Uncle Zac's welcoming laugh and Mable's quite but reassuring nature. Even Ruby smiled more often but it was me, who felt guilty. We were taking up space leaving Ruby having to resort to constantly stay in her bedroom.

I still had some of the money Liam gave me and not having to pay rent was an extra benefit. Unknown to Uncle Zac I would slip Mable a few pound now and then to help with the weekly shopping. So, life was not grand by any stretch of the imagination, but I was happy to be part of a loving and caring family. I thought of the life I shared with Liam and of all the material aspects of our relationship and hoped one day it would all come together. Liam assured me before he left, we still had all our furniture and he would take care of all payments to the storage company. I felt, no matter what, that Brian would have a home when I was strong enough to face the issues in my marriage.

I should have been concerned by the lack of communication between Liam and I and convinced myself he was finding his feet. By late summer anger set in. I did not care if he'd lost his feet to frost bite. He should have at least thought about Brain. My plan was to wait until after Christmas find work and build a life without Liam. I still loved him but loving my son was my first priority.

Six weeks before Christmas someone knocked on the front door, a man whose head almost reached the skylight stood on the step picking his teeth and grinning. 'Zac in?' he asked. One of the man's feet almost covered the large coconut mat. Uncle came out and embraced the man. 'Do you mind leaving us for a while, love?' he said. 'Me and my mate have a talk'

I closed the door. I heard them talking about Liam. 'He loves the ladies and a drink,' the stranger said. 'But we've found the yanks, if you still want anything sorting.'

Uncle Zac came to see me after his friend had left. 'I'm disappointed in myself for not recognising how different you and Liam were,' he said. 'You seemed to be devoted to each other.'

'Uncle, Liam had a life before he met me you know.'

'Alright, Bess, let's leave it at that. If he ever hurts you though, he will have me to deal with.'

Uncle Zac hinted his friends were ready to act against

the yanks. The two Americans had become regulars in a well-known drinking den. 'Bess, you can come with me if you want?

Mabel's knitting needles clanged together, and she sucked her teeth at his suggestion. But I found myself nodding. Even if it didn't bring Liam back, me and Brian would be safe.

Our feet crunched and slipped on thin layers of ice as we made our way towards Upper Parliament Street. We shielded our faces from windswept snowflakes falling all around us.

'Come through, Zac,' said a man at the entrance to the club. 'Long time no see.'

'Well, you know when you're this good looking the wife wears the trousers,' Uncle joked.

We walked through the door into the room full of people dancing to a three-piece band. They strummed a Frank Sinatra song which helped turn the smoky atmosphere into a cosy and seductive scene. Decorations and Christmas lights flickered in dark alcoves. The bass player grinned intently, hypnotized by the sound each instrument created.

'Good to see you again, Zac,' the barman said.

'You too, Iron Face. Just pour me half a glass. I want to keep sober, anything could happen tonight.'

'You want a drink, queen?' Iron Face asked me.

'I'll have a brown ale, please.'

We went over to a small group, who rearranged seats close to the bar and wiped the table before we sat down.

'That's them,' one called Snake Eyes said to Uncle. 'Those two yanks.'

'Do your usual patter, Joe,' Uncle said to another of the men, leaning over the glass-laden table. 'Make sure they don't suspect anything.'

Joe had the kind of face that made woman swoon. He was dark, tall and handsome with a voice that sounded smooth and reassuring. But with all his star qualities, he seemed the most approachable of the group. He went over to the men drinking at the bar. We listened in.

'Are you alright?' he asked them.

'Yes, man, we're fine,' the American answered, willing to strike up conversation.

'Where do you come from? You sound like Canadians.'

Turning to get a better look at Joe, one of them said, 'No, man, we're from New York. We're here on holiday. You know, slumming.'

Joe edged nearer. 'What brings you to this club then? Usually it's the All Nations club down the road that gets all the trade.'

The music was too loud to hear much of the conversation, but Liam was mentioned and then Joe excused himself saying he was going for a slash.

The smaller of the Americans put his hand into the inside pocket of his suit. 'Slash, man! What motherfucking bad arse is going to slash us?'

Joe laughed. 'In England it means going for a pee. But take it easy, man. Don't make any false moves in this place or you will be dead.'

'Weird words, man,' the American muttered.

Joe walked briskly to the men's room and gave the nod for Snake Eyes to follow. Joe was grinning when he returned, leaning over me. 'Snake Eyes is ready to batter them. He's coiled like his namesake. Tell Zac it's all set. We're going on the Avenue. Those yanks think we're taking them to another club. Tell him to stay here, let me and the boys take care of things.'

On hearing violence could be involved, I panicked.

Then I was angry with Liam for inflicting the problem on me and it was too late to change my mind. Hoping for the best outcome, I walked over to Joe, ready to do my part. I my arm around his waist and kissed him on the lips. The charade was meant to give the impression to the Americans that Joe was my man. The kiss felt as though he was, but the feeling of his soft lips soon faded as we walked down the steps of the club.

33

Joe slowed the pace as we walked in the opposite direction of the Rialto, where in their younger days Uncle Zac and Joe danced to rock and roll every Thursday night trying to make contact with pretty white girls.

'Young women,' Mandy had once told me, 'eager to defy the racist views of their parents, whose hatred of black people spread from the Labour Exchange to the Rialto ballroom.'

But once the dance was over and they'd had a quick fumble in a back entry with only rats scurrying around to see them, they would return home as dutiful daughters and portrayed no desire to sample the forbidden fruit beyond that. I imagined Joe felt alive on those nights. I bet he was always the best dancer. He must have rose above the silent resentment of others as he twisted and turned to the music.

As we walked into a side street, one of the Americans began to panic.

'Hey, man,' he said, positioning himself to run. 'Where is this club? This street's dark, God dammit.'

The row of lock-up garages, with their creaking tin doors, had the hallmarks of a trap. Snake Eyes and Iron Face loomed in the shadows, while others blocked any exits.

'So,' said Joe softly, 'You're looking for my mate Liam? Why didn't the mob send real men instead of you two little shits? Move your fucking hand now before I slice the little piece between your legs.'

The blade Iron Face produced glistened in the frosty air giving the America second thoughts about reaching into his pocket.

'Frisk them,' Joe commanded.

Iron Face moved towards the men with military precision. In the moonlight I could see damp patches appearing on one of the American's as Iron Face ran his hand over his body.

'Why can't we take these mother-fuckers?' The other American said. 'They're only a bunch of old cronies jumping around like the guys in the States. We can deal with them.'

'Fucking hell!' Iron Face shouted. 'That guy's pissed himself.'

I'm sure he could see the warped look in Iron Face's cold eyes. Their lives depended on quick thinking.

'We only wanted our money,' one of them said. The other nodded his head in agreement and managed to babble a few words that we could hardly understand.

'So, where does the mob fit in then?' Iron Face demanded to know.

'I never rode anywhere with them mother fuckers,' one mumbled.

'What racket were you running then?' Joe asked, cracking his knuckles.

'The boss,' the bigger of the two explained, 'sent us to England. We were told to visit the Cotton club in London. A man called Melvin would approach us. He would give us a packet, and we would smuggle whatever it contained into the States.'

'What about Liam?' Joe demanded.

'He was meant to be a runner, but he stole our money.'

'Go on.'

'We managed to get Liam's address after having a

drink with his buddy. Then we came to get our money back, made Liam think we were part of the mob.'

'Let me get this story straight,' Joe said, edging nearer. 'You mean to fucking tell me, you are not part of the mob?'

'N-no,' one of them stammered.

'You two bastards have come to Liverpool to give my spar aggravation. Fuck them!' Snake Eyes said. 'Cut their fucking bollocks off.'

'We'll give you money? Good money. Just let us go, man.'

'How much have you got?' Snake Eyes muttered in the darkness.

Both men dipped frantically into their pockets and handed their wallets over. Snake Eyes grinned and within seconds he had a handful of gold chains

'Now,' Joe said. 'Start running. Run for your fucking lives.'

The men bolted to freedom with the frosty wind on their already taunt skin. The laughing and jeering Joe, Snake Eyes and Iron Face gave the Americans the abilities of world class sprinters.

The three men were jubilant. So was I, yet a part of me felt disgust at being there. With mixed emotions I tried to wipe the image of the terrified Americans from my mind. I focused instead on Brian and relished in the peace I now felt. I was sure Father would have understood.

We headed back, climbing the club's slippery steps and helping each other avoid thick blocks of ice that were frozen around the concrete slabs. Snake Eyes gloated over the spoils – a twenty-two carat ring and the hangman's rope of a chain almost touching his waist. Iron Face rubbed the face of a watch and Joe kept a tight grip on the money.

Uncle Zac was propping the up the bar. 'I've already been given a garbled account from Snake Eyes about what went on, Joe. Give me a beginning middle and an end in English, will you?'

Joe rocked on his heels. 'There is no fucking mob for a start. Those two hillbillies were trying it on.' He sucked his teeth. 'Liam should have known better. Anyway, let's have a drink. They won't show their arses around here again. I done it for you and that lovely niece of yours, not that arsehole Liam.'

34

It had been a while since I had sat so close to a man, and I hoped Joe hadn't noticed my unease. There was no way he could hear my heart beating when I tried to avoid my leg touching his as the cab jolted over bumps in the road and skidded on pockets of ice. It was only a five-minute drive from the club to our house but enough time to gather my thoughts and stop fantasising about Joe.

Mabel was waiting as the taxi pulled up. 'Thank God,' she said. 'He's only smashed out of his head through drink and not by someone's fist.' She hooked her arm underneath Uncle Zac's shoulder and both of us struggled to get him indoors. It must have been the crashing sound that brought Joe back inside after paying the taxi fare, to find Uncle sprawled out on the floor.

'Here,' Joe said. 'Leave him to me.' Effortlessly he pulled Uncle up by his arms and helped him upstairs. We followed and watched as Joe slipped Uncle's shoes off, threw him on the bed, turned him on his side and left him to dream.

'You must know after tonight's episode your feller has nothing to worry about,' Joe said to me. 'And neither do you.'

'Thanks, Joe. Without your support I don't know what we'd have done.'

'That's okay. I wanted to do it. You know why, don't you?'

'Joe, I'm a married woman.'

He stood up and walked towards me. 'I understand

that, but something tells me you want more,' he said, brushing his lips on the back of my neck.

Desire made me feel weak at the knees as I pushed him away.

He smiled. 'Nothing will put me off you.'

I slammed the door behind him. My head throbbed. I wanted to tell Liam to come home as Joe's words rang in my ears. But Liam didn't care about any of us, particularly Uncle Zac. I tried to recall how happy we were on our engagement day, when me and Abigail had danced around the flat in sheer bliss. I wished she hadn't gone to Canada. I missed Mandy as well, despite everything.

I hoped when the New Year arrived, things would be different, that Liam would come back and accept Uncle Zac as his own.

35

Walking through the door with the wind howling behind him, Uncle Zac took off his coat and filled his pipe. In between sucking on the stem and letting out a haze of smoke, he announced, 'It will be Christmas soon.'

Mabel sighed, no mood to be reminded, and walked over to the sink. 'Anyone fancy a brew?

'I'll make it,' said Uncle Zac, kissing her on the cheek.

This brought a smile to Mabel's face and she sat beside Uncle, drinking her tea. My thoughts turned to Mother and who I should spend the festive season with. I knew from my last visit that she would only tolerate me being with her on Christmas Day for the sake of Brian. I had to find a compromise and quick.

I was concerned about Mother's neighbours. Her purse was always on view with money scattered over the table. Neighbours would make cups of tea without asking. The washing machine was always crammed with children's clothes. The children themselves were running up and down the stairs and turning taps on in the bathroom.

It was as though Mother was paying for their company and letting them take advantage. Recently when visiting her, I'd snapped and threw them all out of the house, leaving Mother frothing at the mouth.

My actions opened a can of worms in the form of the verbal abuse Mother hurled at me. She stomped her feet and demanded I leave. Unable to intervene in Mother's affairs again, all I could do was wait until she came to her senses.

Meanwhile I received news from Liam.

> *Dear Bess,*
> *I hope you are okay. I have enclosed some money for you. I will put some more in the bank after the holiday. The good news is I am working. So, if you need anything in a couple of months I'll send you some more. I hope that Brian likes his presents. Please kiss him for me and take care of yourself. Love Liam xx P.S. say hello to your mother*

I counted the hundred and fifty pounds he'd sent, and I shoved the money into my housecoat pocket. There was no mention in Liam's letter about coming home. I heard Uncle Zac moving around upstairs. Taking out Uncle's and Mabel's cups from the cupboard, I waited for them come down. It was the weekend and Brian was still asleep, so we could all take it easy for a change.

'Good morning, girl,' said Uncle Zac. 'Did you hear Ruby come in last night?'

I shook my head as he sat down and yawned. Mabel appeared, smiling. She had seemed so much more relaxed with me lately. I made a pot of tea and sat around the table.

'I'd like to give you something,' I said, and I put the money on the table.

Uncle pushed his chair back. 'Look girl, we're family. We won't take it.'

'I want you to have this money, so for once you can buy yourselves something without worrying about the cost.

Uncle had a stubborn expression on his face. Mabel put her hand on his.

'Zac, Bess only wants to give us a present. She is not

doing it because she's living here. She loves you.'

'Alright, alright. Give it to Mabel, girl. She will know what to do with it. And thank you.'

I knew that Uncle Zac wasn't intending to spend any of it himself, especially when he brought a Christmas tree home a few weeks later. We watched as the branches almost poked his eye out and he disappeared into them.

'It's for Brian,' replied Uncle Zac. 'And it was going cheap.' He brushed the pines off his hat.

'They must have seen you coming,' Mabel said. 'The bloody thing's already half dead.'

'Well the other half will be alright then,' he answered, smiling. Within seconds we were all helping to pull the tree indoors. Mabel was like a squirrel gathering nuts, as she picked up the fallen needles of the tree and put them into the pocket of her apron.

Uncle rubbed his hands together. 'Right now, all we need is the deccies. We'll sort them out after our tea.'

Mabel served the meal. 'If you find your food full of little green things, it's not my fault, blame bloody Father Christmas.' Winking at me she added, 'Who also calls himself Zac.'

After we'd finished eating, Mabel washed the dishes and I gave Brian a bath and then sat him in his highchair watching his uncle tinkle with the decorations. Brian was memorised with the tiny glass lights and tried to grab one of the golden lanterns hanging from the lowest branches. After a couple of hours of shaping and reshaping, the lights were on.

Uncle Zac stood back with pride. 'Well, it's going to be a smashing Christmas.' Using brute force and the heel of his shoe, the tree was finally stuck in the corner of the room.

'Fancy a drink, girls?' he asked. He poured the drinks

and raised a toast. Ruby popped her head around the door, closed it again and banged upstairs.

36

Early in the morning on Christmas Eve, I left Brian sleeping and found Ruby sitting on the floor wrapping the last of the presents. Mabel had already been up and made the fire. It was as though she'd waved a magic wand to transform the room. Everywhere had extra sparkle. The curtains were wide open, and I could see rooftops thick with snow reminding me, for a second, of Shakespeare Road. Not wanting the past to cloud the wonderful scene before me, I started to put my presents for everyone under the tree.

'Morning,' I said to Ruby.

'Thanks for the money. Dad told me what you gave us,' she mumbled, giving me a small smile. Even when she pouted her mouth or screwed up her forehead she was stunning. I didn't reply but sat beside her. Unexpectedly, she asked me if I'd like a cup of tea. It was a nice moment between us.

Later in the day Uncle Zac helped Mabel to stuff the turkey. The radio played seasonal and chart music in the background. My heart was filled with peace. It felt like no one could spoil my happiness. I laughed at Uncle Zac with Brian in his arms dancing around the room.

I went to bed that night without overloading my brain about the future. I heard Mabel singing to Brian and Uncle complaining she sounded like a cat. I would always remember that Christmas Eve. If Father was watching I was sure he'd smile too.

I was first up the next morning. After I'd prodded the

turkey to see if it was cooked, I turned the oven down and lit the fire. Putting on my boots, coat and hat, I braved the torrent of snow blinding my vision and went to the phone box to call Mother. 'Merry Christmas!' I said. 'I'll bring Brian down tomorrow to spend the day with you.'

Surprisingly I didn't need to keep the phone at arm's length when she replied, 'Same to you, love. We… I'll look forward to seeing you.'

Her being happy was more than I could ask for. I skipped back to the house, like a child, not caring if I toppled over in the snow.

After we'd opened the presents, Uncle told me to spend the morning doing what I wanted. 'Ruby can take care of Brian, me and Mabel will do the rest.'

I decided to take a bath. As I lay back and relaxed into the water, something Mother had said came back to me. '*We* look forward to seeing you.' At the time I put the slip up down to her age or missing Father. Finishing my bath, I crept along the hall wanting to get a sneak preview of the Christmas table. I opened the door inch by inch and peeped in.

Brian was in his chair munching on a chunk of bread and jam. He kicked his legs to the music playing and laughed at Mabel dancing in Uncle Zac's arms. She was enjoying every moment as Uncle, with a paper crown on his head, twirled her around in one of his Fred Astaire moves.

'Call our Ruby and tell her dinner is nearly ready,' he said, spotting me.

After our meal, with a tea towel draped over his arm, Uncle Zac acted as waiter. 'Do you require any more wine, ladies?' he asked.

Mabel and I covered our glasses

But Ruby, with a grin on her face said, 'More wine

please, waiter.'

'I knew you wouldn't refuse. He laughed and refilled Ruby's glass.

After dinner we all helped to turn the kitchen from a warzone back to how Mabel liked it, then settled in front of the television. There was a constant ruffle of sweet wrappers, as we chewed, drank and sang the day away.

This was in contrast to my short time at Mother's on Boxing Day. I arrived with Brian to find all the neighbours sitting at the table, finishing plates of food. A deliberate snub. I vowed never to set foot in the house again. Tears stung my eyes as I pushed the pram away. I tried to unravel the motive behind Mother's logic of bringing those individuals into her home and showing how she preferred them to me.

37

With the bite of winter gone, spring allowed me to become surer of myself in Uncle Zac's neighbourhood. I loved their vibrancy of its people. Watching them, I slowly changed my introverted nature, edging nearer to becoming independent.

Uncle Zac and Mabel tried everything they could to discourage my decision to find somewhere to live. But it seemed like a great adventure. Blinded to the reality I'd face, I grasped the chance and flew with my dream.

Trudging through the streets looking for rooms to rent was a task. I had furniture and wanted somewhere unfurnished. After weeks of searching I found somewhere in Percy Street.

'You can move in once you pay a week's rent,' the landlord told me. Full of plans, I rushed home to give Zac and Mabel the good news.

But my plans were dashed the following day, when I learned Liam had sold everything we owned. The big sunny room I'd imagined that Brian could scamper around in was out of my reach. Squashed in spirit, I cried myself to sleep.

It took a week of knocking on doors before I found somewhere else to live. It wasn't far from Uncle Zac's, in a street where there was no competing to have the best net curtains or the cleanest doorstep. I felt a connection straight away with the smiling faces of the women gossiping on their doorsteps, and the hub of humanity in a street with no more than ten houses either side of the road.

Walking behind the landlord who jangled a set of keys, I did not expect luxury accommodation. But nothing could have prepared me for the dimly lit room, sparsely furnished with a bed, a table stripped of varnish, four backless chairs, something pretending to be a wardrobe and two armchairs.

All that mattered, I told myself, was that Brian would have enough room to play. The high ceilings could heighten my aspirations for the future, maybe even stop the feeling that everything around me was suffocating my optimism.

'I'll take it. When can I move in?'

After the tour of all the basic amenities, I was given a key to the front door. I knew I had enough money to buy food and pay the rent for a month, but it was imperative I found a job and put Brian in nursery as soon as I could.

Ruby was the only one smiling when I gave the news of my departure. I'd no intention of using Uncle Zac and Mabel as a safety net. Yet I knew the moment I fell, they'd be there to catch me.

Next morning, like an army of ants, we scrubbed, cleaned and fumigated my new home in hours. By the time evening shadows crossed the sky, we were having our first cup of tea.

Mabel had tucked Brian up in my bed. 'He'll feel better sleeping with you tonight,' she said. 'Come on, Zac. We'd better be getting home.'

Watching them walk away brought a smile and a tear. They were so different but oddly compatible, and this reminded me of my mother and father.

The house became a hub of activity from the moment I opened my eyes. Footsteps echoed through thick walls, squealing children played outside my window as their mothers brushed yesterday's rubbish down the long hallway. They'd sing, out of tune, to a crackling record player or a radio. At least this always gave me the will to get out of bed and put my plans into action.

Standing as a visitor on Uncle Zac's step felt strange. I wasted no time in pushing the pram in the hallway and explaining to Mabel I was off to the Dock Road to look for work. Mabel bent down and picked Brian up. 'I'll have him until you find a nursery.'

I hit the Dock Road in earnest. I didn't have any concept of how dangerous it was until I heard the rumble of vans, tankers and handcarts loaded with freight. Some pressed their horns to warn me from their path. It was like walking through a maze, until I found the warehouse I was looking for. I was surprised that they asked when I could start, instead of brushing me off.

Work in heavy industry wasn't my ideal vocation but it paid enough to keep a roof over my head and food on the table. The only criteria needed was strength, which I had in abundance.

I spent the first day lugging yards and yards of wool, cotton and silk thread, pushing the tangled mass through a machine, which left my body stretched to capacity. Dragging one leg in front of the other, I managed to walk to the bus stop, lift my leg far enough on the step and board the bus.

That night my body burned like a fire had been lit in my bones. I fed and washed Brian, sponged myself down and climbed into bed.

For a while, trudging through the streets pushing a pram to the nursery wasn't a problem. It was finishing work and taking a bus crowded with people, mostly well dressed and clean, that bothered me. I'd be covered in enough dust to grow potatoes. If I sat next to anyone I could see their noses twitch with disgust. They'd do that anyway, but now something of colour could actually rub off onto them. I'd find myself at the edge of the seat trying not to sit too close to the other person, praying they'd move and I'd have a space to myself.

I'd arrive home to my dismal room, light the fire and attend to Brian. Every week I'd promise to buy something to brighten my surroundings. But after the landlord snatched the rent and I bought food, fed the gas and the electric meter, I had nothing left. It was a blessing that we had Sunday dinner at Uncle Zac's.

Sadie, a neighbour who lived upstairs, was my only other beacon of light during this time. 'Hello,' she said the first time I saw her, her handbag over her arm as she passed me. 'You live in the front room, don't you?'

'Yes.'

'Come up any time,' she said. 'We can have a cup of tea and a chat.'

But despite Sadie's friendliness, I felt helpless in the conditions I lived and worked in. I was neglecting Brian because I was always flopping in the raggedy chair and falling asleep after work. I would spend my time arguing with other tenants to use the stove or whose turn it was to clean the toilet.

But there was a fighting spirit slowly taking over my placid nature.

38

One morning Brian took ill, shivering with a runny nose and damp with sweat. I rang the office and told them I would not be in that day.

The woman seemed indifferent to my circumstances. 'I hope this won't be something that happens all the time?' she said.

It did the following week, and I was given the sack. In panic, stepping on half eaten lollypops and toffee papers, I walked up the stairs and found Sadie in the kitchen talking to another tenant. She turned around when she heard my footsteps.

Since leaving Uncle Zac's there had no improvement in my status and when I thought of Liam selling all our furniture, I kicked out at the bandy-legged bed in anger. Next, I drew a knife and carved chucks of matted fibre from the warped settee. I roamed around the room looking for things to destroy. Tossing the unhinged wardrobe door on the floor, I stepped over it and walked towards the bed. Tearing at paper thin covering, I ripped, slashed and stabbed the mattress until the knife slipped from my hand and I fell to my knees.

Sadie knocked gently at first then banged her fist, shouting at me to let her in. Finally, I found the energy to stand on shaky legs and open my door.

'The show's over,' I heard her say to the other tenants who milled around the hallway. She asked me to come to her room. Until then, I hadn't noticed how strikingly beautiful Sadie was. Her dark skin enhanced the blueness of her eyes and her fine features were framed by a mane of nut brown hair. She was three years younger than me but much wiser.

'I lost my job too, and I've got a son as well, you know,' she confided. I'd often heard the patter of tiny feet overhead but hearing children play was nothing unusual. I told Sadie about Liam and how I had no money to pay the rent.

Sadie went over to the bed, which gave me time to look around her room. It was so nice. She had a lampshade of pink satin dangling overhead, comfortable armchairs, and lino with all the colours of the rainbow. Her wardrobe didn't need to be propped up with cardboard and there was no musty smell.

'Here,' she said, coming back over and shoving five shillings in my hand. 'Tomorrow go to the social, tell them your feller has left you, and they will give you some money for your rent and food.'

I was unable to thank her because of my tears, as she put her arm around me.

For a couple of months, Monday was my payday. I woke up early to be the first in the post office queue, then scurried through empty streets, to the nearest shop to buy the essentials.

On Monday morning Brian tossed and turned on the bed as I hopped around the room looking for my shoe. There was a knock on the door, but I ignored it. Then there was a bang which startled me, so I opened it to a man in a suit.

'I'm from the National Assistance Board,' he said. 'Can I come in?'

'No.'

'I must see your home,' he said.

'What for?'

'You know the reason Miss… Mrs Marshall. I have to establish if you are cohabiting.'

'Cohabi…what?'

The man tapped on the book he carried. 'Mrs Marshall, once again, will you allow me to follow our procedure?'

Digging my heels in against the intrusion into my life, I refused.

'Then I need to see your payment book.' He waited while I rummaged through the drawers. I'd thought there was no substance for the visit, but I was startled when I handed him the book and he tore it apart and handed it back to me, before marching down the stairs. My only source of income had gone.

With the responsibility of a child and rent to pay, I had to go and sort this out. I asked Sadie to mind Brian. Full of despair, I trudged my way through town and reached the dreaded office.

'Please God, don't let me see anyone I know,' I whispered, entering the large room. The shame attached to living off the state and to be seen collecting your handouts was like you had committed a crime.

'Elizabeth Marshall,' a woman called. 'Booth ten please.'

Crossing the room, I tried to look dignified. I sat on the chair and waited for the interrogation to begin.

The person behind the desk eyed me carefully. 'Do you have a man living with you?'

'No.'

Peering over thick-rimmed glasses, she added, 'Are you quite sure? We have had information there is. You also refused our officer access into your home. Why did you do that?'

I looked into her eyes. 'Shame, I guess. My son was

hungry, and I was in a rush to get out and buy food. Now I have no means to do that.'

I'd touched a nerve. The clerk looked down and scratched hurriedly on the file. 'Your new book will be sent to you. Sign there, please.'

The woman's voice sounded far away. 'That's all, Mrs Marshall, you can go now.'

'You mean go back to hell?' I blurted out. I waved my hand and stood up. 'By the way, your perfume stinks.'

I could tell by her faint smile that she knew I did not mean the bitchy comment. I was just angry.

I walked back home along Catherine Street, shoulders hunched thinking about my life. No solution came to mind, but I remembered what Sadie once told me. How she didn't care what people said or thought about her and one day I'd wake up and think like that too. I needed and wanted to see my Mother. I hoped we could get past our differences. I needed her. I also wanted to go back and live with Uncle Zac and Mabel, but pride wouldn't let me.

Brian was still with Sadie, so I took the bus there and then to see Mother.

'Come in, girl. I'm glad to see you.' I was shocked at Mother's appearance when she opened the door. Her hair looked lank and lifeless. She was wearing an old dress frayed cardigan and a pair of slippers with the sole coming away at the toe. She had no gas in the house and boiled a kettle on a two-ring electric cooker.

'Well, you were right. My so-called friends have stripped me of everything. I don't want to go into detail. I know it's my own fault.'

She did not need to explain; it was evident what had happened. I wanted to help her. I still had the money from Sadie, so I went to the corner shop and bought two cans of soup, bread and eggs.

We sat for a while talking and she kept repeating how she had been kind to the wrong people. It was almost too much to bear.

Before I left Mother said, 'Thanks, girl. God bless you.' Then she kissed me. The kiss seemed to wipe away some of my pain.

39

I was desperate to see Sadie and find out about her lifestyle. She wasn't dependent on others or scrounged for cups of milk or slices of bread. I needed her advice.

She was on her way out when I got home, but said she'd give me a knock later. I'd never been so happy and had Brian washed, fed and tucked up in bed by nine o'clock. Then I brushed the floor and gave myself a quick wash and watched the clock until I heard the click of Sadie's heels coming down the street.

She didn't need to knock on my door, it was already wide open.

'You can't go on like this, Bess,' she said. 'But then again I don't want to push you into my world either.'

Anything was better than what I had now, I told myself.

'Just help me understand,' I said. 'What do you do to survive with a child to look after?'

'I'll show you,' she said. 'Be ready tomorrow afternoon about twelve o'clock.' She paused and looked at me. 'Smarten yourself up. Put a bit of lippy on and we'll hit the club.'

It was all so fast - club, afternoon, lipstick? I reminded myself that I was the one asking for help and should put my trust in her.

In bed, the reality of what I was about to do dawned on me. Like most times in my life, glossing over the truth is what I had always done. The time had come to rip away any preconceptions of childhood dreams. I was about to take off the cloak of respectability, chuck it next to the empty sack of coal, and be brave.

In the club the next day Sadie told me our only interest was in the size of the men's wallets.

'All you have to do is lay back, open your legs and count the money you'll make,' she told me. I managed to hide my shock.

We sat at the bar and waited. It was difficult for me to look composed because I felt so scared. The jukebox played in the corner and soft lights flickered over an array of bottles stacked neatly on glass shelves.

'You're nothing without a few bob in your pocket,' Sadie whispered. 'Be brave, think of your babe.' She ordered two bottles of beer and a packet of cigarettes.

The man sitting next to us edged nearer to Sadie. 'What the hell is that in your glass?' he asked.

'Brown Ale.'

'Well for a start,' the stranger said, 'I'll buy you something a little more up-market. By the way my name is Bobby. What's yours?'

'Sas.'

The man smiled broadly. 'Have a drink on me.' He ushered the waiter with a flick of his hand.

Before long two men in suits were looking in our direction. They had receding hairlines, protruding stomachs and left the spell of Old Spice aftershave and Fiery Jack rubbing balm wafting in the air. The taller of the two winked at me.

'He must have something in his eye,' I joked.

'I know those two. They're not bad payers,' Sadie replied, looking over. But they can be shifty.' Before she could explain, they were next to us.

'Want a drink, Sas?' One of the men pulled out a

handful of money. 'And whatever your friend wants.' He smiled at me.

I watched as Sadie made light conversation. I turned my face towards the crowd, silently wishing someone would ask for a dance. Even the alcohol could not quench my panic.

'What do they call you then, kitten?' The man who had been staring at me finally asked. I made no reply but pointed to my nose.

'Come on now!' the man said sharply. 'Are you a business woman or not? You are treating me like a schoolboy. So, what is your name? And have you got somewhere to use?'

Sadie nudged me.

'Bess' I said.

'I'm Bill,' he replied. 'I thought you were giving me the brush off there.' He gulped his drink and waved to his friend like a traffic signal showing a green light. 'Ready then?' he said, taking me by the arm.

Secretly surprised at my boldness, I stood up.

Sadie grabbed hold of my hand. 'Now don't forget money first and use protection,' she hissed.

I swayed slightly and nodded. A business woman. That's what I was. That's what this was. Business.

Calling a stranger darling and sweetheart was odd, but Bill seemed amused with my playacting and clutched me to him in the taxi, like he owned me. He paid the fare and followed me up the steps. Hurriedly pushing the key in the front door, I prayed no one would see me. We tiptoed the few yards to the privacy of my room.

There was a faint smell of baby soap and talcum powder, but the waft of dust and decay couldn't be eradicated. Drawing the curtains, I stood against the window, poised but provocative.

'What's the charge then?' Bill asked, sitting on the bed.

Sadie had told me to be aware of haggling clients. 'It's fifteen pound for sex with a full strip and ten pound without.'

'Give you twenty, if you give this a kiss,' he said, unzipping his trousers and holding what looked like a paralysed worm in his hand.

I put my hand over my mouth to stop the vomit getting out before shouting, 'No, just leave it! Get out I've changed my mind!'

He made no attempt to leave. 'Okay, it doesn't matter. Come on, I will have a strip. Sit down, here is your money.'

I could see the crisp notes and wanted them in my grasp. I calmed my breathing and shut myself down, so it was like watching myself from outside my body.

'Are you sure it's not inside-out?' Bill laughed. His eyes glistened with amusement as he lay back, watching me struggle to keep the condom in place.

Rolling down my panties and opening the buttons of my blouse, I leaned towards him. My breasts brushed against his flesh. I felt his wet lips on my nipple. I thought only of the money.

'Are you enjoying it?' Bill asked.

'Yes,' I managed to say.

He jerked up and down for a few seconds more then collapsed into the pillow. He got up and checked his watch, not interested in conversation or caresses. Did men think giving women money was an excuse for them to become insensitive? Were my lovers only being polite when they'd hang around after?

'Can I see you again?' he asked, which surprised me.

I agreed on my terms only. Pulling on my frayed panties, I said I would meet him at the club and never to call at the house.

He pushed an extra five pounds in my hand, 'Here you are, love. You were worth the twenty pounds anyway. See you next week.'

Within the hour I was in Granby Street. The windless breeze mingled with the smell of freshly baked bread and cakes and gave me an appetite I could now afford to satisfy. Standing in the queue of the drapery store there was no need to search in the lining of my bag hunting for loose change, because now I had money to spend.

I resisted choosing anything at random. There would be plenty of time to buy clothes, food was my main priority. Instead of choosing the usual, basic items, I bought treats and came out with my string bag bulging.

I told myself that there was no need to hide in the shadows like a demented bat. I could be more like a trapeze artist, reaching for the highest bar. Even if this had come at a price.

40

I came crashing back to earth one Sunday while unwrapping the leg of lamb I'd taken to Uncle's for our lunch. I handed it to Mabel. Her eyes shifted from my face to the package and back to me again.

'How can you afford this?'

'I've met someone,' I lied.

She slammed the joint back onto the blood-stained paper. 'You're a married woman, Bess!' She shouted for Zac who came into the kitchen at once.

'She's met someone, Zac.'

'So?'

'But she's a mar-'

Uncle Zac put up his hand. 'He left her on her own. Sold all their belongings. He's a rat, so good luck to her.'

I suppose Mabel was only thinking of me and my reputation. As long as I could, I'd keep what I'd become to myself. If necessary, I'd pretend Bill, who came regularly now, was my boyfriend. Hopefully he would not be invited to tea. I wanted to ask for their help, to get me out of this mess. But I was so proud of being able to support myself, that I stayed quiet.

The meat roasting in its juices smelt delicious. But I knew with each mouthful, I feel my guilty secret suppressing my appetite. I was no better than Liam, lying to those who trusted me. Yet there was no way to change the sequence of events. It was either rot in a hellhole of a room, work for unravelling oil-soaked rags, or stand up to my ankles in water packing in some frozen food factory. Worst of all, those options meant I would have no energy to take care of my child. I needed to remind myself of what I'd left behind. Grasp the future in both hands and live.

Even though my neighbours sniggered and pointed at me when I passed, I held my head high. The other tenants covered their pots of food whenever I was in the kitchen. But I'd ignore them and concentrate on my juicy steaks while they pricked big thick greasy sausages and stirred pans full of beans and toasted slices of mouldy bread.

There was no contact from Liam, but he was often in my thoughts. Brian was thriving. It was a joy to pick him up from the nursery, have his meal ready, and take a stroll each evening to a little park not far from home.

I'd rented a television set, bought new curtains and other things to brighten up the room. I'd covered all the battered furniture but most of all I loved my tablecloth. Covered in bright yellow flowers spread across the table at meal times, it gave me peace of mind. Now I felt like the caring mother I'd always wanted to be.

41

Even though the electric meter was never empty, and my stomach ceased to rumble, I was still unsettled. Having a cup of tea in Sadie's cosy room one evening, I told her that it was time for me to move on.

Her words spilled out in a rush. 'But everything is being demolished. New flats and houses are springing up everywhere. Stay around here for a bit longer and you'll get somewhere good to live.'

I shook my head.

Sadie poked the fire. She lifted the lid of the coal bucket and began to rearrange the coals on the flame, a small shovelful at a time, as though she was inwardly rearranging her life without me.

'Sadie, you'll see me all the time.'

She looked up. 'People say that, and you never see them again.'

'You soft cow,' I laughed. 'I've already seen what I want. It's only a few doors down. Our landlord owns it.'

'The rent will be high, girl. He's a thief.'

'The house is better than this. At least we can have a bath, you as well.'

'I forgot about that.' Sadie threw her head back and laughed. 'Girl, you're rich.' Then she looked me earnestly. 'I'm glad for you.'

I needed to do something to put my plans into action. With my own bed I could argue I held an unfurnished tenancy rights. But my new career had told me that I might need something else.

Hours before the landlord Mr Smith was due, I dipped myself in a baby bath, creamed my skin and brushed my hair. As I adjusted my suspenders, there was a knock on the door.

'Coming.' Wearing a blouse opened to the navel and a skimpy brazier that exposed everything but my nipples, I opened the door, slightly.

Mr Smith's wife stood there.

'Oh… Mr Smith usually collects the rent,' I said, glad that she couldn't see my outfit behind the half-closed door.

'He's busy. Have you got the rent, please?' she asked in a stern voice.

The landlord called the following week, and I was waiting for him. I was wearing the same outfit as the previous week. I opened the door fully this time.

'Can I have a room in number four, please?' I asked.

He stroked his chin. 'I…don't know about that. It's not usual practice.' He looked at my cleavage, mopped his brow and blew his nose on a discoloured handkerchief. He turned around and walked away.

'Mr Smith!' I called. 'You forgot to take the rent.'

He walked back towards me.

'Bess,' he mumbled. 'I'll think about it.' He gave me a last look up and down before leaving.

After he left, I walked around my room, realising, for the first time, that Liam was out of my head. It was time to move on. I went to Uncle Zac and asked him about the procedures for getting credit in my own name. He didn't think that an unmarried woman would get any credit. But I was determined to try.

Leaving Brian with Mabel making boiled eggs and buttered bread, I caught the bus into town. I walked into a furniture shop and browsed for at least half an hour observing the staff. I eyed the salesman who had a slight twitch and swung my hips from side to side as I walked towards him.

I wanted a bed with a white quilted headboard. I let my coat fall open as I sat down. Then I lay down on the thick mattress turning and rotating over the bed until the salesman looked hot under the collar. 'How much is this?'

'Your husband might want to try it out before we discuss the cost, madam.' He edged at little nearer.

'I'm not married.' I straightened my clothes, knowing I looked good in my mini-dress. I moved towards the electrical equipment. 'Is that a radiogram?'

He opened the lid. 'Yes,' the man said proudly. 'It's our latest model. It has a built-in tape as well.'

'As soon as I have enough money I'll come back for that.' I fluttered my eyelashes. 'I'm also interested in a coffee table.' I could see him calculating the sale in his head. 'I'll pay cash for the bed,' I ventured, watching him carefully. 'For the other items I'd need hire purchase.' I could feel the air fill my lungs waiting for his reply.

'You know,' he said, 'we would need a man's signature.'

Running my fingers along the edge of the mattress, I replied, 'Yes, I know, but I live on my own with a small son. Is there anything you can do to help me?'

'Well, madam, I could give you the form to take home. Would it be possible for me to collect it when you're ready for delivery and in the meantime, you can choose what you want?'

'That will be fine Mr…'

'Robinson,' the man replied. 'My first name is John.' He coughed. 'Shall we sort out the bed and the other items you need now?'

I visualised my room with the new bed in one corner and Brian's bed tucked away behind a partition. I'd put the glass coffee table in the centre and my radiogram under the window. I'd already chosen the lino for my new address - brown, with splashes of yellow stripes and two lamps that kept me captivated with patterns swirling in an oil filled base. John was unwittingly about to change my life.

He arrived a few days later and sat perched on the end of the chair, with a cup of tea rattling on its saucer.

'I've completed the form, John. When will the furniture be delivered?'

'Next week,' he replied, red blotches appearing on his face.

'Shall we make a date for some time next week then, John?' I said stroking his lank hair. 'When my new bed has come. Would you like that?' His eyes were glazed, and I wanted to get rid of him as quickly as possible.

'Yes,' John answered, 'I would.'

'Well, John, next week it is then.'

He stood up like a new-born calf and left the room on shaky legs.

There was excitement in the street when the furniture van arrived. Everyone helped. They hurled bulky items up the stairs supported by two burly assistants. I'd already cleaned the room, laid the floor covering, washed the curtains and removed the old bed.

In the evening, after Brian's bath, Sadie was invited to see the finished result. I could hear the sound of her high heels clicking up the landing. 'It's a palace, girl.'

'Yes,' I replied. 'Because you helped me turn into a wicked witch.'

I saw her face turn serious then. I hadn't intended the comment to hurt her. It was an uphill struggle for her to survive, she'd told me previously. But being a victim did not sit well with her. Sadie never spoke of her parents and I didn't pry, but there was something about them that made her eyes grow dark. Her sadness would start along her brow, down the shaft of her prominent cheekbones and rested on her lips.

I wanted to reassure her that in time she would heal, but it felt inappropriate and a little patronizing. We sat in silence, sipping our tea.

Sadie had the impression we'd nothing in common, but we did. We'd solved our slow decline into a cesspit of squalor and did what we thought was best.

42

There was only a faint smell of paint now in my new room. Along with the aroma of wood, freshly washed curtains and the clock ticking in rhythm with my heart, I was at peace.

Uncle Zac and Mabel came around on Tuesdays. One night, Uncle pushed a letter from Liam into my hand. 'It's up to you, girl, but Brian might want to see his dad.'

Shaking, I opened the crinkled envelope.

> *Bess,*
> *I had a lot on my plate for years and couldn't support you and Brian. I'm okay now and I'd like to make it up to you. Please send me a picture of Brian. All the best, Liam Xx*

I screwed the letter into a ball and threw it on the fire. I kept the envelope with the address. He could have a photo, but he'd lost the most precious years with Brian. Liam could never make up for what he did. Yet I didn't want to rip his head off anymore. He'd done me a favour by being as low as a slimy snail. More importantly, I would not divorce him. I had no intention of marrying again, so why give Liam that privilege? I was a woman of the world now, not the grovelling wife and daughter everyone thought I'd be. I toasted him that night with a bottle of wine.

I replied to Liam's letter without love or bias and agreed to send him a picture. Brian, who was now eight, seemed unfazed when I told him about his Dad. Leaving out the personal issues, I tried my best to explain why we were not together and that Liam loved him.

Brian wasn't happy with the red suit jacket or the smart black pants that I wanted him to wear for the photo and kicked up a fuss. After I promised to take him for a hamburger and chips, he agreed.

That night I went to the club as usual. A howling wind rattled doors, scattering old newspapers and throwing plastic bottles up in the air. The street was empty. Head down, avoiding the dust, I hailed a taxi. I could see the driver looking at me in the mirror. I smiled, wondering if his look was - I'm interested in you, or - I've got daughter your age.

'What are you going in that place for?' he asked.

I crossed my legs and lit a cigarette. He reminded me of Father.

'Because I'm poor and I don't have a white face,' I answered as I left the taxi, hoping he'd think about what I'd said.

Pleased to leave someone with a riddle, I entered the club where no one would question my motives. I brought in the customers and that was all they were interested in.

'Hi, Bob,' I said to the doorman, who nodded and smiled. I went to the toilet to calm my windswept hair and add another coat of lipstick. Walking to the bar, I saw how it was quieter than usual. But in the space of an hour I had to fight my way through a small crowd to buy another drink.

'What you drinking?' said a voice behind me.

I turned around to see a man in horn-rimmed glasses with lenses protruding an inch from the frame, magnifying his watery blue eyes. He was wearing a slate grey suit. The collar on his blue pinstriped shirt was short and out of fashion, fitted tightly around his swan-like neck.

He moved uncomfortably close and I was about to say no, but then he pulled out his wallet crammed with notes.

'What's your name?' he asked.

'Bess.'

We sat at a table and got talking. It wasn't long before he asked if I was a working girl. I nodded and asked him his name.

'Lenard,' he replied. 'Fancy another drink?'

My limit was two glasses of alcohol. The bar staff knew to pour only tonic water into the glass if I went over that.

There were a couple of men looking like they wanted to approach me, and I was growing a little impatient with my present company.

When he returned with the drinks, I got straight to it. 'Look, my time is money. Are you interested or not?

He sipped what looked like wine. 'I don't want sex,' he replied.

'So, what do you want then, Lenard?' I was hoping he wanted someone to talk to, or for me to prance around the room naked. No sex was great.

He ran his fingers around the rim of his glass. 'I only want to see your lovely buttocks. How much do you charge?'

'Thirty pound and you can stay a little longer than usual.'

He agreed to my terms and said he'd get his car, which was parked a few streets away. He pulled up in a Jaguar and I got in, looking around to see if there were any clues to his identity. But there was nothing. I asked him if he was married.

'Oh yes, I'm married,' he said and then went quiet. He

was giving nothing away. Even when I asked him if he went to the club often he replied a basic, 'No.' Nothing I said could draw him into conversation. I sat back calculating the money I'd saved up to date and what the extra from him could buy. When we stopped at the front door Sadie was going into the house and she called me over.

'Don't take him. He's a weirdo, likes to use his belt. Some of the girls told me that he offers them more money to take the pain.'

Gaping in surprise, I watched as Sadie flew down the steps. 'Fuck off!' she shouted. 'Before I get someone to sort you out!'

He revved the engine and was at the end of the street in two seconds.

'Bess, girl, you have to be careful in this game,' said Sadie, touching my arm.

Someone who wanted to hurt another person like that bothered me. It could start as a slap on the buttocks and escalate into murder. Being careful was really no protection. With little time for assessment I wouldn't know who I'd be taking home.

Sadie said I was overreacting. But the incident had shaken me up. How many more creeps might I come across? I had been lucky so far. Never again would I take anyone at face or money value. I stayed in for the next four days.

When I told Bill what had happened he put his head in his hands and kept saying, 'I worry about you, Bess.'

The following week Bill came to mine, smoking a cigar and holding a bottle of brandy. He swayed up the hallway. 'I've had a few. I want to ask you something.' He swaggered towards the bed and then fell face down and closed his eyes.

I hadn't come to terms with my nerves or how I'd face going to the club again. I tried to distract myself by asking Bill if he wanted a coffee.

'No, babe. I want you,' he replied, then fell asleep. In the moonlight, Bill looked so peaceful. I kissed him lightly on the cheek.

'I love you even though you're an old goat,' I whispered. 'But I still need paying before the birds come out.' I turned my back on him, and as the moon disappeared behind the clouds, I closed my eyes.

The next morning, I woke before Bill and went to make some drinks. He was up when I returned and brushed his lips on the side of my face.

'Morning, babe,' he said. 'Give me time to shave and we'll talk.'

I drank my coffee, wondering what he wanted to tell me. He couldn't want to ask for my hand in marriage. Some other poor bugger already had him.

He returned scrubbed up and fresh. 'Don't get mad, love…but I want you to stop what you're doing.'

Oh, you mean making money, I said to myself, and be content with beans on toast for my Sunday lunch.

'Go on say your piece,' I said. I knew in my heart he meant well.

'I want to look after you and Brian. You will have a weekly wage. You won't need to do what you do anymore'

I was taken back by his offer. I'd always thought he was happily married. He owned his own bottling plant with a house in the country and I was just a bit of fun.

'I don't come cheap you know.'

'I'll put a hundred pound in your hand and you'll only have to see me twice a week.'

My mind raced. No more dressing up in the afternoons and I'd spend more time with Brian.

'What days?'

'Weekends only and I promise, lovely lady, no kissing on the lips, on the condition you devote those two days to me.'

'What?' I was now on my feet and felt a burning sensation in the pit of my stomach. 'There is only one person I'm devoted to and that's my son.' I glared at him as he reached and poured two more coffees into the cups.

'Sorry, Bess, wrong word,' he said. 'But you know what I mean?'

'Do you want something to eat?' I asked, changing the subject. The details could be worked out later.

'Yes please,' he said. 'But before that I want you.'

Afterwards, I cooked breakfast and Bill dressed. We ate together, and I didn't want him to go. I loved the way he threw his head back and laughed at the silliest things. He kept me alive. Showering me with compliments and, best of all, I loved to cuddle up to him in bed.

He left, whistling down the stairs, and I knocked on Sadie's door.

'Come in,' Sadie called. 'You look like the cat that's got the cream.'

I twirled my skirt around like a little girl.

'Stop acting daft and tell me what's happened,' she said.

'Bill is going to take care of me.'

43

I learned that Mandy was back in England. She hadn't been able to face me yet, but eight months had gone by.

'I'm only here on holiday. Slim is looking after the little one until I go back,' she said. Mandy was like a politician who evaded the truth. She'd forgotten bad news travelled like the speed of light.

Slim had taken her to court. Mandy fought for custody of their son but lost the case. The desperate fight for her child, and being shunned by the man she loved, showed on Mandy's taunt face. It was lined with early signs of wrinkles around her mouth.

'You look content,' she said to me.

'I am,' I answered.

'I wish I was more like you.'

I wanted to tell her the truth, but I couldn't. Instead I watched my friend, who'd already punished herself enough, fingering some of the items I'd bought. She admired Brian's new clothes, eyed the small but stylish television, and tried squeezing her feet into a pair of my trendy pink wedge shoes. The dainty strap only reached the first hole, but she strutted around the room wobbling from side to side.

'So,' she said, 'I've heard you sleep with men for money.'

'You heard right. Anyway, you slept with the yanks and all you had to show for your effort was a hangover and a tatty head.'

Mandy stood up. 'If that's the way you're going to carry on, Bess, I'm going.' She looked lost and alone. Even with the abundance of love she'd received from her family, she lacked the tools to survive on her own.

'Don't go, girl,' I coaxed. 'Stay for your tea. Look I am sorry for what I said.'

During the meal Mandy broke the silence. 'I suppose your son won't be home until Monday.'

'We can go together to the babysitter on Sunday if you like,' I said, stopping short of telling her about Uncle Zac and Mabel. I wanted to surprise her.

'You're never going to forgive me, are you?' Mandy stabbed at the meat.

'Do you think you I would eat with you if there was no forgiveness? Am I some soft arse?'

'No. Far from it!' Mandy laughed. It felt good to her smile again.

'So, you're not working tonight?' she asked.

'No.' I was telling the truth. Bill wasn't work. He was my friend. Someone I'd allow to play with Brian and hold him when I was busy or when he cried. But there was something in her disapproving tone that got to me. Clearing the table, I slammed the plates together. 'You know nothing of my life.'

When I first met her, with that polka dot scarf tied under her chin, she'd been my only friend. Now she was hurting, missing her child. I snapped back from reminiscing. Mandy's eyes were wide with hatred. 'You always went on like you were fucking miss prim. Even when you were up to your eyes in shit.'

Shocked at her outburst, I was silent until her face returned to its natural pallor.

'Do you think I'm a slut?' she asked.

'Of course I don't.' I sighed. 'Stop being so hyped-up. Let's have a drink and calm you down.'

I walked towards the cupboard suddenly realising she could take advantage and attack me from behind. But Mandy obeyed and sat down as I brought her back a drink.

'Yuk! What's that shit?'

'It's only Rum and Lemonade.'

Mandy sipped it, screwing up her face with each mouthful.

'I regret so much,' she said. 'I love my Mum and Dad and look at how I treated them. But they had no dreams.'

'They were happy,' I replied.

'How the fuck could they have been happy when they were always struggling?'

'Keep your voice down!' I said.

'Okay, but you know people used my parents.'

'You were the main culprit. You gave parties every weekend and must have invited every solder on Burtonwood Air Force Base.' I wasn't letting her off lightly.

'Exactly, Mum and Dad never objected.'

'But that's the way your parents were Mandy, nice people, easy going.'

'They weren't as happy as you think,' she said. 'And it was hard for them, seeing how I got treated growing up.'

I knew that in school she'd been called blubber lips, and the kids would ask why she had hair like wire wool and why she was so black. We'd had the same experiences growing up.

'That's why I went with Slim,' she said. 'I wanted a boy who knew what it felt like. It was so hard before him, even most of the black boys believed that I wasn't the definition of beauty.' Mandy laughed suddenly. 'I used to get my own back when a white woman became pregnant with one of them. I'd tell them that the baby could come out as black as coal.' She swirled the drink in her glass.

I'd seen this too, how worried the white women were about having a baby that was too black. How their mothers would tell them they could visit anytime, but they should not bring their nigger kids with them. Some were okay with that arrangement. But their children weren't a part of their white grandparent's lives - from the cradle, to the grave.

'Fancy another?' I asked.

'Yeah, don't give me that weed killer. A real drink if you please.'

I crossed the room and reached for the whisky. Mandy moved her chair closer to the fire. 'We were used by the yanks as well and believed the bullshit.'

'Most of them had nothing just like us,' Mandy continued. 'I thought I was the lucky one marrying a G.I, but it was the likes of you who rose above the hurt.'

'Why didn't you tell me you were so in love with Slim?' I asked.

She looked up at me. 'Would it have made any difference?'

'No.'

I hadn't thought of Slim in a while and no longer viewed men with rose tinted glasses. I saw most of them as predators now. Once they found a woman who seemed lost like a cactus in a desert, they drank the dew. When what they craved for had been used and abused, they'd seek other edible shoots.

I was no cactus, more like a plant who wanted to trap its pray. I didn't want to maim or kill the male species though. To me they had one thing they were good for, to pay for my survival.

I still wished I could have crushed Slim. He would have loved the woman I'd become: strong, bold, with a no-nonsense attitude and someone who no longer wore pyjamas in bed but lace panties and matching bras. I'd make him beg for my attention. When he'd sampled a little of what he'd lost, I'd toss him aside like a used tissue.

Mandy left promising to return the next day. I never saw her again.

44

Brian seemed to change overnight, from a happy youngster eager to sit on my knee and say he loved me and let me wash his hair, to a boy who locked the bathroom door and told me to stop fussing. Gone was my little yappy chap with the voice that rang like a well-tuned bell, now it sounded like sandpaper being rubbed against his vocal cords. He refused to go anywhere with me.

He told me that he was a Mod. For a while I thought it meant Ministry of Defence and wondered if he'd go in the army. I was so proud. I even bragged to Uncle Zac that we were going to have a soldier in the family. But Uncle was onto it. 'Oh, he will be a soldier alright, but he won't be fighting for king and country.'

That was when Fred Carter appeared on the scene. Brian had brought Fred home for tea. The small boy sat staring at me with large bluebell colour eyes and jet-black straight hair, with a fringe almost touching his Roman nose. His pants had more holes than a fisherman's net. The wild look in his eyes sparkled with enjoyment as he munched on shepherd's pie, mashed potatoes and green beans.

'Thanks, Mrs Marshall,' he said politely.

Brian overcompensated for the lad's company. He fussily stretched his model train track across the room, dragging out a boxful of signal boxes. Fred's dirty fingers toppled and moved the trains, while Brian sat enjoying his friend's captivation or serving lemonade to him like it was water.

I left them alone and went and knocked on Sadie's door. She had a roller in her hair holding her fringe in place. Making two cups of coffee, she set them down on the glass table.

'I saw Brian with that Fred Carter,' she said. 'Keep an eye on him, love. I know the family.'

I was just happy Brian had a friend he liked and had had enough of gossiping in Shakespeare Road. 'They are only kids,' I replied, putting the cup to my lips.

Over time other boys joined Brian and Fred. 'The little group of bandits,' Uncle Zac called them. But with no concerns about Brian's capability in school, I wasn't worried about the antics of his peers. Brian was not the sort to be easily led, I told myself. That was until the police brought him home one night.

I was told to take him to the police station the following day as they wanted to interview him.

'Can you bring your husband with you?' the policeman said.

'He's away.'

The policeman scratched something in his notebook 'Okay,' he said. 'Your son must be there for ten in the morning. He's been seen robbing a shop.'

Brian clung to my dress shaking. 'Mum, I didn't do anything.'

Looking straight at the policeman, I drew Brian close. 'I believe you, son.'

That night I thought of what Sadie told me and tried to question Brian. Only stopping when I was fearful Brian could become hysterical. He was already slamming doors and kicking the furniture. It was late when he finally calmed down after I gave him a warm drink of milk and tucked him up in bed.

Uncle Zac came with us the next morning. He was not allowed in the interview room and I could hear him kicking up a fuss. 'I hate you lot!' he shouted. Then I heard a scuffling and Uncle yelling, 'Get off me, you bastards!'

The door slammed and two policemen carrying notebooks entered the room. Brian told the truth, about how Fred and the others had planned it. They let him go in exchange for the evidence.

At home he became moody and withdrawn. Door slamming was his favorite pastime and he often gave me the silent treatment.

When I saw Uncle's black eye and swelling to his face after our visit to the police station, I didn't ever want Brian to be in that position. Losing friends like Fred was something of a blessing. My son didn't see it that way.

'Brian's writing to Liam again, Bess,' Uncle would tell me.

I found him in the front room with some paper and a pen in his hand, covering the letter when he saw me.

'I want to spend a weekend with my dad,' he told me one evening.

I wasn't shocked by his request, only hurt by his timing. He wanted to see his father and I wouldn't stand in his way, even though I wanted to separate them by as much land and sea as possible.

'Okay, son,' I said, almost choking on my words. 'But you'll have to wait until your school holidays.'

Talking to Liam on the phone was hard. It was about our son, not about us, yet Liam rattled on and on about our relationship.

'Let's back to the reason I called,' I said.

'Bess, it would be nice if he could stay for a month.'

'A month?'

'Why not?'

I hated him. I knew he would worm his way into Brian's heart and I would end up as the bad one. But Brian wanted to go.

The four weeks Brian was away from me would be more like four years. I could see Liam with a big smile on his face parading around, showing what an attentive father he was and failing to say how he'd left him for years.

Before Brian left, I made a fuss of him. I took him to the pictures where we'd eat popcorn and drink lemonade. To Brian's amazement, I even kicked footballs with him.

The night before Brian left for London I packed his case and had a sleepless night worrying about him. I cooked breakfast in floods of tears. But I had to laugh when Brian arranged all his toy soldiers on the mantelpiece and said, 'They will take care of you, Mum.' That childish action helped me to bath, dress and accept four weeks would soon pass by. Then he would be back and away from Liam.

When we arrived at Euston Station, Liam was waiting on the platform and ran towards us when the train stopped. Only glancing at me quickly, he lifted Brian off his feet and held him.

Liam was still handsome. He wore a tailored suit, soft leather shoes and gold cufflinks, which flashed in the reflection of the sun shining through the windows of the stationary trains.

'You look well, Bess.'

Tightening my grip on the case, I looked down. Thanking Liam for his comment would give him an opportunity to have a conversation. Brian's welfare was what I was concerned with. So, where Liam lived, where he worked and whether gambling was still his source of income were the questions I asked.

'Self Employed.' He grinned.

If there was anything I'd learnt from the man standing before me in the slate grey suit, it was to believe very little of what you see and nothing of what you hear. Gambling was in his blood.

I let Brian go with Liam quickly before I changed my mind and caused a scene. Kissing him and giving some last-minute instructions, I bit my lip as I walked away.

45

I arrived home alone wondering if Brian was okay. After a cup of tea and slipping into a comfortable dress, I fell asleep on the couch. It was dark when I woke up and ran to the phone box and dialled Liam's number.

Brian's voice was in the background when Liam answered.

'How is he?'

'Fine. We've just been for a meal.' Liam said. 'Son! It's your Mother on the phone, come and say goodnight. He won't be a minute, Bess. He's just putting his new clothes away.'

Brian sounded breathless on the phone reeling out what Liam had bought him, how they had eaten in a Chinese restaurant. It was all 'Dad done this, and Dad done that.'

Eventually, I asked him to put Liam back on.

'Look after my son.'

'*Our* son, Bess.'

'It wasn't always that way,' I said and put the phone down. I returned home feeling empty and alone. A stone hit the window and when I looked to see who it was, Bill stood there grinning.

I opened the window wide and shouted that Brian had gone away and I wasn't in the mood, before closing it again. Another stone hit the window, so I stormed to the door and let him in.

Holding a large blue teddy bear, a bottle of wine and a box of chocolates, he took me in his arms. 'I've come to cheer you up.'

Only Bill would think I'd need something to cuddle. I smiled.

He didn't try to make me laugh that night, but he kept me company. We drank the wine while I talked about Liam. He quietly listened as I poured my heart out and he left just as daylight changed the black sky to orange and white. 'See you soon, sweetheart,' he said closing the door.

The twenty sixth of August arrived and Brian was due back around teatime. I'd make sure Liam returned to London soon after they arrived.

Brian stepped off the train with a smile on his face, but when it was time for Liam to kiss him goodbye, he wiped away a tear with the back of his hand.

'I've missed you, son. Are you happy to be home?' I asked him in the taxi.

Keeping his head down, he mumbled, 'Don't know.'

Liam had accomplished what he'd set out to do. Brian loved me, but Liam must have been like an eagle to him that might fly away. I suppose Brian wanted to hold on to the father he adored. But I was the mother who'd always been there.

Brian settled until the school holidays ended. Then one morning another bombshell shattered me. I'd got up early and found Brian sitting crossed legged on the floor. The rays of the sun danced on the walls making a halo of light around his head, which looked quite spiritual. His hands were clenched into a fist. He pulled away sharply as I touched him.

'Brian, if you don't tell me what's wrong I can't help you.'

'Can I live with Dad?'

It took me a while to digest what he'd said. I knew Brian was unhappy. I sat beside him, hoping a grown-up conversation might swing the pendulum in my favour.

'Love, will you think about it for a while? Won't you miss me?'

He hung his head. 'Yes, Mum, but I hate it here.' He pouted his lips and fidgeted nervously. 'I don't have any friends.'

'Alright, son. I'll talk to your dad and work something out.' My next thoughts were of Uncle Zac and Mabel. If Brian decided to live in London, I didn't know how they'd take it. I sought advice from Uncle Zac before I told Mabel.

'Girl, as much as I loathe Liam, Brian would have a good start in life.' Stirring a pot of rice, he turned the gas down. 'Look at me, girl, an old man with nothing to show for my life. Let him go. He's already on the wrong track and he knows it.'

Mabel gave me the same advice, but she wanted to know if I could visit Brian whenever I wanted to.

We agreed that Brian would move to London at the next half-term.

'It will give me a chance to secure a school, wallpaper Brian's bedroom and take time off work,' said Liam. I thought about how he would probably end up on the bloody board of governors, sit with them without dunking his biscuits in his coffee. Then he'd turn up with a present of a school bus with his own graphic design plastered all over it. 'I can charm a bird out of the trees,' he often boasted.

At least Brian had a father who knew how to get things done. I was still in the elementary school of life and Brian deserved better. Yet it was the saddest day of my life when Brian waved goodbye to me. The train window had been pulled down and I could still see his hand as the train turned into the tunnel. It felt as though he'd been torn from me. I questioned what I had done. How did I know what the future held? Had I been too weak to find out and passed the responsibility over to Liam?

It was no use fretting and worrying about my decision to let Brian go. In the end, it was better for my son. My heart would take time to heal. And there was also the practical side of being a mother. It was simple things, like a half-full washing basket with no little t-shirts or school uniforms to wash and iron, that had me in floods of tears.

I stayed in bed and smoked ten cigarettes before I got up. I've always had Brian to take care of. Now it was only me to care for and it wasn't enough. I have to change my life as well, I told myself, but the will wasn't there.

Bill wanted to have fun, but I just wanted to be a mother and a housewife. Hands on mothering had been snatched from me.

'It's a new dawn,' Bill said. 'The eighties are just around the corner. Don't you want to be here and be part of it?'

Once I remembered how far I'd come, it was less of a battle for me to convince myself Brian would thank me one day. He would never experience lugging bags of coal on his shoulders or have to suffer the consequences of having a black mother. Liam had seen the deprivation. He'd seen the hopelessness of being black in Liverpool at this time. Would the eighties bring any change?

One thing I was certain of was that Liam would never allow his son to miss out on the security education brought. He would use his skills of survival to shuffle, gamble, manipulate and push Brian to his full potential- Whenever my mind strayed from being positive, I would try to remind myself that one day Brian would be a man. He was already on the way and I'd had the best years. Knowing he was loved would stay with him forever and living with Liam would never change that.

Baby Love was being played on the jukebox when Sadie, Bill and I walked into the club in Upper Parliament Street. Sadie was in front of us in the queue, her lime green suit like a beacon.

Bill and I followed her trail. It was the first time, in a long while, I'd been inside a club without a feeling of exposure. There were no clients scrutinising my face, so my fine wrinkles no longer mattered. The false eyelashes were left on my dressing table with my wig beside them.

For the foreseeable future I wouldn't be for sale. I'd saved enough cash to last me a while. And I had Bill.

Putting his arm around me, Bill asked if I was okay.

'Yes, thanks to you.'

Sadie looked sophisticated as she glided across the dance floor. She found a table and we sat down. Bill stood up beside me sucking on a large cigar and puffed his chest out.

Sadie looked at me and smiled. 'He looks more like an overprotective hen than your fella,' she laughed, dragging me on the dance floor. My soft pink maxi dress caught the lights as I started to dance. Bill clapped his hands at our steps. He nibbled my ear when I said down, paid me compliments and told me how happy he was.

When he'd drunk too much though, he'd become obnoxious. He'd cut in between the man I was dancing with, take me by the arm and stomp his way through the song.

It always happened at the end of the evening. So, I was quite happy to bungle Bill in a taxi, undress him when we reached home and toss him onto the bed and hoped he'd had enough excitement. Tonight, was no exception. Sadie was ready to go as well and helped with the drama.

'You hold one cheek and I'll grab the other,' Sadie laughed as we pushed Bill up the stairs. We finally managed to get him into the lobby when Bill announced in a soberer tone than I expected, 'He'll be outside now.'

'Who?' I asked.

'My friend Robbie is going to take us to Manchester.' Sticking a cigar in his mouth, he searched for a lighter. 'I fooled you both,' he said. 'I'm fed up being tucked up in bed.'

Sadie and I couldn't walk to the car for laughing. We had to stop and hold our sides. Sadie was even crossing her legs.

'Crafty old bugger,' I said to Sadie.

Sadie and I sat on the back seat. Robbie turned around and shook hands with us before he switched on the engine. Bill fiddled with the car radio. 'You don't mind, do you?' he asked Robert.

'Not at all. I love music.'

'That's good', said Sadie, smiling at Robbie. 'Because you're going to have a good time tonight.'

Tuned into a decent channel which played soul music, he drove to the East Lancashire Road.

'Anyone want a drink?' Bill asked, pulling out a flask from his pocket.

46

We drove into Manchester. It was like the middle of the day, with people everywhere, either moving from one club to another or jumping into taxis.

'Is it nice where we're going?' Robbie asked, wiping his windscreen.

'You ever been to a Shebeen?' I heard Sadie ask Robbie.

'What's that?'

She put her arms around him. 'Somewhere we can rock the night away.

Robert looked at Bill. 'Don't worry, you'll love it.'

We walked through a dark lobby with people lining the walls smoking, then into a room with spotlights shining in the corner and made our way to the makeshift bar.

'What the hell is this?' asked Robbie.

'The best place on earth,' replied Sadie.

'Welcome, sister,' a tall man said. 'Nice to see some Liverpool here.' He handed Bill a joint. 'Smoke, man, and enjoy.'

Sadie found some seats next to the speakers and we listened to the music we'd travelled miles to hear. In Manchester nobody watched what you did. If someone wanted to dance on their own, then they could. No one commented.

Bill and Robbie took it in turns to supply us with more drink than we could handle. Sadie and I slung our shoes in the corner and danced till dawn.

The sun was peeping through the windows when the last song played. Sadie was in a dark corner dancing with Robbie. Bill managed to stand, take me in his arm and did the best he could not to stamp on my feet.

Stepping outside into the cool air and watching the crowd disperse, Bill put his arms around me. 'Hungry, love?'

'Starving.'

'When Robbie drags himself away from Sadie we'll find somewhere to eat.'

Robbie and Sadie finally joined us.

'Looks like you're in love, Robbie,' Bill said.

Robbie smiled. 'I think I am.'

We left the car and walked a couple of blocks and found a customised caravan selling food to the crowd gathered around the open hatch.

We ate fish and fried dumplings in the fresh morning air and then set off, reaching home about eight-thirty. I felt like Cinderella returning from the ball but still dressed in my beautiful gown.

I took a good look at the place I called home in the morning light. The house looked like it was about to crumble into its foundations. The paint was scorched by time and hung like loose skin around wooden window frames. Rags for curtains flapped around broken glass. I'd known for years the house was a hellhole and hugged Bill as we walked down the long hall. He had thrown me the lifeline I'd needed.

'You're not drunk, are you?' he asked, laughing.

'I've never been more sober in my life,' I replied.

I visited Brian the following week. Liam and Brian met me at the train station. Brian ran towards me, his face beaming with pride. He'd grown and almost reached my shoulder. He wanted to tell me everything at once and bobbed up and down reeling off all he had done with

Liam and how he was enjoying school.

'I got top marks in my exams, Mum, and in maths too,' he told me.

I thanked Liam in front of Brian, but I was still resentful that I was not there to support my son. We had a wonderful day together and as the train pulled away from the platform, my heart sank.

At least, I told myself, when Brian visits me I'll have a home he'll be proud of. From that day my heart was set on leaving the street. I needed to be away from this place where tenants were expected to bath in rust-crusted baths, where rats scratched for scraps of food in over spilling bins. I'd had enough and was determined to find a home of my dreams. Anything would be better than what I had now.

I'd kept the house hunting to myself, knowing Sadie would be distressed at my leaving. It wasn't long before a house became empty in Beaconsfield Street and a viewing was arranged for the following week.

'I thought you were going miles away,' said Sadie with relief. 'Or back to your mother's area.'

'Don't wish that on me. I'm going to view it on Tuesday. Do you fancy coming along?'

'Try stopping me.'

The mid-terraced house had gleaming windows and a front door that closed properly. It already felt like home, somewhere to shut myself away when I wanted to without the trauma of other tenants squabbling. I'd miss the mandolin player though, on those cold winter nights when I'd close my door against the elements and sit by a roaring fire.

The landlord stood nearby with papers in his hand ready for me to sign the agreement. The place was ready for someone to stamp their own personality on. It was perfect for me. I signed without hesitation. Sadie's mouth was wide open, and she only spoke when the landlord gave me the keys and left.

'Girl, it's lovely,' she said over and over, until I managed to playfully push her out of the door, still looking over her shoulder as we walked away.

Uncle Zac and Mabel were having tea with me that night. Sadie volunteered to cook. I suggested we'd dress up and make the night special and give Uncle and Mabel the good news.

Ready and waiting for the guests to arrive, Sadie swirled around in a long blue maxi dress, setting the table and opening a bottle of brandy. Switching on the radiogram, I put on a record by Herbier Mann. Uncle Zac and Mabel arrived, and the night began and ended when the birds started whistling and the moon was overshadowed by the sun. I noticed how protective Mabel was towards Sadie, asking her how she was doing, and did she need anything. Ham and eggs fizzled in the frying pan while Uncle and Mabel dozed on the couch, opening their eyes to a breakfast fit for kings. Giggling on the doorstep about being out all night, Uncle and Mabel left arm in arm, happily walking down the street.

I was elated too. I'd crossed the final hurdle. Everything within the walls of my new house was mine. Now I could call it my own home.

Sadie often found me on my knees scrubbing the step or cleaning the brass. Then she'd drag me from domestic bliss and encourage me to mingle and not hide myself away.

I was happy with Bill. On summer evenings we'd stroll to the park, Bill with a bottle of brandy jammed in his inside pocket and cigar dangling from his lips

He'd lie on the grass looking up at the sky. Topping

up cups of lemonade with brandy, we'd plan the evening ahead. We argued about what club to go to later on, but most of the time end up staggering home, having something to eat and staying in. Often after midnight we'd hear the music and people walking by.

It wouldn't take us long to wash and dress, walk over the road and join the party. Bill would be okay standing in the corner stomping his feet, but I would go into a world of my own and let the music reach the depths of my being.

47

From the time I moved to Beaconsfield Street at the end of the seventies, there was a change in the air. We began to listen to others around us. The ones talking about politics grabbed my attention. Granby Street was a place we aired our thoughts. Even people like me shed conformity and my true self emerged.

Poets and storytellers helped stoke my imagination. They told the truth, through rhyme and verse, while others challenged those in power. A feeling of unrest pumped through my veins. I blamed the generation before, not realising my parents had no power to bring about change.

I'd just finished cooking myself some lunch one day during this time and smelt smoke. Rushing back into the kitchen, I found the fire was not in the house. It wasn't long before I'd found out the flames were only part of the raging furnace, a riot.

I'd only ever witnessed one-man demonstrations outside places like picture houses, where someone would have a billboard strapped onto their back shouting, 'The end of the world is upon us.' But nobody took any notice.

This time they did.

We were bombarded with good doers wishing to put things right, trying to give the community the opportunities we'd been denied. When the dust settled, Toxteth was reborn.

Taking the bus into town not long after the riots was one of the happiest days of my life. I felt like I'd burst with pride. It wasn't the burning and destruction which gladdened me, but the recognition.

Soon after, I saw Joe again.

I wanted Joe to remember me as I was. Forget what he'd heard. Erase from his memory that I was a prostitute. The look on his face as he strolled towards me told me that this might be possible. Looking up into his face and his bronzed skin shining in the sunlight, I began to tremble inside. I was ready for a new beginning too. Bill had been my saviour, but we couldn't continue.

'Good to see you,' he said.

'You too.'

Quickly making an excuse to hurry home, I walked away with sweat trickling down my back. I couldn't resist turning around, and I saw that he was watching me. I turned the corner and ran the rest of the way.

Running a bath, I took off my clothes and stepped into a sea of bubbly foam. Holding my hair above the water, I sunk lower and lower, eventually resting my back against the bathtub. The doorbell rang. Dripping with water, with only a towel wrapped around me, I opened the door.

Joe was standing there grinning. 'Thought I'd come and say hello properly.'

For a moment I was dazed. 'Come in,' I said, tripping up the stairs in my haste to escape. 'Go through the sitting room I won't be long.'

Taking a cigarette, I lit it upstairs and took a long drag, letting the smoke go deep into my lungs. Finally, I came down and entered the sitting room. 'What are you doing these days, Joe?'

'Thinking of you,' he answered.

My heart thumped against my chest. 'Don't be silly. It's been years since you've seen me.'

'So, what difference does that make?'

I'd heard a lot about him. He was living with a woman much older than him. She had a good job and owned a house in the country.

I changed the subject. 'No kids then?'

'Not yet, but there's still time.'

He left an hour later.

'I'll be back,' he said, then kissed me on the cheek.

Joe slipped a note through the letterbox the following week: *See you Thursday night.*

It had been a long time since I'd snuggled up to someone young and vital.

Sex with Bill was different. He tried desperately to fulfil my needs but to me it was always about the money. The hurt I'd suffered in the past hardened everything below the waist. He was unable to break the invisible seal I'd created, so he gave up trying.

Joe knocked around nine thirty and we had a meal and a couple of glasses of wine. The small talk lasted until his hand accidentally brushed against mine. His velvety soft fingers traced my face. 'I've wanted you from the first time I saw you,' he whispered. The sky was starless and wispy white clouds draped the moon like a bridal dress.

We went back to mine. Taking my hand, Joe led me to the settee. He loosened his tie and unbuttoned his shirt. I leaned back, and Joe moved closer. As his hands roamed my body, gently tracing his fingers around my breasts, my breathing changed. A tingling sensation came, and I let it take over. I could hear his sounds of pleasure as he entered me, and in the light of the moon our black silhouettes moved in rhythm.

'You're as sweet as sugar,' I said in Joe's ear. 'Don't stop, baby. I need to give you something that I thought was Liam's.' My prize for him was on the way. Sinking his fingers in my hair, he gave me his prize at the same time.

The man beside me was overcome with emotion. It was like looking at a past mirror of me, when I was the needy one, the one always looking for reassurance. Now I had this man in my arms begging to see me again. It felt powerful. Joe was in a relationship, but I didn't care. It was a dangerous place to be, being the other woman. Neither one was going to let Joe go, for different reasons.

The sex was good, and I could have him whenever I wanted. But my heart would never be his. I knew what he was. Beautiful and conceited, he thought he could have women falling at his feet. This woman had fallen so many times, but like a gladiator she rose up to fight another day.

48

'Penny for them,' said Sadie, as I sat down. She pushed a bread roll filled with cheese towards me. 'You look like you haven't eaten in days. Eat that and I'll get you a drink.'

I bit into the roll. 'Thanks,' I said. 'I've met someone.'

Sadie laughed. 'Been there, done that and worn the knickers.'

I was in no mood for joking. I had to end it with Bill.

When I told Sadie that there would be no more afternoon sessions for me and him, she stopped eating and looked at me open mouthed. 'How you going to manage giving everything up?'

'I'll manage. I'd gladly go back to the bag warehouse before I sell my body again.'

She smiled. 'Good on you, girl. I wish I could. Maybe when I fall in love like you I will.'

'Who mentioned the word love?'

'You're a woman after my own heart. No love no hurt.'

Plucking up the courage that weekend, I went into a deep explanation, trying to tell Bill it was over.

'Stop right there, Bess. I love you but I'm also in love with my wife.'

I couldn't believe what I was hearing. No tears, no promise of undying love, my Bill giving me up without a fight. He told me he was happy for me.

'Love,' he said, 'is not just about sex. Real love is what you feel when someone leaves you.' Taking another drink, he added, 'If my old girl left me I'd be lost.'

My own losses came to the forefront of my mind. Outwardly everything seemed to heal. I'd moved on, but the memories never fade. 'You okay, love? You've gone pale.'

I stood up and held onto the back of the chair. 'I'm okay. I just need a glass of water.' The water was cold and clear, and I drank slowly.

After Bill almost drained the bottle, it was time for our final farewell. His eyes were moist but so were mine. He'd been part of my life for so long; he'd be missed. He opened his wallet and wrote a cheque. 'Here,' he said. 'This will help for a month or so.' It was for five hundred pounds. Choked at his kindness, I walked with him to catch a taxi.

I smiled when he told the driver to take him to the little club in town. He stumbled in the cab and waved.

Goodbye sweet, I said to myself.

That weekend I stayed in my housecoat and threw my mule slippers under the bed. I dragged out the ones with bobbles on the front and tied my hair in two bunches and played music all day. I had a snack of crusty bread cheese and pickle. Sometime later Sadie visited. Uncle Zac was already in the house.

'I can't stay too long. I just wanted to see how you were,' said Sadie.

'Did Joe stay with you last night?' Uncle Zac inquired. 'If he's in the area it would be better for him to stay at yours. It's mad out there, police everywhere.'

'No. He was with Iron Face and some of the others. I'll be with you in a minute. I'm just going to put the kettle on.'

I heard him talking to Sadie in a low voice. 'God knows why she lets Joe use her. He's already got a woman. She's a bit of a head case, but I like her. She's been good to Joe.'

I returned with a tray. The white bone china cups edged with a gold rim looked expensive on the black lacquered tray.

Uncle Zac filled his pipe and put it down while he poured his tea. 'Well girls,' he said. 'What happened in Liverpool 8 will be in the history books.' He leaned back in the armchair. 'If things don't change after all this, God help us all. But I've got a feeling they will.'

'I'm thinking about taking a foundation course,' Sadie told us.

'Are you?' I replied with surprise.

'It will only take a year to complete. If I pass it would put me in a good position to apply for the Black Access course.'

'What's that?' I asked.

'It's the ordinary Access but Black History is covered in detail,' she explained. 'We could both do it together if you want. Do the foundation course first.'

This would be a chance to brush up on what didn't sink at school. 'Let me think about it.'

'Don't take too long, the new term starts next month,' she said, picking up her coat from the back of the chair.

'You seem good,' I told her.

'I'm not in love yet, but I'm learning to love myself.'

I knew what she meant but Uncle Zac scratched his head. When he had gone I thought about the advantages of doing the course. It might give an insight into my capabilities. I wanted to express myself but struggled with the words. My brain knew what I wanted to say, but somewhere between my vocal cords and tongue, the words were lost. I wanted to enrol with Sadie and find the words and maybe myself. When I saw Joe, I told him what Sadie suggested.

'I don't want you studying. What about me?' When

he bent down and kissed me, all the talk of courses and books went out of my head. I'd been waiting for him, longing to feel him next to me warm and sensual, him taking my clothes off layer by layer.

But when he'd gone, I thought more about my future. Brian was doing well in college and Liam had promised to buy him a flat. Most of my troubles were over now. Maybe I needed a job. The peanut factory was walking distance from my home. It was nine to five, so plenty of time to pamper myself for my Joe.

I wondered if the need to be loved was my downfall. Yes, everything was going my way. Joe was my fairy godfather. But the price was too high. My life was being wasted, tangled up in the bedsheets. It was the need to feel wanted which handcuffed me to the past.

His pupils would dilate when he saw me wearing my black stockings, with a dainty suspender belt, bras with my breasts leaping out of the cup. And panties, yes panties were his favourite.

I would often become hot and feeling sexy every time I thought of him. Often, I'd have to leave a message for him on his friend's phone. Urgent, I would say. He knew what urgent meant. He'd arrive and give me what I wanted and was more than happy to do so.

Heavenly I called it. Sadie called it madness. My enthusiasm for my life after the riots was lost in Joe's embrace. Before meeting Joe again, I thought positive, like Sadie. Now I was ignoring a chance to better myself by making my sexual needs a priority.

So, the peanut factory it was, with its sickly smell that always made me nauseated.

49

I'd often meet Joe in our hideout, which was any club that opened late. Dark and cave-like, the space was designed for lovers to dance close.

I'd cook breakfast Sunday morning and spend the day in bed. Sunday night was always heartbreak, not for me, but for Joe. He would bath and shave, have something to eat but keep looking at his watch. He had to leave, he'd say, show his face, as he'd put it, to the little woman waiting for him at home. It was the price I paid for a few hours of joy.

I kept myself busy. Apart from Sadie, Uncle Zac, Mabel and Ruby, I had few friends. Again, it was the way Joe wanted it. 'We are keeping a secret,' he'd say. 'The less people who know the better.'

Two years into our love affair, holes began to show when Joe started to make excuses on why we couldn't be seen together in the clubs.

Finally, I snapped and started to follow him. One night I stood watching the entrance and saw him and a girl pull up in a taxi. She was well-groomed and beautiful.

There was no part of me feeling jealous, just annoyed that Joe could not tell me the truth. I felt sheer delight when Joe saw me walking in. He turned a deadly shade of grey as I passed his table and sat by myself.

Within seconds of ordering a drink I was asked to dance. Yes, I thought, it was time to make him sweat. Not only did I have the power, I will show him he did not have any control over me. I danced, laughed and flirted with the men, taking a sneaky look at Joe sitting with his partner and watching him trying to look calm and collected.

I was still laughing when Joe turned up the next evening.

'What the hell do you think you are doing?'

'Teaching you a lesson,' I answered.

He didn't understand how he was not the centre of my universe. If he wanted me, it would be on my terms. I was playing with fire, but I was making sure he would feel the blisters. He wanted the best of both worlds. Having him wondering if he could tame my independent spirit, but watching him struggle to find a solution, gave me the greatest thrill of all.

Sadie called one afternoon in her lunch break. She'd changed so much in a short time. She wore a duffle coat, long skirt and a bag over her shoulder. She looked studious.

'Bess, I don't have the love and support of a family. You have all that, so why are you wasting your life with Joe?'

I had no answer to her question. How could I explain that deep down the hurt of the past dominated my actions?

'It's not too late,' Sadie said. 'You can still do the course.'

Taking no notice of her concerns, I continued my affair with Joe. I buried my head, not only in sand, but in mud.

A foggy day in January changed my life. Joe still had me, but I was in control of my senses. Sadie inspired me to get my self-respect back. I knew her well enough to know that encouraging me to educate myself, was in my best interest.

Joe, on the other hand, wanted me to stay dumb. He made the mistake of telling me we would part if I joined the course. But I was ready. Amidst the gloom of the atmosphere inside and outside of my house, I could see a ray of sunshine. Now I know the glow came from me and my determination to better myself.

Joe stormed out of the house on hearing my news. He put a note through my door telling me he wouldn't be returning.

I laughed and disregarded the scribbled note. He'd be back when he needed me and longed to lie next to me in bed. It might take a while but the tension inside of us both would build up. Then he would come crawling back.

Being on the foundation course was like going back to school. The main difference was though, most people were black. What I'd learned at school didn't come flooding back. I'd retained nothing, except to read and write. But I walked into a classroom of adults and felt welcome. Now was my time to take in everything I was taught, and I did. There were no glowing reports. I was average. The marks were good enough for me though.

Joe tried punishing me with his lack of contact, hoping I would react and cause a scene. I didn't dwell on his mind games. I was focused on reaching my goal and nothing could change that.

Spending most of my days in town visiting the library and meeting Sadie, gave me less time to think of Joe. The course was detailed, disciplined and hard work. It was like being submerged in an ocean of discovery without a lifejacket. There I was, taking an active role in debates around social issues of past and present. I had entered another world. My brain felt as though it would explode with all the information. The curriculum brought rage, disgust and sadness within the group. The teachers sat back and let us air our thoughts.

Now I knew more about Daisy's plight working for the Richardson's in South Africa and of my own disadvantaged life in more detail.

I completed the course fully equipped for work with one of the biggest employers in Liverpool and chose to work in the library. I was used to the environment and the ambience of the building and was able to continue learning. Finally, I reached where I wanted to be many years ago, working in an office.

I remembered those words in school. Hilde telling me, 'You'll never work in an office.'

Brian was overjoyed at my achievement and was celebrating his own. He'd passed his exams with distinction and guaranteed employment after training. Liam had bought him a flat. But before I had the chance to visit Brian, my life took a dramatic turn.

Success hadn't dampened my raging desire for Joe. I still waited for the tap on the window or a late-night call. Whenever it happened, and he would stand under the light in the hallway, my heart would skip a beat.

One such night he came, pulled me into his arms, dissolving anything I wanted to say about our fragmented relationship. In the early hours there was a banging at the door.

Hastily pulling on my housecoat with nothing underneath me, I went to the door, expecting to see a neighbour needing my help. Instead I felt pain as a woman's stiletto heel struck the side of my temple. Falling to the floor with blood streaming down my face, I saw a woman hovering over me.

Joe rushed out and restrained the woman from doing further damage. The woman was his girlfriend. I couldn't remember much of what happened afterwards. I woke up in my bed, alone and scared. Sadie came around and helped me bathe the congealed blood from around my eyes. She told me Joe had rung her and said I was in trouble. I wept at the thought of Joe leaving me in a state, not caring if I was severely injured or needed hospital treatment. It was then Sadie told me what I had done.

'Bess, you beat the woman to a pulp. Joe managed to drag you away, but you still managed to grab hold of her hair and start fighting again. She's gone to the police.'

It was the mention of the police which frightened me. I would have a record. All my hard work would be for nothing. How could it happen and why had I reacted so violently? She had attacked me, but I didn't even want Joe. That woman must have been in the firing line for all my pent-up rage at Mandy, Liam, Mother, and those teachers at school.

'You'd better get out of here for a while, girl,' said Sadie. 'Joe's woman doesn't know anything about you except for where you live. If the police pick you up now while they're punishing people for the riots, it'll be much worse for you.'

I felt differently about Joe after that. He would spend the rest of his days cooped up in the clutches of someone who owned him. But I know he'd have made excuses to hide the fact he had no ambition. He was happy to be someone's sex object and pampered like a child. He was the one with no self-respect.

Sadie packed some clothes into an overnight bag. 'I'll take you to a friend of mine. You can stay there a couple of nights, then decide what to do.'

Before I left my home, I put away old photographs of

happier times with Joe and vowed to let them fade over time, just like my father did with his memories. Joe was part of my past, now the future was staring me in the face.

50

Back on the train, back to the modern day. Brian twitched and opened his eyes. He stretched and seemed to uncurl but his movements were restricted, forcing him to adjust to the cramped seat. Then suddenly, like he'd been jabbed with a needle, he was awake.

He scanned the table for discarded crisp packets, even screwed up sweet wrappers would enlighten his day. Brian moaned when I left toothpaste tops on the bathroom shelf or dented the middle of the tube. He saw red at scraps of paper, or out of date magazines cluttering the coffee table. Now with no litter to pick up, disappointment edged on his face. I observed him with gritted teeth. I munched fiercely on a sandwich to keep my angry words in.

After sweeping away microscopic crumbs, Brian took out the phone and tried to call Sadie, moving to get a better signal. I opened a bag of peanuts and I popped some in my mouth. I chewed contentedly.

Brian returned twirling the phone in his hand and shaking it as though he was testing a light bulb, 'Still no signal,' he said. 'I'll keep trying.' He paused. 'You'll be okay if I go for a drink, won't you?'

'I'll be fine. Take your time.' I put back my headrest and closed my eyes. The heat soaked my pores in sweat, leaving my skin damp and moist. My eyes danced around my skull as my body slumped forward. The sun hid behind the clouds and cooled the atmosphere. As it reappeared, a golden glow bounced off the windows.

Eventually the journey was over. Brian shuffled with the cases to the nearest exit. The distant light in the distance looked like illuminated sunflowers.

'It won't be long now, Mother, before you see your old crowd,' he said.

'Yes,' I answered, looking out at the blackness. But I knew I'd taken too long to return. My heart began to pound as the train reached the spot where home was less than two miles away. It was like coming through the birth canal. I'd soon be part of the world that gladdened my heart with memories too precious to abandon and too important to forget. I left Brian with the luggage and stepped out of the train in shock.

Standing on the platform were three smiling faces. Uncle Zac leaned on a walking stick with Joe and Sadie stood nearby. Uncle's sunken eyes, hollow and dim, had lost their twinkle, but his smile was the same. As he encircled me in his arms, I could feel his bones. He gripped me with affection and love. 'Girl, I'm so glad to see you. My Mabel-' He was heartbroken. He walked slowly, shoulders hunched with grief.

Even through her sadness, Sadie glowed. She wore a smart suit, high heels and had a black leather bag. As she walked towards me, my love for her welled up inside me. She was my best friend. The one who had brought me from the ashes when Liam had dumped me. All I could do was hug her. Words were not necessary.

Joe had lost his slim-toned body. Now he was gaunt and slightly stooped. My heart didn't leap when our eyes met like it did in the past. It was a quiet reflection on the time we'd shared. I liked the way he was now cool and composed but without the mystery of the younger Joe. He kissed me tenderly. There was no passion, only gentleness.

'I'm sorry that I drove you away,' he said. 'I wanted to be here now for Zac…and for you.'

'All is forgiven,' I said, and I meant it.

I put my arm through Uncle Zac's and guided him to the taxi stand.

'He's doing well,' Uncle Zac told me, nodding towards Joe who walked a short distance behind. 'He goes to college as well.' Uncle must have thought he was whispering, but his voice carried like a loud speaker.

Joe laughed nervously. 'It's only a night course.' He said it as though he expected me to be dismissive of his achievement and brush it aside.

'Good for you,' I said. My thoughts turned to Mabel. Sadie had already told me she was not expected to live. Brian didn't know yet. We thought it best to break the news in Uncle Zac's.

The house seemed empty without Mabel. The coldness was the first thing I noticed, and I shivered when I went into the kitchen. Her pinafore hung on a nail and the tea-stained cups and her broken spouted teapot looked out of place without Mabel there to welcome us.

Joe and I took a taxi to the hospital. Brian insisted he'd follow on.

'I'll stay with Uncle Zac,' he said. 'Anyway, I want to see Auntie Mabel by myself.'

I smiled. How could I deny the intimacy Brian shared with his auntie? He must have wanted to tell her how much he loved her and become her little boy again.

'I'll stay in the waiting room,' said Joe. 'Give you some time on your own.' I wanted to talk to him, but the worry of Mabel's serious condition had overshadowed everything else.

Mabel looked pale and I reeled with the humid smell of the small side ward, which was private enough but isolated. She waved her skeletal hand. I bent down to kiss her.

'Sit by me, girl. Bring the chair over,' she said. Her voice trailed weakly as I pulled out a chair and sat down.

'It was not your father's fault,' she said in a hushed voice.

'Do you mean the fallout between him and Uncle Zac?'

'That's part of it,' she replied and then asked for some water. 'We never told you the full story.'

Gently lifting her head, I put the plastic beaker to her lips. She sipped slowly. Moving her into a more comfortable position, I plumped up her pillows and laid her head back.

'Sadie's mother was our friend, and your father was her first love. When your father met your mother, it broke her heart.'

I never heard Sadie talk about her family much. Maybe she knew what had gone on and left it that way.

'My friend fell apart when your father left her,' Mabel continued. 'Zac begged your father to go and see her, tell her he was sorry, make her feel better. But he said no.'

I didn't want to hear what happened next. 'She died in a mental institution and Sadie was brought up by her father, who eventually abandoned her.' Mabel closed her eyes.

It was all falling into place. My mother's resentment towards Uncle Zac and Mabel. Mabel's resistance to get to know me at first, and her anger at Sadie's lifestyle. She'd wanted better for her friend's daughter. She'd wanted better for her friend.

'Your father,' Mabel continued. 'He wanted to better himself. But he did love your mother. Yet we…Uncle Zac told him he was just turning his back on his black roots.'

She coughed. Blood was coming from her mouth. I rang the buzzer frantically and a nurse came quickly to the room. She wiped Mabel's mouth with a damp paper towel. 'She's alright. She's had some medicine to clear her chest. Don't worry, she is okay.'

The room felt airless. Mabel was asleep now and her face was relaxed. It was as though a burden she'd harboured was gone.

I sat at her bedside for a while and then Joe and I caught another taxi and we went back to Uncle Zac's.

Mabel died early the next morning.

We hadn't been able to track down Ruby, who had deliberately left no trace of where she was. She would regret not being at her mother's bedside, I thought.

Sadie put her arms around Uncle and held onto him, easing him towards the door, away from the sadness in the room. Brian was inconsolable, on his knees weeping like a child. Joe helped him to his feet and slowly walked him through the corridor.

I stayed with Mabel in the silence of the room, looking at her face, peaceful and free from pain. Bending down to kiss her forehead, I promised her that I would look after Uncle Zac. It was left to me and Sadie to be strong and organise where Mabel would rest. I thought of my parents. I hadn't been in touch with Mother about Mabel and I wasn't quite ready to.

51

It felt like death was everywhere. The limp leaves of Mabel's plants hung low through lack of water. Dirty dishes were scattered on the worktops as Mabel was not there to scoop everything up and hustle them out of sight. The unlit fire brought no comfort to the surroundings, even the clock had stopped ticking.

Eventually Joe sprang into action. He took off his coat, rolled up his shirt sleeves, cleared the ashes and lit the fire.

Brian announced he was going to see Mother. I wasn't ready for that.

'Okay, son. But don't expect too much.'

'What do you mean?'

'All I'm saying is, she can be a bit funny where Zac and Mabel are concerned.'

'Even now Mabel has died?'

I didn't answer. Brian left, and I drew back the curtains and turned the key of the clock. With the first movement of the hands and light from the windows, it was like a colony of ants had begun work.

We sat Uncle in his chair. Sadie took the dishes into the kitchen and the sound of the whistling kettle brought some normality to the house. We drank tea and sat with our own private thoughts.

Mine was remembering the first time I met Uncle and Mabel. How Mabel's dark eyes seemed to look into my soul. She scared me with her no-nonsense approach, yet she had a softer side that I soon got to know, and love.

A few neighbours and friends came to support Uncle. In their company, he became his old self and talked about the past. Only when Ruby was mentioned would the sadness in his eyes return.

Mabel was taken to a funeral parlour not far from their home. We were led over a cobble-stoned courtyard. The tomb-like room with a flagstone floor felt rough and uneven underfoot. A dim light swung above our heads as we stooped under the low beams. The freezing temperature chilled my bones. I was not at ease with the tiptoeing assistants walking in and out of the room.

'I want her out of this God dammed place,' said Uncle. 'Take her home where she belongs.'

'No, Uncle. We'll bring the flowers and her picture. That's what she would want.'

Looking crushed, he bent his head. 'Okay, girl. I'll leave it up to you.' He wiped his eyes. 'Find my Ruby, girl. She should be here.'

There was nothing I could say to comfort him.

An elderly woman who turned up with a small bunch of violets, pulled me aside. 'My Granddaughter might know where Ruby is.'

'Don't tell Zac yet, he might get his hopes up.' But the idea of giving Uncle Zac his wish filled my heart with joy.

The morning of the funeral, we got a special delivery of flowers. They were a mixture of yellow and white with a card placed in the inside. I handed the flowers to Uncle Zac and helped him retrieve the card. He seemed unsteady on his feet, so I took his arm and made him sit down. 'Ruby, Ruby,' he kept repeating. 'She sent them.' He dabbed his eyes with a handkerchief. 'I knew she hadn't forgot us, girl.'

Even though Ruby had not come home, Uncle Zac

was happy to hear from her and I was happy for him. We didn't talk about why she wasn't home. Everyone had moved on with their lives, so maybe she was at a stand-still and ashamed to come back.

Meanwhile, a small crowd gathered outside the house waiting for Mabel to arrive. The hearse drew up outside. The funeral flowers were laid neatly around the coffin and Uncle proudly placed Ruby's flowers next to them. He stood by the car upright and head held high. We took our places in the procession of cars. I saw Iron Face and Snake Eyes and nodded my head.

The attendants, wearing top hats and gloves, escort-ed the mourners. Everyone was in a reflective mood, remembering those who'd passed away who had taken the same journey, and one day it would be our turn. We were taking Mabel to a church close to where she had grown up in Scotland Road.

It was strange going to an area I'd heard about but never visited. People walking in the street turned their heads to look at the black faces.

Pulling up on a grass verge, the bell tolled as the priest stood by the entrance, his white, gold and black robe flapping in the light breeze. Smiling, he bowed his head as we filed passed him taking our place in the aisles.

A group of people sat at the back of the church. Their marble faces seemed three dimensional against the dark wooden beams and benches. No one knew who they were until Uncle Zac said, 'That's Mabel's family.' Then suddenly, giving me no time to stop him, Uncle Zac vented a verbal condemnation on them.

'You lot,' he said in a low determined attack. 'Left my poor woman all by herself without any family support other than me.' Lunging forward, froth formed around the corners of his mouth. 'But I did my best to make her happy, and she was.'

There was no response from her family. Someone intervened and put an arm around Uncle, urging him to let it go.

The service was simple but moving. There were no dry eyes as the priest gave an account of her life. When the service finished, and the coffin was carried out, the sun shone through the stained-glass windows. Mabel's family slipped out through a side door.

We continued our journey to bury a much-loved wife, mother and friend.

52

Uncle Zac gave his final farewell to Mabel by placing a rose on her coffin. He left the graveside in tears, being supported by family and friends. We returned to Uncle Zac's house to have our own kind of memorial for Mabel. Opening the curtains to brighten the room, the table was already set with food. Everyone wanted a cup of tea then started to nibble on the pork pies and salads.

The attendants joined us and were given a glass of wine and something to eat. The elderly told stories about Uncle Zac and Mabel. They made everyone laugh, which stopped Uncle from withdrawing into himself with grief.

His eyes lit up as he bobbed up and down showing Mabel's dance moves and brought creased pictures he'd found. With trembling hands, he traced the outline of Mabel's face.

A neighbour's daughter came to see Uncle Zac. She was beautiful with jet black hair and eyes to match. Brian could not take his eyes off her.

The night ended around ten o'clock when the mourners dispersed. Only Sadie, the young woman, Brian and Uncle Zac were left.

Sadie cleared the table of empty drinking glasses and food. The young woman and I washed the dishes and Uncle Zac sat quietly crying over Ruby.

Brian disappeared with the young woman, but I could hear them talking by the front door. It seemed an intimate conversation. Maybe it wasn't their first meeting and I was not going to ask. It had been a long time since I'd witnessed Brian so relaxed.

I knew Uncle needed all of us to be strong so he could draw on that strength, otherwise he might sink to a depth where there was no way back.

He reminded me how my father kept anything to do with his health a secret. Uncle would not have the opportunity to create a smokescreen because I would watch for the slightest change physically or mentally. But I would not be in Liverpool for much longer and pondered the idea of taking Uncle Zac back with me. I knew it was too early to look at the situation long term. If I could get Uncle strong enough to cope, he could always return to Liverpool.

I told Sadie this and she rubbed her temple. 'Let's see how he copes here first.'

But Uncle had problems from the onset. He would refuse to go to bed and fall asleep on the couch. A few days before my departure, Sadie, Brian and I decided the question about leaving Liverpool was to be put to Uncle Zac.

'Uncle, would he like to come and live with me?' I asked.

His eyes lit up and for a moment he was happy, then he looked worried. 'What about my Ruby?'

'She would be welcome to live with us in London when she comes back.'

I didn't want to be angry with Ruby, but I couldn't help myself. She had parents who adored her. If only she'd stopped and thought of them, she would be here now.

'What about you, Uncle?'

'Yes, yes, okay, girl. Sadie can stay here and maybe sort out the council house offer I got a few weeks ago.'

Patting his arm, I was delighted. 'So, my dear Uncle,

you're coming to live with us.'

He clapped his hands like a child. 'To the Big Smoke.'

The smile on Brian's face told me all I wanted to know. He'd also put his demons to rest. He'd been so worried about facing Fred Carter, but now a woman had taken centre stage and I was sure Brian would cope with any events that came his way.

I had coffee in town with Joe the day before I was going back to London. It was four o'clock in the afternoon. The sun burnt the leaves brown and the light wind scattered them like sparrows wings on the pavement. My life was uncomplicated now.

Being away for so long stopped me from remembering the bad times with Joe. Even though I was older and much wiser, I thought of being in his arms and missed having him around. But I was not going to let him know how hard it was for me to go away again. My life had turned around. There was no way I could throw all my hard work away.

We talked about local issues and his view on things. He used his hands for expression and furrowed his brow when deep in thought. It wasn't my Joe sitting there. I liked the rogue Joe. The change was better for him though.

In respect to Mabel, we didn't talk about anything personal. He kissed me on the cheek before he left, and we both went our separate ways. It was like my soul was free.

The time came to sort through Mabel's belongings. Uncle Zac kept the dress she was married in, carefully wrapping it in tissue paper. He wanted the rest to go. Mabel didn't have many clothes, but what she did have were always washed and ironed and neatly folded. I put her blouse to my cheek. I could smell a hint of her perfume. I put it in my bag and closed the zip.

Brian had already visited my mother. 'She has a good network of friends around her,' he told me. Sadie also called on Mother regularly to stock up her fridge and pay bills. Mother wanted to see me, and I decided to visit her before I left Liverpool.

I walked down the street to her house, remembering how I'd pushed Brian in his pram and crossed Princes Road, how I was in floods of tears when Father died, and Uncle Zac became part of my life.

Uncle's house would be smashed to pieces in the near future, leaving the memories of happier times scattered amongst the pieces of bricks - flattened to create a pathway for more crammed housing estates and the ever-present poverty.

The soul had disappeared from the area. The old houses were gone, with their crumbling walls where weeds sprouted between the cement and tiny yellow and purple flowers blossomed. I traced the same places where sadness, happiness and despair hugged me like a shadow.

Most of the clubs had gone too, and the hustle and bustle left a silent hush. The roads had the bumps and lumps temporarily levelled, just like the promises made after the riots.

I'd returned to Liverpool under unforeseen circumstances; stopping me from daydreaming and romancing about the past. If I'd have returned to see Joe, the daydream might have blighted me from reality and stopped me from realising what I already had.

As I arrived at Mother's, I could see through the glass pane in the front door how frail she looked. Yet she walked down the small hallway swiftly for her age. I kissed her on the cheek and she put her arms around me.

'So sorry about Mabel, girl. How's Zac?'

It was the first time she'd mentioned their names with compassion; an opening for me to tell her of my plan for Uncle Zac. Breaking the news, I held my breath.

'It's a good idea. I know how lonely he must be.'

Hearing those words from Mother, it somehow made the past not matter to either of us.

I left feeling we had all come full circle in our lives. We had all learned the hard way, but now the path would be easier. I promised to come back to see her regularly. There would never be long spells of absence again. I could be the daughter I always wanted to be, and I could be me.

As I was getting ready to leave, Sadie told me she'd met someone.

'I love him, girl. We're thinking of getting hitched.'

Hugging her tightly, I said. 'Sadie, I want you to enjoy these years. You have cared for Uncle Zac and Mabel like a daughter. So now it's my turn to help.'

'I'll miss him,' Sadie replied. 'But you do need to spend some time with him, and he needs a chance to grieve. A new environment could help that process, but I expect you both to return for my wedding.'

'Try stopping me,' I laughed. Uncle and I would return for Sadie's big day.

I thought about my own love life. I thanked my mother for my early years, which toughened me up for the bad times I'd face. It had all been done and dusted. For the first time in my life, I felt free from the past.

When we caught the train later that day and waved goodbye, I knew my life would change. I'd longed to return home for so many years. Now I was leaving my city behind but taking a part of Liverpool back with me.

Acknowledgements

My sincere thanks to the following people who have supported me on my journey to publish *Bess*: Mike Morris and Madeline Heneghan, Co-Directors of Writing on the Wall, and to and all members of their team past and present. Without their support over many years, my novel would probably have ended up in the attic. They never complained, read all my drafts and always gave feedback with compliments and encouragement and organised and produced the final version of the novel you hold in your hands today; my first editor Jenny Newman who helped me organise, with support from Arts Council England, my then jumbled first draft. Jenny went above and beyond with her support, and I was still seeking her advice up to a year ago, so thank you, my dear friend; to Dave Evans who was so complimentary about my writing when I entered WoW's Pulp Idol novel writing competition; my neighbour and friend Caroline Ihiekwe, whose involvement and support in helping me with structure was invaluable at a key time in the development of the novel; to Clare Coombes and Matthew McKeown at The Liverpool Editing Company, who did such an amazing job on the final edit and proof of the manuscript; to Janet Johnstone who first introduced me to Writing on the Wall some years ago - I will never forget her enthusiasm whenever we discussed my novel, but most of all, I really value her friendship. A special thank you to my family, friends, neighbours, taxi drivers, shop owners and all those people I bombarded with my novel. You are the ones who kept me writing, wanting to know when my novel would be published. Finally, I can say, it's here done and dusted.